A Woman's Jurisdiction
By A. Joseph

This is a work of fiction. Similarities to real people, places, or events are entirely coincidental.

A WOMAN'S JURISDICTION

First edition. October 7, 2024.

ISBN: 979-8227668226

Written by A. Joseph.

Chapter 1

Tamian Paigelo had been stripped naked so his body could be smeared with thick, gray-blue clay found in abundance in the region. His more vitally positioned solar plexus remained bare, an area the size of the hand of the man who had smoothed clay around it. A puckered male teat at its center ... the one distinguishable mark that the mudman being hoisted into the trees was human. Tamian despised the smell of damp clay. It made him nauseous to the point of near unconsciousness. Bloating leeches, beneath hardened clay, smothered his feet. The Spanish explorers he had traveled with had grown up despising Jews. Now at sunset, while he swung high in the treetops, creaking on ropes, he prayed they would not forget him or leave him there on purpose. He groaned with pain. The thought of uncertainty coupled with the fear of abandonment weighed heavily on him.

Tamian had seen them earlier in the morning while they had prepared for him to be pulled up into the tree. The Spanish explorers had torn through open caskets, shredding the protective straw to eagerly remove amphoras of wine from the Iberian vineyard that the trading supply ship had delivered the previous day. They planned to leave him hanging in the tree for two nights in the place now known as 'The Everglades.'

He strained to look below. A crust of dry clay on his neck broke, flaking away. He strained to watch a collection of conquistador helmets of their military escorts sway off back into the jungle. They had hoisted a fruit basket beside him, filled with rations of known-to-be-edible fruit, water, and salted red meat that had been cured onboard their vessel for months at sea. The hum of mosquitoes grew louder the closer sunset came.

Tamian struggled to relax, but ropes cut in around his armpits. He let out a loud scream to release his physical pain. He closed his eyes to sail in his mind around the long peninsula they had begun to circumnavigate. The only way to ease his pain in conjunction with his racing pulse was to envisage his charcoal poised in his fingers, ready to trace the coastline's shape. He found the new continent the greatest challenge for his map-drawing ability yet. Since he had become the New World's chief cartographer, nothing in his past career could compare to this undertaking, both physically and mentally. What wonders lay ahead of them in this new land?

When the pains in his chest had intensified, the physician traveling with the cartography expedition had prescribed hemoglobin-hungry parasites to thin his circulation. The sting of legions of blood-sucking insects sinking their feeding tubes into the exposed flesh of Tamian's chest while he hung suspended, made him flinch as they fed the frenzy where their initial incisions formed. Their scattered initial bites agonized him, but their undulating bodies tormented him. The wind gathered speed brushing the leaves past him, touching his skin—a welcome brief sensation before it evaporated and the leeches' anesthetic kicked in. Yet the nagging itchiness that followed for hours threatened to unhinge him.

He would have been reassured to learn that he would survive his medical condition to settle down back in Seville, marry, and go on to father four children. Then, generations later, a distant ancestor of his extended progeny would become a citizen of this great continent-to-be and would sit in a prison on the land mass he had sketched onto vellum. Close by the location where he had hung in the tree, today, a bronze plaque read "Near this spot, early European explorers came to shore to document a new continent."

Chapter 2

The state penitentiary door to his cell had been manufactured in a foundry during a century when the word insubstantial was only used in the context of an amoral virtue, when the word 'penitentiary' came directly from the word penitence. And this insubstantial abomination, his sack of bones hunched, affronted the prison doctor's very soul as he looked through the observation hatch in the rived, black iron door. The prison doctor had no real compassion for the dying man he now looked down on. His lack of empathy for this patient made him lean away from the source of his unease as he struggled to stop himself from becoming physically ill. He almost felt guilty to admit to himself that he didn't really care if the prisoner he was about to treat would live or die. The shaky, brittle excuse of a senior citizen in the cell bore no resemblance to the young unformed, pathetic prisoner who had rightfully prompted a nationwide manhunt, inflamed two states clasped in fear, and obligated women and younger folk to be home before dark.

He had seen all of the news reports about the killer. When they had caught him, they had immediately sentenced him to six life terms for his crimes on the clemency condition of revoking the death sentence, if he was chemically castrated, should any technicality in American law statutes change during the duration of his internment. Immediately, this presented an opportunity for a struggling law firm to attract some free publicity by appealing for the 'Beast of New Jersey' to be released. Unfortunately for him, the victims' families came from old money, despite the big dipper Wall Street trends in the nation's chronological economy over the years. The family members with the keenest memories still had the kind of resources that could overturn district attorney rulings to force the state's legislature to pass an unprecedented sentence in U.S. legal history.

"This is inhumane. He needs to be transferred. The man is dying. Why can't we take him to the infirmary?" the prison doctor protested as he entered the prisoner's cell. The doctor looked down at his rotten patient. "Get this patient to the infirmary for life support prep," he yelled at his assistant. The doctor scribbled on a clipboard, tired and eager for his shift to be over. His heartbeat increased, and his stomach fluttered. "And check to see if he has any next of kin. There will be a phone book of forms for this court decision cluster!"

"Already did. No living next of kin on record," the assistant responded as he wheeled the condemned convict away.

Outside, the doctor cringed at the gathered news crews feverish at the prospect of this inmate being connected to life support.

Imbeciles, he deemed as a rolling heat surged through his stomach. He turned his cold look away before he exposed their ignorance. Better to dismiss them than to make a record despite every ounce of his being wishing to belittle them.

Chapter 3

In Santa Monica, positioned back from the coast, hills covered in ferns and other vegetation were cliffs left behind from Ice Age shifts in tectonic plates that caused the ocean to recede. Now, houses stood, alongside apartment complexes, with concealed underground parking lots. Complexes boasted fountains framed by Corinthian columns, identical to the illustrations of pillars found on each Social Security card, with stairs that led to risen hot tubs beside mosaic swimming pools. Madison often found herself imagining the slow creep of geological time, bleating about human growth amid the misery these ravines and hills so often maliciously concealed—lost.

Her apartment balcony was the lower of four, vertically aligned above the pool. When the marine layer had not crept over to obscure the sky during nightfall, sunlit glimmers from the pool's turbulent surface thrashed in the shadow cast by the balcony above hers in the same way shiny fish do, caught in quantity in a fishing net.

She fidgeted in the frangipani-scented foam bath, listening to the recording of a condemned man's voice expelling from a portable hi-fi unit she had placed left of the bathroom door. The candles around the tub concocted mutating shapes like severed veins and slashed heads that closed in on her soaking body. The barometer of her mood shifted to a drop in pressure.

Now, the variations in the pitch of the harrowing description recounting each one of his dismembering crimes became inexplicably syncopated to the wicks' flames of the five aromatherapy candles that flickered around the walls to the comfortable cleansing of her intact anatomy. Madison imagined blood in the water. She saw her body dismembered while she still lived. Death had not closed her eyes yet. The whole bathroom was embossed in blood, an illusion created by the candlelight's quiver. She sat up distraught at the vivid, haunting images her mind contemplated. She fixated back on the voice to the one statement that overrode all he said.

Fifteen words of his had whittled down a thousand of poised, shocking narrative. "A woman is still a virgin until she has undergone one of my cosmetic procedures." Living proof that even a disturbed philosophy counteracts a catalog of verbs, nouns, and adjectives that summons wounds a serial killer had inflicted. Acid reflux from the red wine broke in her throat as a prerequisite of vomiting at the horrifying recorded vile subjects. Her stress level increased, making the vein under her eye pulse.

She had promised herself from the beginning she would never let it get to her. She would be resilient to graphic photographs and revolting coroner reports of how the hacking and slashing of innocent victims took place. She had first realized back in the spring of 2004 that the valve she had envisaged that filtered out impurities, tucked in behind her main coronary archery, had like a fountain pen in her top pocket unexpectedly leaked, leaving a dark, visible blemish around her indestructible approach to her work and clouding her sense of duty. She lay in the bath, revolted by humanity.

It was the child murders that had torn the thin membrane on the seal of her confidence. Now, for them, in light of the fact, she produced none of her own. These were now her children as far as she was concerned. Writing books about why killers kill might help soothe the relenting torment she harbored for their purest echoes asking for justice. A cause she felt nobler than creating children of her own to place in harm's way. Her murdered orphans grew into her books. Her fervor for unsolved child murders became her endless pursuit to find them justice. Her book research made her delve into the depravity of killers' minds and their complete disdain for their innocent victims especially women and children.

This kind of research was slowly taking a toll on her mental well-being. She sometimes wondered how nice it would be to have a job that didn't confront her with the worst society had to offer, but her inner voice left her no choice but to continue on her relentless quest for justice. It was a calling she couldn't escape.

She had gone from a master's degree in forensic archaeology to an internship, working on homicide departments' forensic teams that had inadvertently become a full-time profession. She had successfully helped the L.A.P.D. and S.M.P.D. on cases that had been as deeply buried in departments' unsolved computer database systems as they were chronologically dormant in sequential preference. Brushing dirt from human remains in a shallow pit began to feel every much as run-of-the-mill as it would for someone working in an office or a bank.

Always the same thought came, like it was fresh. *Bone can retain contagious viruses for hundreds of years. Who knows what landed on the coast of California before harbor authorities regulated ships.* She had been delivered into the world prematurely. To date, this made her health an unreliable factor in the building of a career to evaluate whether or not it was wise to examine all kinds of found remains.

She had been endowed with an uncanny aptitude for understanding a killer's mind. Though not formally trained or educated in criminal psychology, she began by identifying bones from those with suspected foul play that were not so old. Her last book *A Grave History-The Telegraph Hill Murders* had reached the number one position of every major newspaper's best seller list for non-fiction. Her literary agent had urged her, to the brink of begging, to try her hand at writing a novel. This had prompted her to listen to a backlog of taped confession interviews packed with psychotherapy material, searching for snippets of reality that would spurn forty-five suspense-filled chapters.

The cosmetic surgeon's voice continued. He had derived a perverse pleasure from making incisions in his patients to begin with, but he had matured into a gory, grotesque adult game of mix and match. In his basement, police found composite bodies—hacked-up corpses he bound using parts from separate bodies based on the most perfectly proportioned person he could imagine. The national obsession with procedures to a better way of looking had driven him insane, causing one journalist to christen him—how all American serial killers are given a nickname—The Frankenstein Murderer.

She couldn't bear to lie in the tub any longer, the candle flames flickering as truth oscilloscopes measuring his voice pattern. She jumped from the water in a panic to switch on the light. She reached for her robe and went into the hallway. Madison bent down to pick up the local paper that had been delivered through the cat flap in her door. The last tenant, presumably, installed this feature, and the paper was delivered there because her mailbox was full.

The headline "Terrier Kills Santa Monica Woman" caught her attention. A woman in Madison's apartment complex, so the paper reported, had been driving into their underground residential parking lot while she listened to *Splendid Harmony*, a New Age CD that contained subliminal messages to calm stress and promote her peace of mind. Unfortunately to canine ears, it had sounded like something entirely different. When she had driven up to their parking lot's open gates, Truffles couldn't take the subliminal noise anymore. He went ballistic, attacking her face from around the headrest, causing her to delay her entry. Then, the car sped off blindly to smash into the slow, self-closing gate. The low-speed crash contained enough impact to kill her. Had she been wearing a seat belt, like she had moments before, she would have survived.

The intercom buzzer made Madison jump, almost causing her to drop the front-page story of the pet lover's bizarre demise. Its button-pusher expressed an impatient annoyance.

"Hello!"

"Hi, I'm Anton Winter. I found your credit card."

"Okay, come on up ..." *That was months ago*, she thought.

A tap on the door made her engage the security chain. She peered out of the gap. All she could see, filling her vision, was her credit card.

"Where did you find it?"

"In a video I rented."

"How did you get my address?"

"There are ways and means."

"But wait, how did it get into a video?"

"You know the kind of video box you squeeze at the opening to get the tape out? You must have forced it into your coat pocket, or your bag at the open end, and your card slipped up inside, wedged against the case and the video tape." Anton demonstrated by putting the card in his pocket. He rammed the video he had found it in after it. He withdrew the cased cassette and squeezed the open-ended grip points on either side. The tape fell out, ejecting the card.

"Thanks anyway, but I canceled the card and got a replacement weeks ago."

There was a pause before Anton reread the back of the video case. "Makino's *Silent Samurai*. It's a cinematic masterpiece, a legend of a movie."

"I'm sorry?"

"The movie you rented. I rented it too," he said, sticking the video case in her face. "Over the period of one year, the girl in the rental shop said the two of us were the only people to rent it out, but you didn't watch it."

"How do you know?" Madison answered, feeling defensive. She wanted to slam the door in the stranger's face, but something inside of her decided against it.

"You don't DVD, then. Me neither," he said, changing the subject, a sure sign of a manipulator.

"How did you know I didn't watch it?"

"Because you would have found your card if you had."

"Must have waited too long to watch it and returned it," she replied, relaxing her stalker-phobia defenses.

Other people in the corridor got her attention, and something made her push the door and slip off the security chain. She swung her apartment door open. The sight of Anton standing there made her step back. She hadn't really noticed his attractive face during the conversation. The defensive female part of her thought he should learn that there was a difference between being inquisitive and being intrusive.

With her arms folded, she stood in a stance that would give a polar bear the chills. Again, she had forgotten her warding-off signal by not putting her fake wedding ring on. She pulled her robe together at her knees, visible through the crack in the door. This exchange took a fraction of a second.

Powerful waves of truth pounded at the sandcastle dam of her manner, exposing the truth of what she really felt. She had known him from another time and place, another existence. His forehead's shape, the way his hair slightly kinked to curl, and the glint alive in his dark eyes' core were so familiar, yet they made her uneasy. The voice of her latent femininity knew, as only a woman could, that he had defended her, before himself, against a danger long ago, and she would have bargained with her final breath to save him in a past where savagery had been more brutal, if that was possible.

"Have we met before?"

He looked caught off guard.

"I was about to ask you the same."

She couldn't be sure, but she could have sworn he was trembling.

"Here is your old card, anyway," he said, staring at her, backing away. He bumped into Mrs. Stein, who lived across the way, stooping down to fit her key into the front door. "Excuse me!"

The incessantly bad-tempered woman called after the racing man who had collided with her. The fact that her parents had named her

Phyllis led Madison to believe it was the root of her hatred toward others.

"Come back. Don't be afraid," Madison called after him.

Mrs. Stein looked up from the keyhole with an expression on her face that suggested Madison was not only the whore of Babylon but from her diminutive apartment she kept the pornographic industry of America well-stocked with footage of her immoral antics.

Madison slammed the door, then spun around to press her back against it. "What the hell was that?" she said to herself out loud. She never made advances to men she had liked for months, let alone call out after a complete stranger.

For the rest of the day, she jiggled her arms, took deep breaths, and expelled all thoughts of the stranger. Madison rearranged things in a cupboard. She sat when she found an old photo album. She delighted in memories. She thought about her family. Madison loved each captured moment, even though her family only consisted of a mother and a brother who were only hers by law. The only person she really respected was her adoptive great grandfather, an eccentric gentle giant who had helped to maintain the Northwestern Pacific Railroad. Fond family remembrances had it that he would unpick the end of a shotgun cartridge, grade the powder from the shot, then stir the black, foul-tasting explosive into his morning coffee. Maybe it explained how he lived to the age of ninety-two, in perfect health. It was also rumored no man could stand to work behind or downwind of him.

Madison would often study late-nineteenth-century photos of him showing off his strength. Sometimes, especially when she was younger, she imagined holding his mighty hand, him towering above her, while they wandered down miles of railroad track cutting through wilderness. She, in the absence of a father, or real family, would idolize her great grandfather's image, as she imagined him telling her all the secrets of his life and nature he had learned. He was probably one of the kindest men who had ever lived. His surname was Wood, and because of his constantly flushed face, the other railroad workers and foremen affectionately nicknamed him 'Redwood.' She delighted in the other story about him that wild bears would run away from him at the first glimpse of his approach, so he was sent ahead of the others to clear bears from the track.

Involuntarily, her thoughts returned to the stranger who came to her door earlier that day. At least, it got her mind off of her work for the time being. What if she told her literary agent that she couldn't stomach writing about another demented fucker? But she wouldn't. She went to her computer to write but couldn't shake trying to figure out that strong connection to Anton. *Was he really trembling?*

Chapter 4

When Anton Winter had trouble sleeping, he would retrace his steps, toil through how he got to be somebody he wasn't. He would lie on his futon, watching the fan's rotating blades lift the ceiling to fly off into the night torn away by its own mechanical tornado. He would rise up to frozen sparks, hung across the galaxy, to travel through liquid gases, the smudged, raw building-block substance of matter. The only proportionate meditation that made his past transgressions seem insignificant. When pressure built in his head that he could not identify as guilt, he'd distract himself by considering his bed's size in relation to the room, his room in relation to the apartment block where he lived to the layout of Santa Monica—a satellite map of California with a circle around the city, a large expansive atlas page of America fitting in the center of the world's countries—then to the Earth, spinning in immeasurable solar systems, part of endless space.

This was the only time the past set him free because he had killed the same breed as himself. Sometimes in his sleeping-waking boundary travels, he speculated that maybe before recorded history, way back in our origins, an alien planet of ancestors shipped all its criminally insane to a blue-green planet they called Earth, much in the same way the British sent their criminals to Australia in the 1700s.

Now, he extracted Mr. Wrenthrew from the past he confronted repeatedly despite attempts to forget, his ear to the taut strings on the grand piano's frame, tuning it to the sound of four opposingly syncopated metronomes for reasons known only to Mr. Wrenthrew. Always so well-dressed, the elderly man had made his moneyed customers and anyone who had entered his piano showroom feel inferior with his immaculate, suited manners.

One Saturday, then every other day, thereafter, Anton had, after years of odd-job, part-time services, been allowed to dust the deep, thick lacquer varnish on two hundred and nine pianos in the showroom. A job Mr. Wrenthrew had to relinquish when arthritis had finally withered his fingers into the shape of the exposed roots of Anton's favorite old tree in Central Park. The maestro, as Anton had secretly named him, had begun greeting people in the showroom with his hands in his jacket pockets, his good thumbs clipped on the outside of his pockets toward the middle, button-line corners, in a suaver, humbler approach to disguise his worsening condition. The loss of Mrs. Wrenthrew could not have compared to the loss of his ability to play his precious instrument.

The one rare occasion Mr. Wrenthrew had ever mentioned anything other than work to Anton had happened when a Catholic priest came in to look at a Steinway Upright Baby Grand. When he had left, all Mr. Wrenthrew had said to him, still looking at the door the priest had gone through, was, "They want to take over the world. That's why they ban contraception so they can outnumber everyone else."

This single statement had catapulted Anton into months of research in the central reference library. At the conclusion of his exhaustive reading sessions, Anton had practically become an expert on the Catholic faith's history, doctrines, and protocols.

How many times had he gone over the sequence of events that Saturday evening when he had forgotten his bicycle lamp for his ride home? The anger that became blind rage when he witnessed one of the three members of the local street protection racket that had spread into the once-affluent neighborhood holding Mr. Wrenthrew by the throat, crushing his airway, and pressing him against the wall of his small office at the back of the piano showroom. The old man had refused to pay, unaccustomed to such gutter-rat practices. For Anton, this wasn't his boss or even a friend. This was a mentor, who without being pompous, shared knowledge without trying. The protection racket explained the shattered window in the showroom a week earlier. They had already been putting pressure on the old man.

All Anton could remember was charging for the open office door with the U-shaped bike lock in his hand, heavy and solid. Then after a period of blankness, he noticed Mr. Wrenthrew cowering in the corner of his office while Anton still inflicted wounds on the three dead men's bodies, not registering his own stab wounds. A major artery had been punctured and was involuntarily redecorating an office wall with a speckled shade of rhesus negative red. To this night, Anton had never understood how the police believed the arthritic piano showroom owner had slain the three young men.

After Mr. Wrenthrew tightly bound Anton's wounds, he handed Anton a roll of hundred dollar bills that amounted to $40,000 from his safe. Anton's eyes stared away to the distance traumatized. Mr. Wrenthrew gently slapped his face.

"Listen to me. Disappear. Go away. Make yourself a new life. You saved me tonight. I will organize everything here."

Leaning his face into his hands, Anton sobbed. "Why are you doing this?"

"Because ... God gave me the opportunity to feel what it's like to have a son ... I don't expect you to understand this yet, but it's all much bigger than us. Spend your life reveling in mysteries ... The writer Mark Twain was born on the night Haley's Comet passed closest to Earth. Then, he died seventy-five years later, the night it passed closest to the Earth again. Just think about what I said. Now get going."

He'd been thinking about it ever since. Anton closed his eyes, rolled over, and went to sleep in the tail of a comet.

Chapter 5

Madison Paige loved spending time at the Santa Monica Library. It allowed her to do her research while she observed random people doing random things. She belonged to the world of today with its computer-controlled automobiles and DSL. She belonged to the concept of convenience. She fit into the modern way of life in the twenty-first century. She suspected that the man who had stood in her doorway did not. At the moment, neither her research or the people around her could prevent her from letting her thoughts drift to her preoccupation.

She imagined him unable to adapt to a credit card society, awkward in supermarkets, dropping coins while he tried to count them, much to the frustration of the checkout person, coupled with that of the growing line forming behind him. When hunter-gatherers roamed the plains, he would have been a warrior chieftain, sharp and deadly. In the present day, he probably lumbered around clumsily, always looking sad, as if he missed the magic of hearing wild dogs call to the spectacle of naked flame licking kindling while excitement grew for the yellowy silver full moon to climb above geometric pines.

That's why it had been so long since she had surrendered to a lover. This was the only type of man who could transport her. It wasn't about the sex; it was about the joining of two opposites who were meant to fuse together. The receiver versus the giver. The physique of womanhood—fine, perfect, rounded, smooth, close to God. The earthbound goddess, capable of creating other human beings from her insides, skin, eyes, hair, breasts, hips as pure as truth. Him more muscular, different, frighteningly irresistible fueled by a lustful instinct to procreate. Two bodies designed beyond our intelligence to fit together entirely.

Could yours be the face staring up at his?

Primitive, mechanical, pinpointing the meaning of the age-old wisdom that a great lover was not a man who had made love to a thousand women but a man who could make one woman feel loved for a thousand years. That's why she was single. That's why she lived alone.

She recollected close friends, criticizing her approach to dating. "If you sit indoors, not making an effort, the right guy for you isn't just going to knock on your front door. You've got to get out there."

Well ... maybe he just has, Madison thought to herself. She snapped out of it. Reality needed her attention. Stupid, ridiculous ... he was just another unreachable, self-centered guy.

Without lifting her head from her notes, her attention turned to a grumbling couple that stood in the A-C non-fiction aisle. She shifted her eyes a bit to peep surreptitiously and recognized the frown on the woman's face as her partner once again forgot the name of the book she'd asked him to get to save her a trip to the library.

"It's right here!" the woman said, a little too loudly, adopting a challenging tone.

"Well, there it is," he said, smirking. "Now, can we get out of here?"

They strutted off.

Figures, Madison thought.

She loved to be alone to govern the course of her career to serve all the missing children and persons. *Career*, she concentrated on the word, pulling herself back onto the single-track her life ran smoothly on.

By the time the city library had officially closed, Madison needed to affix the lights she carried in her purse above the front wheel and to the side of the back wheel of her bicycle. She lifted her leg to mount her bike when she detected that the feel of its stability was altered. She looked down.

"Oh, crap," Madison exclaimed. The rear tire was flat.

Rain spat in increasing volume. Soon, what was dry sidewalk turned into pools of water. Soaked to the skin, Madison proceeded to roll her bike home, raiding her mind for excuses as to why she hadn't brought her spare tubing. The forecast had inspired her to leave her car in her underground parking space at home, but Santa Monica's weather could foil no amount of million-dollar, weather-modeling computer technology.

The driving rain was no longer a shower by the time she had reached the Lighthouse Diner. Even though she had passed it on countless occasions, she had never been tempted to venture inside, but the storm urged her to find shelter. Her blow-dried, gelled hair was now lank, unflatteringly flattened, dripping from the downpour that her safety helmet had let in through its ventilation slats.

She slid along the deep foam, vinyl-covered bench seat, looking out on the street outside through raindrops caught on the glass of the window that refracted streetlamp beams, distorting the evening's reality. Nobody seemed interested in asking her for her order. A man at the table in front of her laid strips of dried bacon in a line on an open paper napkin. The concentration with which he arranged the rashers caught Madison's attention. The process took almost ten minutes until the bacon was wrapped as carefully as a piece of diamond jewelry in neat folds of a paper napkin.

The young man looked up, seemingly embarrassed at Madison's engrossed expressions at his to-go ritual. He returned to his own closed-in attention span after giving her a look communicating that she had exceeded the given period of time in the accepted unspoken rule of staring impolitely.

She took the hint but found herself drawn back to the way he buttered before he slowly massaged a plastic single-serving, foil-covered cube of preserve thoroughly into the porous surface of a precision-cut sourdough roll. Madison had never seen a person take a quarter of an hour to spread a roll.

He caught her again staring at his latest edible endeavor. A waitress bailed her out by breaking the Mexican standoff of him staring back at her. "Are you ready to order? Or do you want a minute?"

Madison considered how long she'd waited. The young man's appreciation for food was so humbling the diner had taken on a new meaning for her. She studied the menu. Her imagination probed each description of the different dishes like a microscope moving into the molecular structure of the protein crystals that produced the food's makeup.

Madison glanced up at the impatient waitress and put her order in. She decided on a burger with large fries, something she hadn't had in years, as she seemed to be constantly on a diet. While she was waiting for her food, sitting alone at the table, she got a sense of how lonely her present life really was. She purposely kept herself overly busy with her work so she didn't have to deal with the fact that she often felt isolated and disconnected in her personal life.

Bob Capistrano the Third, practically five years ago to the day, must have experienced a sensation of macho inferiority. That day, the financial advisor had stood surrounded by so-call friends, also in the investment consulting business, at the no-holds-barred gun show, eventually giving in to their male, goading pressure for him to buy the South-African-made pistol that he kept getting drawn to. He didn't even like guns. He especially didn't want one in his house.

Now, he stood holding it, loading the safety off in the pouring rain before the lengthy Hot Yoga Studio window. In his mind, he had already heard a stammering spate of hollow pops dulled by the downpour shattering the glass in a wavering line of shots. He pictured ostentatious yoga people, whose heads remained fixed on their frozen poses, whichever way their bodies turned, fly back compressed when a bullet struck one of them. It seemed to him that, even in death, they would be perfectly choreographed. He wasn't sure what to do: kill everyone in Jill's yoga class, then, when she was the only one left alive, he would scream "I love you" before he blew the top of his skull off, or wipe out the couples doing yoga poses, then turn the gun on himself. Bob had been known to go to great lengths in the past to prove his point. Now, unfortunately, the quiet, unassuming man who had never really been known to get angry, was just that, for the first time in his life, and he was fit to blow his top in more than one way.

He had hoped by the time he had reached the multi-story parking lot, he would have taken some deep breaths in the car, then turned around and gone home, but no, jealousy had taken him right to the edge. Now, he watched, like a hunter, as men who woke daily to apply a skin moisturizer busily twisted their bodies next to their partners through their routines. Partners who were the kind of women whose faces had aged considerably faster than the firmness of their fine-figured bodies. The thought that perhaps these were the type of couples that frequented swinger weekends in Florida hotels, taken over for that purpose, made Bob raise the gun once more, and maybe this was one of the aspects that had made Jill turn from their marriage.

On the wall across from her, Madison noticed an old, overly colorful photograph of the city she lived in, reminding her of her initial impressions of Santa Monica's burgeoning mélange that covered clusters of rolling hills. She remembered her sense of foreboding that somewhere so green, built on a collection of hills, was in fact the equivalent of a neoclassical city.

She had learned, in a musty inner-city classroom long ago, that Rome, Athens, and Jerusalem had all been built on seven hills. Santa Monica sprawled past about six and a half based on her early count and some artistic license. She had decided it would be her home, indefinitely, after an incident when it had seemed as if the sea breeze whispered through flowering wisteria plants on lattices on her tiny balcony garden: "Time like innocence once lost can never be regained."

She had curled her body to the side featly elongated on the sun lounger. Her book had opened flat on her stomach. She had slept, dreaming that the same sea breeze read the wisdom in the books, streams of linear text, to her bloated ovaries embedded in-between her hips. The tiny, bleached skull of a sacrificial goat that would, in a matter of weeks, dissolve into her chosen method of sanitary product. From then on, she had supposed that perhaps every flower Californians called the Bird of Paradise—because it looked like the head of an exotic bird of plumage—eventually pointed toward Santa Monica to pay homage to the misty domain of the sea breeze philosophers. But no one had noticed or knew, except her.

Turning from the loud photograph of Santa Monica, the sea breeze blocks away dominated by the petrichor, Madison caught sight of the strange, bacon-wrapping boyish man across the rain-swept parking lot. He looked up from controlling his bike, pushing it toward the Hot Yoga Studio by holding the handlebars' counter with one hand. Madison did a double take when she saw him throw down his ride to run, stooped down with his arms held out rigid and moving in a zigzag formation. She let out a sound of amusement when he leaped back, like a dancing aboriginal person, from another figure in the rain.

"Wow, he was weirder than I thought!" Madison whispered, looking down at the table at a flaccid low-density, foam-rubber pancake breached on every side by paper containers full of calorific dairy spread and synthetic maple syrup that the waitress had placed before her without her noticing.

Madison's unheard comment that "this was not her order" was proceeded by the loud sound of gun shots that shattered the west-facing windows. In such a situation, Madison had often imagined she would drop to the floor to crawl over to the nearest available firearm and defend the innocent. At least, that was what she had done during courtroom dilemma training. During a simulation, a defendant, who was really a tactical cop, had snatched a courtroom cop's gun, then had proceeded to blast the prosecution stand. Madison had lost fifteen points in the exercise because she had crawled over to a supposedly deceased courtroom cop to pull out his genuinely loaded department-issued firearm to retaliate to the blanks with live rounds.

Now, confronted by the real thing, she sat in shock, staring out into the stormy night. While her now dry hair was Medusa-excitable, everyone else in the diner had screamed, revising or altogether creating original obscenities as they dropped for cover. Madison pulled herself into action when she saw one figure through the sodium-streetlamp-charged raindrops squatting down in a black, long coat, the type suit-wearers put on in the city. With his hands clasped over his head, the bacon-wrapper lay upward over his fallen bicycle.

After carefully stepping over hiding diner customers, Madison ran into the stormy night. She reached the boyish man and bent down to perfunctorily examine his body for bullet holes. A wound bled, diluted by rain, on his face. He gargled, stretching to reach something lying in a puddle by his bike. The back of his pants leg was torn around another cut that dripped pink waterdrops down from his leg.

The neatly-folded rashers of bacon soggy in the napkin lay away from the bike in the puddle, which also contained the reversed reflection of a moving neon sign from a nearby shop front that read 'Doggy Style.' It had been a bone of contention, so to speak, with the Santa Monica Chamber of Commerce for some time. Especially the flickering graphic that propelled the rear end of the upper, mounted dog toward that of the lower, standing animal. Even though it was just a harmless dog-grooming emporium, its sign's controversial nature had caused locals to deliberate.

Madison squinted in disbelief at the copulating canines reflected in the pool of rain. She read the words glowing in the puddle, and, despite the seriousness of the situation, she found herself laughing.

"Um! I can think of better ways to spend the evening ... Can you get my rashers, please?" the boyish man asked with a peculiar voice.

Madison was so taken aback by his intense way of speaking that she stood staring down at him.

"Go the other way. Avoid him. He might still want to end his life," he rattled off, as if this kind of thing was a regular occurrence. He lifted his head awkwardly, lying across the bicycle. "That's what you were laughing at," the boyish man acknowledged, noticing a corner of the neon-reflected sign in the puddle. "Are you a lawyer?" he snapped.

"No, but close. In that area," Madison answered reluctantly, not understanding where this conversation was going.

"You work with the dead, then? You are too casual," he spouted.

The shooter sobbed.

Madison crossed over to the squatting, distressed man in the woolen, long coat.

"I wouldn't do that! Can you help me up?" the boyish man, crucified on his bike, called out.

She ignored him, focused on a shuffling sound as Bob got to his feet. "It's okay. I know some great people who will get you out of this." Madison's voice sounded unconvincingly feeble even to her own ears.

"You don't know anything. Damn it all!" Bob exhaled completely, miserably defeated.

Madison closed her eyes, anticipating what he meant to do. She settled her imploring eyes back on the boyish man for support, but he had crossed his arms to shield his head. Her gaze returned to Bob.

She was glad he had put the machine gun down. Instead, he pulled a two-piece resin equator-round grenade from his coat pocket, and oddly, she found the grenade less threatening. He slid his finger into the ring pin. "I'm sorry," Bob apologized, unable to control himself.

"Wait!" Madison screamed, elevating her pitch and gasping to control her breath. She couldn't think coherently as adrenaline shot through her entire system. A numb tingling filled her toes and fingers.

"Bob! What's wrong, Bob? I love you!" a woman's voice called out.

"Shut up, just shut up, Jill. It's too late. I know everything," her husband, Bob, answered. He shook, shuffling around, almost collapsing into himself until his breaking voice made him cover his face with his hands.

"What the hell do you mean? He is my yoga instructor. Your jealousy has gone too far this time. You know we've got too much going on for this."

"Put it down, and the two of you will still have a chance of working this out," the boyish man called out to Bob, with as much compassion for the situation as the two of them had.

Surprisingly enough, Bob's hand, holding the grenade, dropped.

"I'm not that way inclined, sir," the instructor called out, as tactfully as possible, from behind Bob's wife.

"What do you mean?" Bob called back in the pouring rain, regaining some anger.

"He means, that scientifically, as a species, we are all referred to as 'Homo erectus.' He is saying he is more than comfortable with that label, Bob," the boyish man interjected.

"Oh Christ! What have I done?"

"You're guilty of being human, Bob, that's all," the boyish man added.

Bob's wife ran forward while Bob slipped the grenade into his coat pocket. "I love you, you idiotic romantic fool." She sighed, holding him.

"It wasn't real anyway. I'm in the shit with the diner, though, and I punched that guy lying on his bike."

"Don't worry. When the cops get here, we'll work it out," Madison said. She went over to the boyish man to pull him up off his bike, which his jacket was trapped in, preventing him from standing up. "What's your name? I am Madison by the way."

"My name is Mat," the boyish man yelled out.

Instead of accepting Madison's help, he pulled her on top of him and with amazing strength and skill, flipped her, the bike and himself over, so that she was at the bottom of the pile.

"Get off me!" she cried.

"So, you took the dummy grenade out of the display case in the living room?" Bob's wife asked.

"No, from the metal case in the safe."

"Oh, Bob, you are so forgetful. You don't remember what you told me to remind you," she muttered.

Madison gasped.

"I saw the ring pin glisten in the light and snag around the guy's coat pocket. He accidentally pulled the grenade pin out," the boyish man confirmed, still protecting Madison.

In days to come, the local papers described the incident as one of the most tragic in Santa Monica's history.

It wasn't until the inquest weeks later that Madison saw Mat again. They went to Le Jardin, a coffee boutique and bookshop on the opposite hill across the valley from Madison's neighborhood. Spring sunsets ignited the windows of hilltop condos across from the valley and the apartment complex Madison lived in to the south, giving a view from the northern coffee shop of the built-up area on the hill five miles across the valley. It took on the appearance of a smoky, twilight palace filled with reserves of gold that shone, supernaturally, from the windows. Its spectacle made Madison doubt she lived there.

Madison pushed Mat's wheelchair to a vacant table. "They took down the emergency boards from the yoga studio to put in new glass today," the boyish man said while they attended to their coffee requirements.

They swapped a jug of half-and-half for a squeezy bottle filled with honey, shaped like an opaque bear.

"I was shocked to see you in the courthouse in a ..."Madison felt too uncomfortable to say the word.

"A wheelchair," he finished for her.

"Well, I've always been lazy, so if I can keep it up, I can get pushed around for the rest of my life, and to think I was sick of people pushing me around before," he continued, highly amused by his own offbeat humor that made Madison feel uncomfortable. "I'm not so bothered about walking. It's if I can still paint and draw."

"Did the tragedy affect you psychologically, you know haunt you, afterwards in any way?" Madison asked, treading on conversational eggshells.

Mat changed the subject. "Bob Capistrano the Third! Jeez! What a name. The clumsy oaf I call him was my, well I say it without proof, perhaps he was my only living relative. I had been watching him for weeks. That night, I almost got the courage to knock on his front door to discuss his family tree. When you're an orphan, anybody with a drop of the same blood will do. I followed him out to the diner, then I watched him go out to the dance school."

"I know ..." Madison replied compassionately.

"What?" Mat responded, his smile slipping a little with a pinched expression.

"About the orphan thing," Madison continued.

"Really?"

"Yep. Tomorrow, tomorrow, maybe tomorrow and all that." Madison sighed heavily.

"So, you know how difficult it is to track anyone down. Agencies go out of their way to stop you. All I knew was Santa Monica," he exaggeratedly announced, waving his hands like a conductor.

"Um, not much to go on." Madison adjusted her position in her seat, bursting to ask him more about the wheelchair.

"So now, as you can imagine, it really sucks that I have to sue my dead 'possible' cousin," Mat announced, almost bragging.

"What?" Madison was so taken aback by what she had just heard that her facial expression turned to anger.

"Relax, it's what I do for a living," Mat responded.

"What? Law?" Madison responded while still trying to digest Mat's announcement.

"No, I'm a ..."—he put his hand to his chin and scratched it—"I don't know what the job title is. I'm best described as a professional suer. I give a whole new meaning to the expression, 'you've got a mind like a suer.'"

"Oh, I see, you're basically phlegm in society's lungs. You're a con man," Madison responded. What she had just learned disgusted her.

"Yes! Incidentally, the guy who invented the television set was called Logie. And you are calling me a loogie? No, no, how rude! There is no skill in that. No!" He pulled back his shirt collar to undo the buttons. "Nineteen eighty-nine burns, from falling on a broken sidewalk on 51st Street, New York. Settlement $97,000, paid in full. When you're an orphan, you're hard to trace. The records are kind of vague. A year later, Chicago, the Windy City." He pealed back the opposite shoulder of his shirt to reveal a dizzying scar. "I filed for damages from Macpherson and Sons Construction Company under a different name, a faulty, badly affixed hard hat area sign took flight, almost slicing off my shoulder. Out-of-court settlements: $86,000. Florida 1994 under another assumed alias a defective bug fogger I purchased." He lifted his shirt to reveal his stomach crisscrossed with deep, lacerated skin graft tissue. "It blew up my bungalow, setting me on fire in the process. Forty-five percent of my body burnt. I even managed to incorporate the old neck burn from New York into that one. A quarter of a million settlement, superstore chain and manufacturer." He smiled, genuinely proud of himself. "A simple con man fakes his accidents, limps without pain, whereas I, the master, am part illusionist, manipulator of inanimate objects, and I am an expert on anatomy. I train my body to heal." He stopped talking when he looked at Madison's expression. She looked at him how a fish does out of water.

"So, you travel across America, amassing a small fortune, to look for ...," she said, grasping for the right choice of words, "your long-lost family by self-mutilating and maiming yourself."

"You could see it like that. I like to think of myself as a modern form of a claim jumper. A jutting curbstone ... a pavement pothole are pure nuggets of opportunity to me."

"You're possibly the sickest individual I've ever met. And you're telling absolute strangers about your conquests? How do you know I won't go back into that courthouse and blab on you?"

"Because I am in a wheelchair from catching shrapnel with my spinal cord to save your ass and your traditional, altruistic upbringing, going back to the Quakers or whatever, will prevent you."

Madison stalled like a single-prop engine aircraft in the air. She dove about 700 feet, then regained some stability. "So, what did they say at the hospital?"

"Oh! I wasn't really listening. I could just hear settlement figures coming from Bob's worried estate attorneys. I am working on the angle that blood tests will prove that I'm his sole beneficiary. I tried to stop him but was injured in the process. It might be advantageous for his attorneys to award me his last will and testament, instead of going for a drawn-out battle in the courtroom," Mat continued, boasting about his schemes.

"You're more like a mercenary than a claim jumper. I never believed people like you could exist," Madison replied, looking away in complete disgust. It was hard for her to fathom how far people would go for monetary gain. It reinforced her cynical view of humanity.

"There's even a tribute website for people in my line of work. You remember the woman, way back when, who burned herself on a fast food chain hot drink? She got an out-of-this-world settlement. I wake up in the morning for one reason and one reason alone, and that's to come up with a lusher like that one. So, am I emotionally distraught by what happened? No, I'm positively elated. This is my 'caution ... the contents of this cup are extremely hot' wisher. I'll retire on this one."

With that, Madison got up to leave. "Well, it's been good seeing you again."

"You liar, you cannot stop lying either, can you?"

"Look, I am flattered you risked your life and limb for me, but it was obviously a good day's work." Madison started to rush out of the coffee boutique.

Mat followed her, walking as fast as she did unhindered. "I get it. You're insulted. You really thought I was a Christ, knight-in-shining-armor type guy. You wanted me to prove I cared about you."

Madison stopped mid-sentence because he had blown his cover. His ability to use his legs was up to about 100% effectiveness.

"Ummmm, don't you think you might be jeopardizing your claim by dancing about miraculously cured?"

"Oh no! I only needed to go to the hearing in that thing. I stole it from the hospital anyway. I will have both legs in a cast when the time is right. It's just going to hurt, like a son of a bitch, when I push those fragments of metal under the skin of my lower back."

"Right, that's enough. I'm out of here. You're unbelievable." Mat's statement repelled her. She lurched away from him as quickly as she could to clear her head.

"Oh, come on, I risked getting out of the chair for you," Mat yelled from a distance.

"Fuck off!" she called after him. A sudden feeling of cold heaviness expanded within her. She had never said that to anyone before assertively, especially in a public place, in a real-life situation. She tripped and fell headlong into a rival coffee shop's outside tables.

The man and woman who sat at one of the tables jumped back alarmed.

Madison lay on the floor. Blood trickled from her head. She grabbed her head, trying to get up but lost her balance in the process.

Mat caught up with her. "You see, you're getting the hang of it already. It's almost addictive. I would go in low, for about twenty-five K, to start with. Then, I would check out your shoes' manufacturer," the boyish man whispered seriously.

Madison slowly opened her eyes. Her vision was out of focus. She could make out Anton's shape, gawking down at her before she fainted.

Madison lay on Anton Winter's couch with an aquamarine gel, cold compress wrapped in a bandage, draped across her brow.

"I'll call you tomorrow. Yes, I'll make sure a doctor looks at her. Bye," Anton told the woman he had sat with at the café before Madison's grand entrance. The front door closed.

She pretended to be asleep. He strolled into the room. Though she was desperate to open her eyes, she faithfully played opossum. Madison was convinced she felt his eyes crawling across every square inch of her skin and covered body so intently it became almost an internal inspection. Something dropped onto the carpet with a recoiling thump. Her guesses featured various objects, then settled on a knife. A cold blade's point stuck into the soft skin of her throat. His rasping voice revealed a man who seemed to be at conflict with himself.

He told her, "One scream would give me the reason I need to give you a Colombian necktie." Once he described it, her body grew rigid picturing her tongue being pulled down through a tear under her jaw.

The darkness closed in on her. She leaped up and bolted upright on the couch. Anton jumped back in fright.

"Where am I?" she asked, knowing full well where she was.

Anton held a wooden-handled kitchen knife in one hand and a partially peeled apple in the other. "What's wrong?" he asked.

"Nothing. A bad memory, induced by a concussion, I guess."

"There are some things I've got to ask you," he said.

"The platform is yours," she forced out, rubbing her neck muscles.

"Who was that guy you were with at Glenducies?"

"Where?"

"The coffee shop where you swan dove into the table I was sitting at."

"Oh! To tell you the truth, I have no idea ... Secondly?"

"What?"

"You wanted to ask me more than one question."

"Did I? How did you know that? Okay, whatever! Did you feel anything? Peculiar sensations in your doorway ... the night we met?"

"When ...? Oh, the night you knocked on my door? Was that you?" she lied. Secretly, she had driven around the city the next day, looking for him. She had even considered searching for him in Santa Monica's bars and restaurants. "No, I never really gave it much thought," she added.

"Good. That's good."

"Why do you ask?"

"Oh! It's nothing. I've just had some second thoughts, some nagging doubts about a prior engagement after our chance encounter."

"Wow, you're on the verge of getting married. Congratulations!" she feebly exclaimed, failing to disguise her disappointment miserably.

"Not imminent. A month next Saturday," he corrected, expelling any misunderstandings.

Before she could stop herself, Madison's mouth involuntarily exercised her submissive alter ego. "So, there's still time for an independent woman of the world to fuck some sense into you, before it's too late."

"I beg your pardon?" Anton recoiled, almost falling over.

"I can't believe I just said that," Madison replied.

"No, neither can I."

"Don't you think the country is becoming more dysfunctional because people never follow through with what they really want to do?" she blurted out, hoping to regain his distracted attention.

"Most definitely." Anton nodded his head. He still seemed absentminded. He ran to the basin, swiped the faucet, and filled his cupped hands with water to douse his flushed face. Anton then turned to confront Madison again. "I'm sorry. I just had the urge to—"

"Think nothing of it. I was hardly overtly suppressing the opportunity to stop being promiscuous. I hope you can always keep your urges under control," Madison responded, trying to keep her emotions under control.

"What do you mean?" Anton replied in a slow, low firm voice, fixing a stare at her.

"Your inability to distinguish between desire and destruction. The look on your face, I wasn't sure if you wanted to drag me into the bedroom," Madison remarked. "What's wrong? Don't you know how to react when your dirty little secret is out in the open? Seriously, Anton, if you want me to help you, you are going to have to learn how to open up to me. For instance, when you watch a woman's backside or look at her dressed, you're doing so in an unsexual way. You are, in fact, imagining how the saw will cope with the tissue and bone, the curves of her hips, how you can cleanly bag it, then dispose of it without a trace." Madison's position altered on the couch, like a bad edit. Anton's body movements and expressions froze. He took a moment to compose himself.

"Are you okay?" Madison asked, looking up from a nasty graze of her arm.

"Just a bit of sun stroke, I guess," Anton fumed, bristling.

"In Santa Monica, that's a first," she replied, leaning into the hard edge in her voice and engrossing herself in scrutinizing the gritty deposits apparent in her injury. "I think we're attracted to each other because we both fear our own twisted expectation of others."

He stared at her as if she were an edit in an amateur short film.

"You see, conscience makes us all a victim of our own capabilities. For all I know, you could harbor dark, grudging fantasies of debauchery."

He stared, and stared, but she did not flinch. "I always imagine, if I let go, let down my guard, someone close to me will want to snuff me out, because I'm happy ... Pew! I've never been so intense with a stranger before."

"Maybe, we are not such strangers. Maybe we are perfectly adjusted to a warped society, obsessed with the negative. I fulfill your needs, you mine." Madison had moved closer to Anton. She wanted to touch him, but she resisted the temptation. Madison noticed Anton had missed a patch of stubble on his chin when he had shaved. She could smell a cologne but wasn't sure if it was his or his female companion's from the coffeeshop.

"But, how could we tell from the beginning?"

She wondered if Anton had also not noticed that during the conversation they had gotten closer and were staring into each other's eyes. "But it's so unhealthy," Madison remarked.

"What is?" Anton interjected.

"You are making me think and speak in ways I have never enjoyed until now. Let's make a pact. No matter how much we want the other, to disappoint the other, we won't let it happen and we will have a duration of time to explore the depths of our respective illnesses. Me the victim, you the victim of your weaknesses, so that we conscientiously seal each other's fate." Madison found the tension unbearable. It was hard for her to keep her focus. She couldn't understand why this awkward conversation made her more attracted to him.

"Will there be any sexual strangulation practices?" Anton asked, his eyes sparkling and gleaming.

"No, none," Madison replied shocked about where this conversation was going.

Anton's face dropped in disappointment. "Your suffering will be explicitly exquisite."

"I still cannot believe this conversation is taking place," Madison exclaimed.

"Neither can I."

They got closer to kiss, then POW ...

Madison stared out of the window, absentminded. Using the computer screen for so long had made her eyes ache. She had been typing out the story for over nine hours. She wasn't sure if she was happy with what she had written or not.

"Maybe I should give fiction a miss," she muttered to herself. She giggled, picturing her image as that of a Santa Monica Cartland-style dame, who attended media events in blood-spattered garments, carrying life-like severed heads made by a Hollywood theatrical department. She scrolled to the scenes where Bob shot up the dance studio. She studied her fiction carefully.

Um! It needs work, she thought.

She decided to use her own name for the female character, then she would change it when she found one more suitable. She skipped over some parts of the story again, switched off the screen, shut down the disc drive, and left her apartment.

On the walk up to her building's roof, the post office billboard that always came to mind haunted her. The faces of grinning children, shown one after another, feared missing. Some dated far back and loomed in her recollection. Two or three times a week, she would stare at their photos. Passersby would politely look away. Sometimes, they realized she was crying.

In the distance, the outline of palm trees pushed up beside timber power cable poles that in low cloud cover or dense fog crackled, suggesting to her a hidden, mysterious world lay beneath the ordinary layer of every day. She wished she had the power to control the electricity to make it seek out the lost children, beyond the realms of normal human comprehension. It could move through buildings, covering cities at the speed of light. Go from Santa Monica to Boston, bringing to life appliances and necessities. It could if it knew their faces and voices find them in seconds.

Chapter 6

Martin Thompson stood in the alleyway off of Third Street Promenade in Santa Monica. He lifted a super-sized burger chain cup he had found in the trash from his waist level, did up his zipper, then placed the lid back on the cup. From the available options, in a selection of unused dimple indicators, he pushed in 'other' instead of coffee, tea, juice, or soda. He tossed the cup of warm urine into a nearby dumpster next to the parked surveillance car his partner sat in as he surveilled the alley. Only last week, someone had committed suicide in the alleyway, and they were still trying to figure out the Jane Doe. Despite seeing a ton of dead bodies in his time as an officer, the young girl's face smacked him behind the eyes like a sinus problem ever since. She was still there in the alley in her yellow sundress, wearing at least seven strands of necklaces and the highest heals he'd seen in a while ... in mauve no less ... despite the alley being empty. He blinked his eyes, hoping to rid himself of her image.

Martin turned toward the car. Eddie was struggling to do up the top button of his shirt.

"I hate lukewarm stakeouts like this. I feel like a gypsy, Eddie," Martin complained through the open car window.

"Plenty has happened in this alley. You know that despite a lot of it being people masturbating, junkies, or drug deals. And if you're gonna complain about a glamorous profession like ours, then you're just plain spoiled," Eddie answered, still struggling to do up the collar of his shirt.

"I'm not sure that suicide was junkie-related, seemed sadder somehow like a lost soul who headed here and had no breaks," he speculated, his eyes dulled. He scrunched his face at the site of Eddie munching. "You've got to cut back on the junk foods," Martin said between bites of the last weekday-bargain cheeseburger that they had bought in bulk to last the night shift. He winced thinking of all those who'd taken a Greyhound to LA metropolitan to make it, away from intolerable families, who didn't have the wits needed to outrun smarm.

"With a partner like you, I have to do a lot of comfort eating."

"Hey, Eddie, it is true. When you were in heaven and God was handing out chins, you thought he said gins and asked for a double."

"Yeah, and if wit was shit, you would be constipated."

"Not a bad response. I would have expected something more original, like are you sponsored by PrepH?"

Eddie ignored him.

"No, why?" Martin prompted rhetorically in a dumb way.

"No, why?" Eddie muttered, dragging out the question.

"Because you're a pain in the ass."

"Next time maybe." Eddie looked at his watch. "Look, we were so engrossed in our stimulating conversation, it's time to go home."

"No, it's fine. I put us down for a double," Martin said.

"You're kidding, right?" Eddie replied, rapidly blinking.

"No, I need some overtime to pay for that new pool pump I just had installed. You're always bitching about money, so I took it upon myself to book us in for double duty. I have to finish this and meet Miss Paige in the morning," Martin continued, knowing full well his partner wasn't happy with his decision to put them down for a double shift.

She opened the top box in her spare room first thing in the morning, having finished listening to the entire cosmetic surgeon's recording and having done some more research on a specific child murder. Kate Glass, only seven years old, had been missing for a year. A neighbor, only a few houses down the street, had found her body in the log pile, logs pressing down on her from every angle. She opened the file and pulled it out. This box only had a few files in it, bodies that had been found, despite the killers remaining on the loose and likely feeding their hunger for taking out their depraved state of being on innocents. She added some of her notes to the file. She hoped she'd still find the killer.

Kate was only two years younger than the neighbor's girl, Mila Brown, who used to come over and show her pictures to Madison when they were growing up. Madison had still been living at home with her adopted mother and brother. Mila would draw them and get so excited when Madison would post the ones she gave to them on the fence that separated their homes. Especially since Madison was five years older than her. Often a tough crowd to please.

Madison had decided to leave them on the fence ever since the day she had turned on the news to see a picture of Mila reported missing. The disconnected newscasters' voices sounded like they were far in a tunnel as she doubted their report that Mila had been missing since the day before. Madison hadn't seen Mila the day before, but Mila didn't stop by every day, so nothing stood out to Madison as strange.

That night when she looked over at Mila's house, her parents were meeting with streams of people trying to help find her. She had run over to help. The search had turned up nothing. Within a short period of time, the Browns moved, too pained to stay in the same house without Mila. Everywhere they looked reminded them of her. When Madison moved, she left Mila's fading drawings on the fence.

She closed the lid on the top box. An enduring sense of loyalty—formed from an inbred duty ethic that bordered on obsessive—kept Madison from disposing of the cardboard boxes that towered above her in her spare room. Each box contained files on how a living, breathing person had been discovered butchered, strangled, or shot indoors, outdoors, afloat, above or below ground. Each file represented a life's demise that remained, as yet, unsolved by one of California's homicide divisions. Her idealistic notion that she would eventually get around to reducing the stacks of unsolved investigations into a compact set of computer discs that would easily fit into a transparent, plastic case the size of a pint of strawberries, on her study desk, remained a task she felt at odds with. The task sounded practical, but somehow it reclassified the unavenged homicide from pending to a more permanent dormant stage.

While they were still an obstacle, they were solid, unfinished puzzles that begged resolution. Whenever she contemplated the clutter in her apartment, a glimmer of an internal, self-imposed commandment reverberated from the back of her busy schedule. More idealistically, she delayed downscaling her spare room in the remote, fantastic hope that she might actually solve each box of unsolved, violent crime.

The lunar planet emitted its solitary light in the night sky's choking darkness. A chromium, circular island—fixed at a rejuvenating tilt—beamed from the black heavens ... the only possible cosmic features of an all-seeing deity peering down onto responding emergency vehicles wailing toward some far-off calamity.

The female's torso took on the look of satin in the moonlight's pale glow. The waste ground, where consumer durables were dumped, should have scared her away, but she was too daring this one time as he grinned thinking about her decision. Most who had lived in the area stayed away since being teenagers, scared straight by neighborhood discussions and national campaigns about staying safe, walking in pairs, and avoiding dumping grounds for one thing.

Why hadn't she stuck with her preferred route, the extra-mile walk, instead of crossing the untidy, leveled sand dunes where blinded, smashed television sets had landed for the sake of her daughters who had often accompanied her? Lost her grip on her senses. Toppled strollers—their infant passengers bipedal efficient by now—laid here by whomever wanted their wheels for whatever reason, even though the damaged sign warned that the dumping of trash could result in a multi-thousand dollar fine. Traditionally, migrant workers dumped their unplaceable items that the trash collector rejected. Retired washing machines blotched the few square acres—an open-air museum of domesticities' development—because even somewhere like Santa Monica had its own version of the wrong side of town.

Now, her skin was still warm while the leather brush was dipped in the yogurt container that he used to collect her blood.

Lines of bloody artwork swept beneath the arch of her ribcage below her heavy breasts, taking shape. She was a housewife, a mother of two children, a homemaker; therefore, her killer considered this the most appropriate place to discard her body. She wouldn't ever see her children who would miss her at home. When the blood painting was completed, her killer packed away all the necessary materials he needed to leave sunrise to reveal to the world the sick horror of his spitefully, delightful blasphemy.

Madison sat in her car on the road that led to the underground parking in her apartment complex. She applied a greasy film of lipstick to her naturally full lips. A tap on the car window made her jump. She smudged a line of the cosmetic up at an angle on her cheekbone. Madison lowered the car window and snapped, "Good morning."

"Morning, sorry I startled you," Martin Thompson said.

"Not a problem," Madison answered, tearing open a moist tissue foil packet to rub off the wayward lipstick.

Martin stood up straight, taking in the area Madison lived in. She wondered what he thought of it, but he'd keep that close to his chest. He put his hands in his pocket and leaned forward to put his head back into the open car window. "You know, no matter how hard you try, you can never improve something that is already perfect."

"Compliments so early in the morning. I should keep you around."

"I'm just on my way to a local homicide. I just stopped off to see if you wanted to lend some input."

"I doubt I would get it back. And, I was on my way to do some research. I've got a deadline on a book I am writing."

"That's great. I can give you some ideas. You can give me some ideas."

Madison thought for a while, hoping Martin would leave. When he didn't budge, she capitulated. "Okay! I'll follow you in my car."

Madison pulled up behind Martin. She looked to her right through the torn-back wire fence at the jump-suited forensic team, tiptoeing around an obscured object. The same feeling she always got in the pit of her stomach fluttered down past her pelvis. It told her there was a body at the center of their attention. She could never get used to it.

"The world of people is a poorer place than we would want to believe it is," she muttered, rising from the car seat.

Martin walked briskly beside her, almost in step with her. His protective manner was just about to smother Madison into visible annoyance when he lost his footing in a rut.

"Fuck!" he yelped through tightening teeth and lips until his clenched jaw high-pressure suppressed any further revisions to the pain of straining his ankle. He stood balanced on one foot, rotating the other foot from the ankle.

"I never knew you used early police acronyms, though I suspect there's only one corpse," Madison said, walking on.

The bruised look that Martin gave her confused her. He substituted the look so quickly to anguish, staring down at his injured ankle, that she questioned if she'd ever seen the momentary look.

He hobbled behind Madison. "Early police what?" he asked. She detected in his dismissive tone that he was intrigued with her complicated way of thinking but recoiled from the slight hint of a superiority complex.

"When Scotland Yard was founded in nineteenth-century London, and couples were found murdered in a possible crime of passion, the first detectives would write in their reports that the deceased were 'found under carnal knowledge,' which was later abbreviated to F.U.C.K."

His cunning smile instigated her.

"What, Martin?"

"Nothing," he said, shaking his head and averting his eyes. "Just my fucking luck that someone else got laid before they died while I'm dealing with a strained ankle and walking up to a dead women's body with you."

Madison smirked. She turned her head and saw the dead woman's body. Her inner radar had already identified it as such. She approached. She had to resist the temptation to become lost in conspiring sea breezes that twisted their peaceful simplicity across the newly established psychological battlefield. She was about to, as she always did, take a stranger's death personally. She knew the procedure but never the outcome. Something irreplaceable was about to break off inside her, never to be returned, because even bringing a killer to justice, with the outcome of a rare death penalty, was not enough to make her whole again, to bring the victim back.

Madison stared at the lifeless body, slumped back on a mound. A daubed, red design had dried tight on the murdered woman's fleshy stomach.

"Get all available help to go around tatty parlors and henna tents down on the boardwalk. I wouldn't be surprised if this lowlife made a living out of this." Madison bent down to take a close look. The fearful stare in the dead woman's open eyes leaped into Madison's.

She stood up quickly, disguising her distress.

Martin pulled out the piece of cardboard that had been spiked through the woman's wrist like an office memo.

Her wince didn't go unnoticed. "Frozen at the epicenter of life's meaning, if the purpose is not to love, then there is nothing," she read from the hastily torn flap of cardboard. The writing was abrupt, but something about it seemed familiar.

"Jesus, you can tell whoever did this loved her very much," said Martin.

"No, I think they are referring to the love of killing in general, not specifically the love of someone," Madison replied, modifying Martin's attempts at trying to get a cheap laugh.

"Maybe we are looking for an Asian or someone who is into Far Eastern religions," Martin threw in.

"No," Madison interrupted. "Oriental dragons have five toes. The Occidental dragon has four," she added, pointing down to the blood-brush-stroked feet of the illustration. "I would be inclined to go with the notion that this is the beginning of a series with this one being our marker. At this early stage, I have to say, I cannot see how she died."

Chapter 7

"Detective Thompson ... Oh! Yeah! About time! What did you come up with? Okay, if you won't tell me now, when? Yep! I'll be there."

As he put down the receiver, Madison absorbed his irritation, registering the stressful fact that the entire exchange was snapped out in a single breath and her "Hey, Martin" and "Eleven" had blipped by like tiny gnats she pictured he had swiped at on his end. Madison hung up like her cell was too hot to hold.

She sped past the open doorway of her spare room but stopped for a second to look at the pile of boxes. Something shone at her, the way a lighthouse beam blinks at the percussion point of its turning. It was an elephant-ear shaped tear of missing cardboard from the lid flap of one of the boxes. She shuddered, dismissing it for being too ridiculous that one of her boxes was evidence.

She stopped off at the 'Rainbow Farm' for a granola bar and some groceries, then drove out of Santa Monica to the Pacific Coast Highway, going north on the winding road. She reached the part of the highway where she always ended up. Even though in the past she had been determined to carry on to see if any other observation pull-off point grabbed her. Pulling over, she turned up the CD player, swung open the car door, rushed to the cliff edge, and let the music fuse behind her induced by the swelling ocean into a single medium of peace. The process of how she put together the killing of Suzanne Gonzales unfurled how a rolled-up flag would, against the sound of "Splendid Harmony," enhanced by the heavy mega system bass of the thunderous Pacific hammering the cliff face far below her.

The sound of Martin pulling up behind her made her close down her gentle, brown eyes to block out the intrusion for a bit longer. Martin's crunching footsteps on sandstone chips stopped beside her.

"So, what's with all the secrecy?" Martin asked arrogantly, void of a shred of tolerance. He backed away cautiously though when the trails glistening down Madison's face caught his attention.

"It's no secret that I cannot do this anymore," she mumbled with a sniff.

"What's happened?" Martin inquired unconvincingly, softening his approach.

"Nothing has happened. It's been happening all the time. I have been prying into the private lives and deaths of the deceased," Madison blurted out, folding her arms to cradle a shiver from the brisk sea air while at the same time, defensively warding off any of Martin's attempts to embrace her. "I'm sick, ill. I'm losing myself. I feel closer, sympathize more with the dead. I'm not interested in the living anymore. I feel like ..." Madison tried to retain the buildup of emotion that grew heavy behind her eyes, but it got free. "I'm dead already."

Coerced by Martin's empathy toward her, Madison got back into the car. Her colleague switched off the radio and produced a flask from his jacket to carefully pour her a drink.

"You see how much better you are at this than me? I call you out to give you my opinion, and you pack a picnic," Madison stammered between chest-crushing sobs.

"Here, it's clean," Martin whispered, sounding almost sincere.

Madison took a handkerchief from his hand.

"Look, it's pretty normal to form an empathy for those who are helpless to demand justice ..." he continued.

His sudden rush of sensitivity surprised her, so she looked up to see a faint look of surprise edge out his usual 'I'm a bad ass' expression.

"But it's work. That's what we do," he continued.

"But you have a coroner at Santa Monica headquarters. Why do you still need me?"

"I need two opinions before I can proceed with my investigations ... Look, if you don't like being a freelance consultant, I can get the forms we need for you to become the official property of the Santa Monica Police Department."

"So you think this is about whether I can get a pension? Fuck you!" Madison roared, her eyes cold and hard.

She threw open the car door to make her way back to the cliff edge railing.

Martin sprung from the seat behind her. She could feel him trying to keep up with her.

"Okay, Clever clogs. I kept you on, so to speak, because I not only value your opinion above that jerk coroner McBride, but because I happen to be completely and uncontrollably in love with you. So, you got it out of me. Well done. And you don't think you would make a good detective."

Madison charged back toward the car.

"Hey, Martin!" she said in a low, even voice, reaching into the car. "I'm sorry I swore at you."

Martin was such a traditional dickhead he couldn't let it slide. "Wow, no colleague involved in the department has ever spoken to me like that before, but due to the circumstances, I'm prepared to call this a private incident."

"Thanks, I appreciate that," Madison humbly replied, knowing full well it was all part of the weird game they played. Her outburst relieved the pressure-cooker in her chest and stomach, so she apologetically climbed back into her car.

Martin said, "Do you ..." He searched for the words like he'd stumbled on a difficult crossword puzzle.

"Do I what?" she asked, peering at him. Her phone played a digital classical remix. She answered it and tossed the phone to Martin. "It's your wife." She smiled for no other reason than her voice was husky from crying but could be interpreted another way. She always got revenge, somehow, somewhere. She knew full well Martin was aching to have her, but she put it out of her mind, filed under repulsive.

"You couldn't get me on my phone. No, my phone is in my car. I'm in Madison's car," he said with a guilty dryness in his explanation that was followed by an uncomfortable silence.

Then, opportunity handed Madison a full magazine of bullets, if by any chance she should need them at a later date.

Martin finished talking and passed Madison her phone with his thumb on the 'end' button.

"There's three rings in marriage," he joked.

Was he trying to disperse the heat in the car? She focused completely on him.

"The engagement ring, the wedding ring, and the suffering," Madison said to herself in unison with Martin's rendition. She knew with absolute certainty that the Thompson household was a suspicious, unhappy one. Probably due to some past indiscretion, perpetrated by Martin that Mrs. T had unpacked. Some remnants of her old self took over.

She leaned forward to pull a packet of tissues from her open purse that rested on the floor of the passenger seat between Martin's feet. As she leaned over, she provocatively rested her elbow on the spongy cluster of glands in his lap. She teased him into cowardness.

"So what's your verdict on the Gonzales case?" he strained to say with an uneasy cough.

Madison checked herself in the rearview mirror.

"Well, to begin with, I had no idea, how Suzanne—"

"Who?" Martin interrupted.

"Gonzales ..." Madison continued, left with no doubt whatsoever as to the extent of Martin's unusual attitude to his work, "was murdered, but then, when I did a preliminary study of her body in the coroner's office, I realized her killer had not intended to harm her."

"You did what?" Martin sneered.

"He killed her, for chrissakes!"

"Yes, by accident," he said. "Okay, hit me with it. I am listening."

"You know how a guy can get the hots for a woman, but she might not even know him, and he is desperate to prove his diminishing manhood to her?"

"Yeah," Martin said flatly.

"But the woman is so unattracted to the guy, she rejects him in an embarrassing hurtful way? Well, in a guy who might not really be in touch with his anger, it's possible he might abduct the woman, put duct tape around her mouth to silence her, not really certain what he is going to do next. It's really just a whim to grab her and hold her captive. It's not premeditated."

"So, what's this got to do with Gonzales?"

"I knew you wouldn't let me finish. It's your way of telling me you don't respect me, but that's okay."

Predictably, Martin stopped sitting in his listening mode position to turn the line of his body toward Madison, looking offended. He hated that she knew him better than he did.

"Gonzales's death was an accident. She swallowed her tongue. Suffocated. The so-called killer did a strange thing though. He used a piece of wire or something similar to pull her tongue back out of her throat to the pallet of her mouth. Then staged this stupid 'I'm the premeditated killer society fears' murder scene. It's like he was upset she choked, but he felt inadequate about it, so he made it look like a genuine murder."

"Jeez, talk about a misplaced sense of pride!"

"Exactly."

"So, how did he think we would think she died?"

"He didn't. I believe he suffered from E.A. Euphoria directly after ... before you ask 'Endomorphin Amnesia Euphoria.' It did not even occur to him what we thought. The whole incident got him so stoked he lost his grip on reality. He posed her, and that was it. I just hope it doesn't turn a tragedy into a killing spree."

"I see what you're saying. An unfortunate incident can provoke a slightly deranged person into becoming a full-fledged wacko."

"Yeah, picture it. A guy full of desire, consumed with lust. When it reaches its peak, it's then you can sometimes catch yourself. Straight after, wondering what all the fuss was about. Maybe the pleasure was in the pursuit of obtaining the desirable sensation or whatever, not the fulfillment of it."

"What if something came along after such an incident that gave you a higher level of indulgence? Something animalistic took over that didn't fade."

"Hold on, that's a scary thought."

"For Suzanne Gonzales, it was a bit more than that," Madison added with an iron fist in a velvet glove.

"Let's drive back into town. My wife wants me to stop off at that fancy bakery on Main Street for a christening cake."

Madison scrutinized Martin, wondering if anything she said actually went in, doing all she could to avoid the sneer forming inside her lips to surface. "Well, it's actually comforting to know something good is going on in the world."

"Is it? Would it make a difference if I told you it's for a squid." He swept his hand toward the Pacific.

"For a what?" *Is he kraken up?*

"A squid ... Most people book a table down at Neptune's Palace and decide if they wanted it with French fries, rice, or a baked potato. My wife and her gang of web-footed marine biologist do-gooders rescue the injured, keep them in a tank, then have a party to give it a name."

"Do they invite kids from local play groups or anything?"

"No. Just from different squid squads." He giggled.

"Yeah, I agree. That's kind of weird. What are they going to call it?"

"Mata Hari won the vote, I think."

Madison broke out into fits of laughter. "You're kidding, right?" Madison forced out between flurries of amusement.

Martin looked on, shocked. She realized that in all the years he had known Madison, he had never seen her laugh.

"That's hilarious."

"Why?" Martin asked seriously.

"Mata Hari, the spoilt calamari."

"Oh, shit, that is funny. I didn't think of that. Good one," Martin managed to get out before he too gave way to an uncontrollable fit of giggles, like someone had filled the car with laughing gas.

"Of all the child substitutes available, a fucking squid, please," Madison howled, taking in another lung-full of air to fuel her amusement.

"Stop, stop!" Martin pleaded, holding his stomach.

"Why a christening when they could have a firing squid? Does she crochet them little outfits?" Madison screamed, winding up to another head-pounding, chest-seizing bout of hysterics.

"Yeah, yeah, when it gets around police headquarters, people will come up to me at work ..." Martin said quickly between intakes of air, "and ask me how my wife and squids are doing."

That was it. Madison flapped her arms, fixed at the elbow, helplessly convulsing. Tears ran from her eyes. She had to wind down the window for an oxygen break. Martin tried to carry on the gags, but Madison held up her hand. "No, no more. Please." She wasn't sure what happened after that. It seemed like one minute she was drawing in sea air, the next she was kissing Martin's stubble-surrounded mouth with a passion that alarmed her. His hand worked its way up her inner thigh. She pulled herself together. "Golly!" she announced weakly, pulling away. "I haven't laughed like that in years."

"Me neither," he said, straightening up and pulling his jacket back into line.

The two of them sat silently, shocked that they had been teenagers again for a few short seconds. Madison wanted to climb on him and take him there and then, but she knew too well married men were not her cup of carrot juice, especially this one. Besides, she would be embarrassed to be seen in public with him. Not only was he old but he also wasn't her type, and he was her boss. Plus, she would end up hating herself afterward.

They drove back into Santa Monica, intent on never mentioning the incident to each other or anyone ever again, apart from when Martin pulled up outside The Bakers Dozen on Main.

Madison pulled into the parking space one car down from his. She wound down the window.

"I'll call you tomorrow to let you know about the christening ... Just squidding," Martin delivered with a dull, monosyllabic tone in his voice.

"Yep!" The magic had already faded. Madison did not find the squid thing remotely funny anymore. "If I get anymore insights on the Gonzales thing," she falsely said, by referring to it numbly, "I'll let you know."

"I'm sorry about what happened back there."

"I'm not. Nothing happened anyway," Madison said, more freely.

"You know my method of police work requires me to lead by example," he blurted out, reverting back to a puckered hole found at the end of a rectal passage.

"Yes," Madison replied, not sure what he was going on about or whether it was just him, dropping a cue, that it was time for her to act like she respected him, or something similar to their old routine.

He turned to go into the bakery. It was then she noticed that she had completely forgotten about a two-quart, self-seal bag of locally produced, organic cream cheese she had bought on her way out of Santa Monica. The contents had spread themselves thickly across the seat of his pants and the bottom of his expensive jacket. She looked down beside her to the passenger seat, intrigued how Martin's weight had pushed the cream cheese through a split in the recycled bag from the damaged inner one as skillfully as a confectioner's decorating piping bag would have. When he had gotten up, out of her car on the cliffs, it must have stuck to his butt, falling back to the seat upside-down because it was neat and clean.

No wonder I didn't notice, Madison thought. She wanted to call out to him, laugh, and hide her head in shame while enjoying a magnificent feeling of satisfaction, all at the same time. She shook her head instead and drove away with a lighter feeling but still ambivalent about the dizzying levels of gruesome thoughts that crossed her mind as she noticed people pushing their strollers and enjoying the sunny breeze. Maybe her interest in the living hadn't faded completely away.

Chapter 8

The next day, Madison got up early to discover fog had rolled in to mystify the California coastline. She avoided the newspaper, then hid the remote control, so she couldn't turn on the TV. She didn't want to know whether the 'Dragon Slayer,' or whatever stupid name the press would end up giving the murderous deranged going-down-the-drain target on the loose in the Santa Monica area, had struck a second time.

Nothing in society has changed since the barbaric days of human blood sports or when executions were carried out to a blood-thirsty public. Except now, it is left much more to the imagination, and the subject slaughtered is more than likely, percentage-wise, an innocent victim, picked off by an unstable, nothing-to-lose hunter. When they have strayed from the safety of inherent common sense that binds the masses together, Madison thought, clutching her car keys.

She was determined to complete her first book of fiction based on facts. Today, she would have yet another day off. She was going to the mountains inland for lunch with Jane who she had not seen for weeks. They used to be good friends. Now, when they visited each other's homes on a regular basis, Madison often found herself wondering why they bothered.

She got in her car and tried to start the engine again, but the battery was dead. She must have left her car lights on when she'd returned from the bakery. Madison couldn't remember the last time she had used any form of public transport. She opted to bus it up to the foothills, past the mall, on the outskirts of town. Then, she'd walk until she got tired and call Jane to come and pick her up from below the mountain. She thought about calling it off, but she could use the distraction, and Jane would feed her plenty of it.

She paid her fare and took a seat at the front of the bus. She sat down, trying not to make eye contact with the other passengers, but the harder she tried not to, invariably, she did. She was puzzled to discover that almost everyone aboard the bus had at least one misaligned eye. Involuntarily, she was going cross-eyed, blurring her vision, because of the statistical phenomenon she was experiencing. The one plausible explanation she could come up with was that this was the only bus to pass the only opticians or eye surgery clinic on the outskirts.

After the bus driver had tried to trap Madison in the bus's exit doors by closing them before she had gotten off properly, she was striding down a country road's less-well-maintained asphalt. Being away from the marine layer meant the choice she had made to wear a summery dress was ill-conceived. She called it that because she said such a summer see-through fabric, summarizing a woman's figure to the world, was the perfect outfit to hike through heat in. By the time she had reached a crossroad junction below the mountains, she was ready to retract the statement she had made about the decision on her choice of clothing.

Another van horn honked. "Hey, gorgeous! Do you want a ride somewhere?" the driver called out while two plumbing colleagues waved to her from the crowded van's bench seat.

This much commercial traffic on a road in the middle of nowhere surprised and infuriated her. *Perhaps, they hide out here when they are loafing,* she thought to herself. She sped up the road, glad it cleared. Now, she could enjoy the trees' rustling leaves, which like her were backlit by sunshine. Normally, the sexual jeers aimed at her by passing vehicles would have intimidated her, but her thoughts had roamed back to earlier when she had been looking for her car keys. It would be more unnerving to know that there was nobody else out here except her and possibly a killer who targeted women and lurked in deserted places.

A commotion in the bushes ahead of her to the left grabbed her focus. A startled rabbit ran into the road. It froze, looking past its twitching nose and her. A slight squeal coming from brakes powered down the vehicle's engine behind her.

The conversation she had overheard outside one of the interrogation rooms in Santa Monica Police Headquarters when she had watched Martin through a viewing mirror echoed in her mind. On this particular occasion, he had broken a rape suspect's silence.

"Look, we both know, a woman really means affirmative when she says negative," Martin had said.

Even then, she'd thought that Martin was probably the leader of a misogynistic version of the KKK, intent on stamping out any woman who independently thought for herself or who supported feminism in any way in Santa Monica.

Why did she think of that one remark panic wire-walking down a country road one foot in front of the other with a vehicle slowing down behind her? Even though it was such a thin veil of denial, she could not penetrate it. She knew the danger involved in hiking alone, dressed in what some might call 'a provocative way.' Had she become so angry with the hopelessness of trying to solve murders without hair samples, fibers, nothing to go on, that she was being flippant about her own safety? Was she, without being aware of it, setting herself up and taking on the role of a decoy? Did she lack the courage to admit to her own sense of self-preservation that she was going out so undercover, even she didn't realize it, to catch the latest social deviant who cowardly snuffed out women?

Madison shuddered, reaching into her shoulder bag for her phone, because by now it was apparent no matter how slow she walked or how far she moved over to the side of the road, the vehicle behind her kept pace, its engine idling, making no attempt to pass her. Then, it occurred to her that she should take note that she, too, was a woman, and maybe, just maybe, she should really think about the consequences of her actions sometimes.

As she lifted the phone out of her bag, she felt the cold metal of the triangular barrel of her 'Desert Eagle' handgun she kept in case of emergencies. The gun Martin had drummed into her to carry. "You live alone. You work with law enforcement agencies. It only needs some creep to notice you with us some day. It's great to have backup," he would say like he was reading her her Miranda rights on repeat in such a neutral, paternal tone that she could imagine all the clogged words and emotions in his throat that he wished he could disclose. It explained the catch in his throat he often cleared when he'd broach the subject. Martin had got her the impossible—a permit that allowed her to carry a fully loaded firearm in California. This was the first time she really appreciated it.

The engine noise edged nearer, impinging on her space, and with it a sense of claustrophobia—the road narrowing and the foothills' spaciousness disintegrating. Ignoring an urge to stop walking, Madison kept moving, unwilling to get pulled into the driver's madness. With no sign of anyone else around, she spun around on her heels, determined to let whoever was violating her privacy that she refused to be stalked. It was a red Oldsmobile. The driver shook, flushed, shiny with perspiration. He sat up from his reclined angle—his right arm still jiggling furiously, his face labored—and sped off. He made a wide turn around Madison who was so enraged she had pulled out her huge handgun and was firing shots at the departing car. The tremendous bucking recoil made her miss the car, but the bullets ensured its driver never tried to pull a stunt like that again in public.

"What a pervert," Madison muttered, trembling and staring up at the empty road ahead before banging Jane's number into her phone.

While Madison waited for Jane and calmed herself down, aware that she hadn't been in such a remote area for a while, she grew restless, letting out huge breaths, and displeased with her unsteady walk. The desire to be back in her more populated neighborhood jumbled her thoughts as she considered whether she'd ask Jane to just take her back to the bus stop or not. *What if the asshole was still watching? I'm out of bullets.* She'd see how it went, pissed that a day off could take such a horrific turn. She rubbed her arms as she scrambled to let nature make her feel better. But only the barrenness sunk in, its dusty deflowered, discarded hills a foul poison, the shrubs and trees anything but a sanctuary away from the rest of humanity or the sun.

Sweating, attempting to hide her face from the direct sun under the brim of her hat but refusing to turn away from the road, she recounted her friend's gentle transformational decline from genuine to fake. It had started in her hair color, then crept into her finger nails, moving up to her bust size, and then into her marriage. It ended up contaminating the fact that Jane always tried to convince people how happy she was, despite the contradictory morning ritual she had of swallowing twice the recommended daily amount of tranquilizers. Madison recalled her own look of disbelief the afternoon Jane showed off her new kitten, proudly announcing to a few of her gathered friends she had named her pussy 'Prozac.' Her thoughts returned to the quiet country road. She dodged thoughts that threatened to turn every shadow she saw into another pervert looking for a cheap thrill.

Before the sun had entirely set, Jane skidded up in the biggest SUV Madison had ever seen, dusting the entire sky and laughing. Madison ripped open the passenger door. "Wow, you're going to yank that door right off its hinges!" Jane laughed, coughing since her window had been open. "I know the price of gas is at an all-time high, but the whole idea of walking sucks so badly, it bursts an ear drum, every time. You look—" She dropped her jaw like she was trying to clear her ears out, and noticed the sweat dripping off Madison. She contorted her face, turning her head away.

"Hi, Jane. It's a long story, and yes, I wore deodorant," Madison said, climbing in.

They drove off back toward Santa Monica. "Well, you can tell me what happened when you're ready," Jane uttered.

"I don't think I will ever be ready," Madison groaned.

"If these foothills could talk, right? Anyway, I've just got to pick up some groceries at the store," Jane declared. Jane's annoying voice resembled nails down a chalkboard. It was husky at the same time, never fluctuating from the same droning level.

Madison shrugged and shook her head. *Not worth getting into it!* she thought, looking into Jane's face.

They clumped in line with their shopping cart, which Jane had filled with the oddest combination of items, and for once in the last hour, Madison held onto a sense of security inside. When they got to the check out, Jane rejected a large majority of what she had placed in the cart to buy. "Now, you dragged out lunch into dinnertime, so you'll get to meet my guest ... well, date really."

Jane's comment made any other response inappropriate, and she wished she had distracted herself from work otherwise. Jane clearly wouldn't even be open to hearing what happened. She had set a plan in motion and hadn't even bothered to think Madison wouldn't want to or that public transportation might take a bit longer. "I don't want to play piggy in the middle, Jane. Just drop me off at my apartment. I've got some perishables that need to get used up," Madison requested, excited to have been offered a way out of spending the evening with Jane.

"No, you can tell me what you think, then I will decide if I want to see him again or not."

Madison wanted to catch a cab from the store when she noticed Jane's wedding ring had gone from her finger, catching Jane's eye as she pushed the cart forward.

"Tony's in Chicago with the youngest secretarial assistant in the world. I'm talking barely legal secretary," Jane said, picking up the most horrendous, ten-dollar-special-offer Hawaiian shirt from the cart that the checkout clerk had begun to scan. "Now, you see, this color brown in the pattern ... it's so plain. I really think it would suit you."

Madison wasn't sure if Jane did it on purpose or if she just didn't think.

"Paper or plastic?" the grocery bag filler inquired, their goods sliding up toward them.

Madison looked down, reaching up to one of her breasts. "No, these are real," she said, scorning Jane's cashmere sweater that contained lampoonish, robust bubbles and dismissively shaking her head, much to the amusement of the blushing teenager who was the only person in close proximity to understand or even hear Madison's swift, witty retaliation.

The drive to Jane's mountainside cabin as she called it, but in reality was a stilted, open-plan mansion as far as Madison was concerned, was conducted in near silence, except for Jane's continual fascination for manually tuning the radio searching for her favorite station.

"You can press auto select, Jane," Madison seethed as they neared a curve on the narrow country road.

The new designer outlet, of course! Madison thought. That time, they had driven separately to shop at the swanky new designer outlet on the other side of Los Angeles, but she had to overtake Jane to verify, to her disbelief, that Jane had been really touching up her makeup in the rearview mirror with the speedometer nudging seventy-five on the freeway.

Eventually, Jane gave up on the radio, turning her full attention back on the road, relaxing Madison momentarily. But she wondered why people like Jane and Martin ever bothered getting married when all they wanted to do was cheat. Or were they the victims, simply doing likewise, succumbing to some spoken or unspoken arrangement, in order to keep the fluidity of their lives constant?

The two women carried the bags into the house from the car.

Madison sat on the chair she liked most, overlooking the steep slope down to land that turned to ocean. Santa Monica's streetlights twinkled before the Pacific Ocean's overshadowing void. A black ribbon, threatening to engulf wavering specks of light that represented the warmth of souls living in the unseen houses. She imagined how many plans were being made down there tonight for dinner. How many people made love at that exact moment? How many practiced an instrument or read a book. How many TVs and hi-fis were on? How many mothers sung their children to sleep or read them stories? Deep down in her feeling of evening contentment, there was somebody out there who contemplated, relived, savored, or fantasized about the diabolical theft of someone else's happiness and plans for the future.

Car headlights swept a patch of white light across the wall, bouncing it back off the windows. Jane vaulted out of the kitchen eating a celery stick.

"Here he is. Now don't mention Tony. I know you're a good friend and maybe you don't approve of my extramarital antics, but this guy is gorgeous, and Madison, as God is my witness, I've done nothing wrong yet."

"Okay, Jane, but just be careful. You don't want someone blackmailing you. Be a bit more discreet."

"Yes, yes."

"Does he know you're married?"

"Kind of," Jane replied.

Madison tutted and shifted uncomfortably. She was beginning to accept that perhaps this kind of situation was synonymous with being single in the twenty-first century. Situations like this happened to her with alarming regularity. It was as if anyone over the age of thirty, who wasn't married, was regarded as a kind of relationship retard by everyone they knew who was joined in so-called "Holy Matrimony." They were instantaneously being relegated to confidant because they were kind of harmless and innocent to the ravages of human nature's cruelest trick.

"Madison, this is Anton."

Madison visibly broke from her daydreaming stare to look over toward the potentially adulterous couple. She did not really say hello because she wondered if they were both adulterous or if only one of them was married, making the other one just an accomplice to adultery.

A long-enough silence made her offer up an unenthusiastic "Hi." The lighting was low, so Madison couldn't really get a good look at the prey ... Jane's new friend. They sat around the smoked-glass dinner table, practically in darkness and silence. Everybody present had stiff, awkward body language with no idea of what small talk to manufacture. They coughed, then fidgeted, aware of the atmospheric tension that took place.

Madison was tempted to call out, "Is there anybody here?" like they were having a dinner and séance combined. In the meantime, she wondered about calling Martin to thank him for drumming her about the gun permit for her fully loaded screw-perverts firearm. Occasionally, as she disengaged from the flirting between Jane and whatever his name was, number four prey, she pictured the Oldsmobile. Had she gotten the license plate? She briefly remembered taking a quick photo, but she couldn't be sure what she had captured. She opened her phone to see. Road blurs. Great.

Madison searched for any glimmer of a conversation opener when more car headlight beams slid around the room. Why hadn't she demanded Jane take her to the bus stop immediately? She had a headache, and this was not how she wanted to spend her day off.

She could salvage it somehow if she just got back to her place. Why hadn't she just called AAA to get her battery started again? Was it AAA? She'd have to check with her insurance company again. She'd get the battery started pronto and go find that Oldsmobile.

Not a good idea, Madison, she scolded herself.

Jane skulked to the front door. Her distant voice from outside the open door confirmed to Madison that Jane's scheduled evening was rescheduled. *Nice.*

"Yes, come in. I didn't expect you home until tomorrow night," Jane strained through her sulk, reentering the house. His expensive suit made the casual dinner seem ridiculous.

"Tony, you know Madison, and this is her friend Anton," Jane lied brazenly.

"I'm sorry to barge in like this. I'm dog-tired. Carry on like I never came in. I need a shower and then lights out," Tony replied amicably and made his way upstairs.

They finished dinner in an uncompromising atmosphere that was far from congenial since Jane had brokered an out-and-out lie to her husband and it hung in the air, reminiscent of the smell produced by Jane's unintentionally flamboyant stir fry. Madison could not wait to get out of her house. She couldn't shoot her the look she so desperately wanted to like back at the grocery store. Jane's table manners were terrible. She didn't know why she invited people over to eat when she proceeded to consume food like a Rottweiler chewing a yellow jacket.

She gauged an acceptable amount of time to pass, then yawned, tired of holding everything back. "Thanks for dinner, Jane. I'd better be getting back. It's late. It's been a hell of a day."

Jane didn't even give her a comforting look, rather a sideways glance at her date as she offered, "I'll drive you down to Santa Monica."

"No, it's okay. I'll call a cab," Madison answered, looking at the fourth empty glass of wine Jane had consumed on top of her medication. The drive up, when she considered her sober, was scary enough.

"I'm going that way," Anton offered.

"Well, that worked out great, didn't it?" Jane said, closing the deal, whether Madison liked it or not.

Anton walked to the wall of windows, overlooking the lights of Santa Monica. Behind him, Madison waved her hands in a furious gesture of defiance at Jane. He spun around. She changed in a blink of an eye to a calm, casual pose, her forefinger and thumb sophisticatedly cradling her chin.

"I'll get my bag," Madison managed to extract from her same-old-hash word pile that lay disheveled in some scratched-up reusable container in her mind.

She picked up her shoulder bag from a breakfast stool in the spacious kitchen area, surveying the back door, debating whether or not to make a break for it. Minutes later, she had said goodbye to Jane indefinitely and was sitting next to Anton in his car on her way home.

"Was that her husband? Or did you vow never to give the game away?"

"No comment."

"It's weird, although she came across as single, I knew she wasn't. Why did she invite me to her house? Why not a restaurant? She is either an idiot or she likes to live dangerously."

"Maybe she wanted to be your friend."

"No, the signals were different."

This made Madison take an interest in Anton. "Signals? Do you think women have to give men signals?" she asked, not wanting to appear ignorant of such things.

"Of course ... I'm talking minor hints a man can't ignore. Nothing that could be misconstrued as a double message."

Madison was still none the wiser.

"You don't remember me, do you?"

Madison did not respond.

"I dropped off your lost credit card last week."

Madison turned to look at his profile in the ambient gloom given off by the illuminating dashboard panel instruments. She found it impossible to comprehend that she did not recognize someone who had made such a powerful impression on her.

"I didn't think short hair would change my appearance so drastically," he continued.

Might have had something to do with where my head was at after being stalked by a perv, she thought. She wouldn't tell him. It wouldn't be appropriate, and what could he do? *Comfort me like Jane had? Not a lot of that to find in either of them,* she thought.

With the streetlamps on the outskirts of civilization approaching, she wanted to get a good look at him. The light would stream through the moon roof, protracting them from one lamp's orange beam to the next. She looked at him from the side. "It's stunning how much your appearance has changed with just a haircut," she said. She started to feel giddy inside but was able to not let it show.

"I saw you back at Jane's house, reflected in the window, trying to turn down my offer of a ride."

Madison said nothing. She was filled with an eager anticipation. The only time she spoke was to give Anton directions to her house, which he knew the way to anyway.

When they pulled up outside her apartment complex, they sat motionless. There was no sound in the car, except the engine clicking to cool down. Anton leaned over to kiss Madison, encountering no resistance. He edged closer to increase the intensity. She pushed him back ever so gently.

"I always expect things to be better than how they actually turn out. This time, I want it to turn out better than I expect. I don't recall giving you any signals," she whispered.

"You threw the book at me, nodded, winked, and gave me the green light the minute I laid eyes on you," he responded with a mischievous, rhythmic humor in his voice immediately returning his mouth to Madison's smiling lips.

Chapter 9

Madison's arrow-like strokes cut through the country club swimming pool's chlorinated lanes, delighting in each stroke like a reward for the wonders that had recently bobbled up out of the crazed qualms infecting her daily life. April was ending. Rain turned Santa Monica lush and green. At the core of her biology, outside the circle of traditional seasons, a prehistoric clause in her reluctant urge to reproduce was vital. Winter had elapsed, a long, lonely set of months. Now, at the peak of physical fitness, a vague sensation of prosperity fed her awareness. She had found a man, who, so far, had reunited her with the wafer-thin possibility that love or something close, especially at first sight, might exist. She just hoped the realization that it didn't wouldn't follow too soon.

Her last relationship had ended as suddenly as it had begun when the man she had planned to live with was fired from the bank where he'd worked downtown. He had been found to be under carnal knowledge with a fellow female employee in the main security vault. While the bank was closed down, being readied for refurbishment, the atomic clock time lock had shut down an hour earlier, due to the shift over to daylight savings time, which in the heat of their passion they had neglected to remember on that Friday afternoon in October. When Monday morning came around and police were considering a missing person's search of Santa Monica's larger bodies of water, another staff member discovered them hungry and frightened. On Tuesday, the *Santa Monica Daily* reported the front-page story with the headline "Safe Sex." Suffice to say, they had even neglected to remove the skimpy pair of women's panties that hung over the prying eye of the security camera in the bank vault.

"There is something about an attractive woman's face when she swims that is too angelic to be put down to mere coincidence," someone called out.

Opening her eyes, Madison acknowledged the fact that a tall figure stood at the poolside in the gargling rush of water in her ear canals. She made out fragments of a garbled statement when they broke from the water, which in turn threw off her stride. She put her arms out as a break, also to stabilize her body, while her feet found the bottom of the shallow end. She stood up straight, pulling back her wet hair.

"When you're dry, you're good looking ...When you're wet ..." Anton said, exaggeratingly gasping, "you're gorgeous."

"What are you doing here?" Madison asked, the tone in her voice about as warm and sparkly as the cold, dull wading pool.

"I was playing tennis, then I thought I would check if my woman was here."

"Is she?" Madison asked, downgrading her tone to a yellow light and varying it a bit like this was a chance for them to experience a functional first encounter minus her doorway, the lost credit card, and the supposed invisible book of signals she threw at him, nodding, winking, and giving him the green light.

"My Monday date is, at least," he answered, joining in with her flippant mood. "Yeah, I call her flippant flipper because she swims better than she loves."

He coughed, standing more upright as people entered the pool building behind him and had heard his last sentence. Madison found his embarrassment highly amusing. She beamed with delight, settling back into the water until she became submerged, hidden from the situation.

She came up out of the water again.

"I'll meet you in the juice bar," he called out, holding his racket and sport bag.

Madison nodded, smiling, goosebumps rising across the top of her arms. The water temperature made her shiver, but inside, something in her chest was about to break open into blossom. She got to the locker room where she had stored her belongings. Before her phone stopped playing a familiar classical microchip recital, she opened the locker door and grabbed the phone from her bag, just missing the call. She checked the number.

Now what? she thought.

Martin drove around the block for a second time. "Where the hell is she?" he moaned, expecting Madison to be available whenever he called. Electronic peeps resembling the "William Tell Overture" made Martin reach in his jacket. "Hello, Thompson ... Ah! I'm glad you got back to me ... Did you know I had a white, creamy substance all over the back of my pants when I left you a few days ago?" he asked seriously, exactly the way he would address a question in court at an inquest or a trial, which Madison had been present at in the past. Martin could have sworn he heard her laugh. "What was that?"

"There's a lot of interference. I can't hear you very well. You're breaking up," Madison shouted.

"Meet me outside your place in an hour. It's important," Martin commanded.

Her long pause aggravated him, but when she responded with "Okay, bye," all he heard was her flat voice.

But Martin said nothing. *Is she pranking me?* he thought, picturing her messing with the speech hole on her phone to cause the interference. *That's my job!* He couldn't help smirking.

"Self-obsessed dork, maybe he realized that his behavior amuses me," Madison said out loud to herself. *No, deep down he begrudges me the right to some happiness.* In the country club's changing room, she realized the odd attraction he harbored for her was nothing more than a constraint device. As long as she was unhappy, she would be looking for some kind of escape that he assumed was him, the fatherly, worldly, wise savior of her fears, not sadly her dreams ...

"Give me a break!" Madison changed her train of thought, remembering to take the pill in case Anton was planning to stay the night.

The last thing she needed was an unwanted pregnancy at this stage of her life. Weeks ago, the doctor had prescribed the contraceptive to alleviate the cramps that frequently made Madison crawl into bed for days with painkillers and a hot water bottle. Although she was not a hundred percent in favor of orally-taken contraception and the long-term effects they had on the female body, she was open to anything that would spare her that particular form of agony.

She had known Anton's intentions after that kiss in the car, even before she had woken the next day to find the 'RE' of an urgent fax that Anton had sent her. An extremely recent medical examination sheet that clearly stated he did not suffer from any form of S.T.D known to the medical profession. This was perhaps the strangest, but most practical, thing a man had ever sent her—reassuring, but nevertheless weird.

By the time Madison had downed a cup of coffee, cuddled Anton by his car, and got to her apartment, she was twenty minutes late. Much to her surprise, Martin was slumped over the steering wheel of his car, asleep. She smiled, turning the wheel of her car to pull around in the road so she could park behind him. She honked her horn, but he didn't move.

"He's been doing too many of those double shifts, I bet," she mumbled to herself, getting out of her car.

She walked up to his car window. She froze. A clumsy mess on the windshield unsettled her nerves. Either he had developed a really sick sense of humor or he was in fact unconscious or even dead. She beat her fists on the window. She stopped when she noticed his hair on the opposite side of his head was matted with blood. She couldn't break the glass. The door was locked.

Hysterically, she rushed to her car to find the gun in her bag. She ran back to Martin's car, pointing the pistol at the window. She pulled herself together, knowing full well how it would look. She decided to feebly hit the glass with the end of the gun's handle, which ejected the full clip of bullets. It hit her foot, sending it spinning under the car. Still, the glass would not smash out.

She went back to her own car to call 911 and to wait. She analyzed the darkened shape of the back of Martin's head. She imagined him walking around, jumpy on a home movie made with a 1950s handheld cine camera, running to a parent's arms as an infant. Then, she saw him as a tiny boy, cranking his neck back to look up at a horse's face. He stared at a cop on horseback. She contemplated how he formulated the idea to become a policeman.

The tragic fleet's distant sounds grew closer. He was dead, but she pretended they would force open his car door, then he would jump up, looking out at her, shouting, "I got you there!" Sadly, shock would not allow her to realize this was real.

An ambulance arrived before the police. She sat in her car as they slid a flat tool down the gap between the window and the door to unlock it. The paramedic leaned in to put his fingers on Martin's neck. Two others wheeled a stretcher close to the car. His limp arm fell out of the Ford, confirming he was definitely not going to jump up to give away a prank.

Chapter 10

The Homicide Division arrived in the guise of Eddie Manfred, Martin's occasional partner. Uniforms soon surrounded him. Madison observed him from her car reprimanding the paramedic emergency crew for disturbing the crime scene before he proceeded to examine the evidence. He knelt down and fished in his coat pocket before he reached under the car with a plastic bag over his fingers. He didn't seem to exhibit a single flicker of visible emotion at his associate's passing.

Madison struggled out of her car. She noticed minuscule things about the apartment complex's driveway, Martin's car, and his crumpled corpse's posture. Then without her permission, the aptitude she received so much praise for, yet feared above all else, took over, similar to a limousine's cruise control. She stood staring into space. In vivid detail, a reconstruction in hindsight as clear as a computer simulation showed the angle with which Martin's car had pulled up to the curve. She saw how he had gotten out to stand impatiently at her apartment complex's gate while he had waited for her to answer the intercom. Behind him, the killer crept, crouching down, working a way around to the driver's seat door to check to see if Martin had left it unlocked. When the handle had given in on its spring-loaded mechanism, granting entry to the car, the killer had slid across the coupe's seat into the back, slickly agile, animal-like, strategically arranging to ready the victim for attack. She saw how Martin had risen from the flat of his feet to his toes, looking around acknowledging that Madison hadn't arrived home yet. He had turned, heading back to the car—the loaded trap.

Eddie noticed her. "Jesus, what the hell is going on here!" he stressed, moving toward her.

The paramedics who stood close by heard him, and Madison cringed.

She blinked, allowing moisture that had collected in the lower rim of her eyes to break, dribbling downward to fly away on gusting squalls, flapping inland.

She ignored him, seeing how Martin had gotten into the car. She passed around the other side of the vehicle, just as the killer had swung upwards with the bone-saw-sided hunting knife that had disappeared into the side of Martin's forehead until it had stopped at the T-section where the knife handle began. She imagined how the killer had struggled to free it, wildly wiggling the knife into the deep wound with the carefree indifference of someone cutting a face into a pumpkin. "Hi, shithead. The blade is mine," the killer had joked. Horrible sounds had come from Martin's wilting body while spurting blood had decreased in volume to subside.

Eddie's hand landed on Madison's shoulder, making her jump back from her hypothetical premonition.

"Get forensics to check the back seat," she uttered, sickened by the casual violence of her imagination's simulation.

The two of them were drawn to the smudged representation of a dragon on the windscreen. A numb Madison looked to her left at the concentration Martin's killer had applied to the bloody-brush strokes. Without removing his gaze from the swirling blood painting, Eddie handed Madison a plastic spatula so she could scrape some of the dried blood off the windscreen.

"Did Martin share this same bad artwork from the dumping ground murder recently?" Madison inquired.

"Yes, he did. I looked into it. There are temples in Serbia that are like pyramids. Very ancient. It's not a dragon. It's a centaur," Eddie replied.

Madison slept on a sagging couch in police headquarters. In the early hours, she woke up to notice Eddie barging his way through the corridor door. He came up to her with a piece of paper in his hand.

"Did you tamper with the evidence we found in Martin's car?"

"Of course not. No, why?"

"It just doesn't make any sense."

"What doesn't?"

Eddie looked at the cop who had followed him into the room. His staunch expression expected Eddie to act according to standard protocol.

"Madison ... much to my disbelief and against my better judgment, I'm arresting you for the murder of Martin Thompson. You may remain silent—"

"You fucking what?" Madison protested. "It's okay. I know the rest," she continued, more annoyed than worried. "You, at least owe me an explanation."

"There doesn't seem to be much of one. I was given a warrant this morning for your arrest. We took a sample of your blood, if you remember, when you started helping us out, so if anything happened to you we could ID you. Just so we could eliminate you from any investigation." Eddie deflated to pinch the bridge of his nose. "The blood, that the killer used to leave us his calling card, on the windscreen ... Oh Christ, I still can't believe it myself."

"What?" Madison asked, convinced a nightmare had spilled over into her waking hours.

"D.N.A analysis could not rule you out. It's your blood, Madison, from you ..." Eddie said, unable to finish what he was saying.

Madison stood up, suspended from any reaction.

"I found a full clip of bullets from your gun under his car. Martin was at police headquarters that afternoon before we found him. He confided in fellow officers how he was concerned that you were acting in an unusual manner. He was convinced you were about to audition at the Santa Monica psychiatric assessment center for a part in a padded cell. He never used to tell me anything, but he told me that."

Madison could not find anything to say in her defense. Instead, she requested to be driven home to pack an overnight bag. Her request was denied. This notion activated Madison's sense of mischief.

"Good, let's get down to the cells. Am I going to police headquarters or the state penitentiary? Figures why Martin turned to me often to help him at crime scenes," she asked, smoldering.

Eddie blinked slowly. "No, what we're going to do is just hold you over in the detention center until we can get some way to work this all out," Eddie said, more friendly.

"I can still get access to the crime lab, right? If it is my blood, I want to know how it was taken from my body to be used to incriminate me. That should be interesting in court," she said, animated, her voice lighter and bubblier as she put her wrists together for the handcuffs.

"But, I've already charged you for this," Eddie replied, trying to reinforce the severity of the situation Madison was in.

She stopped next to him. "Yes, I know, but if I'm in custody anyway, the crime lab is only a few streets away from the detention center. I'm sure you can have an armed guard take me over for a couple of hours ... Shall we go, then?" she added, already taking liberties.

As they walked out, Eddie followed her.

Madison spoke to him with her head slightly turned. "Did you talk to Anton Winter? I was with him at the time I was supposed to have killed Martin."

"We've already checked him out. Anton Winter says he doesn't even know you."

Her eyes widened. Her body overheated.

"What about Jane ..." A series of *Are you sures?* fiended through her mind over and over again. She turned away to gather her thoughts. *Anton?* Her mind scattered before she struggled to refocus. "Mitchell? She knows I know him."

"We're sending someone up there tomorrow for an interview," Eddie informed her.

She held her tongue. A shocked, deeply pained look surfaced on her face as an urge to hit something overcame her. *Is this for real? Had he intended to hurt me all along? What was I thinking letting myself misplace my trust again?* I should have kicked that door closed the minute I saw that counterfeit.

"Jane knows I know him! Ask her!" She glared at Eddie for a moment, then the pounding in her ears and a surging twitchy feeling in her body steered her thoughts to making damn sure she said no more. Someone was hiding a lot more than sex as her mind returned to the crime scene, pressure building to work out Martin's last minutes alive waiting for her. Her chin quivered thinking of her last words to Martin and her long, indifferent pause. He'd said it was important, but why had he told Eddie what they had sworn to confidence?

Although Madison's reenactment was accurate, had she possessed the ability to go back in time, she would have known that a one-sided conversation had taken place between Martin and his killer before he had been murdered. Martin had gotten into the car. He'd selected the ignition key from the bunch he had held in his other hand. He had sat upright, motionless.

"I know you're there," Martin had said calmly. He had smelled the killer's bodywash.

The killer hadn't answered. He remained still.

"It doesn't matter what you do to me. I'm finished anyway, stage 4 finished," Martin spoke calmly, gradually trying to move his hand toward his holstered pistol under his left arm. "Maddy will catch you. I know she will catch you."

A smack was followed by searing pain in Martin's brain. This was the last sensation he felt before his demise.

Chapter 11

He threw down the canvas bag of tools he carried. Nobody had passed him on the road. The sweep of a single set of high beams hadn't picked him out yet. He desperately wanted to continue on his way, but he was a man torn in two, ripped apart. He walked fifty yards, then stopped. It wasn't too late to go back, to undo what he had initiated. The bar, the vodka, the orange-juice-flavored syrup had concocted this plan. He wasn't thinking straight. How would the police ever trace him back to a multiple homicide, ten years ago, on the East Coast? All he had to do was supply the woman he loved with an alibi. His new identity had been solid so far, regarding any official business.

But now, to make matters worse, beyond his own control, something too unexpectedly dark and sick for him to comprehend, an unknown trait in his character, stirred inside him. A diseased part of his ego was enjoying the power he commanded over whether or not the pointless, everyday existence of a cheating, vain, arrogant shit-machine should continue. Just how he had for fun taken that woman, that night, how he had gotten a kick from keeping her in the abandoned farm buildings outside Santa Monica, and how terribly wrong all that had gone. He remembered his panic on finding her suffocated, how she had swallowed her own tongue. How he had thought of painting the dragon on her stomach.

Now, he decided how somebody would decide if they could afford that expensive item or not. Would he carry on letting her life be over, or would he go back to tighten up the nuts and bolts of her destruction? Yes, he had overreacted to Madison's arrest. A factor that had placed a dual purpose of two women's date with destiny. Now, he deliberated whether or not to go back to Jane's house to call off what he intended to do or to go home and rest in readiness for what he had planned.

He sat by the roadside, deciding what to do next while enjoying the feeling of digging holes with a mechanical excavator and trying to fill them back in with a teaspoon. The night continued, evolving into beauty glazed into horror in a spreadsheet creating statistics taking place in its confined duration.

Chapter 12

Madison woke up in a panic, not only because the direction she normally became awake in was different but also because the familiar layout of the room she looked around at was not the same. Then, she realized she wasn't at home in her bedroom. The imbeciles had locked her in a holding cell in the detention center next to the Santa Monica Courthouse.

She swung her legs to the floor to sit on the side of the bed. With a sighing groan, Madison lowered her face into the upturned palms of her hands. She crossed to the corner of the cell, undisturbed by a shiny, black-shelled insect that scurried into a crack when it detected her. Her swollen eyes enjoyed the water she splashed on them at the dilapidated sink. Feeling for a towel that wasn't there, she used her sweatshirt sleeve.

Echoing footsteps coming down the corridor grabbed her focus. The holding cells were in the oldest part of the detention center. Its floors were plank over blocks of desert stone, built at the end of the last century and preserved in small city pride. The cell even had its original full-iron, ceiling-to-floor, 1874 iron bars. Two lamps gave a limited-lit radius through the bars. Someone's body profile crossed the first lamp.

"Has my request for bail been approved yet?" she called out.

The deputy didn't answer. She could not make out his face. He stood in the boundary of darkness between the two lamps' circular reach. A doubting twist briefly pulled her face and head to one side. She sat up to focus on the obscured figure. She strained to listen. She could make out a uniform, supported by the fact that what little light there was beyond the bars caused a gold sheriff's star on the left side of his chest to stand out in the gloom.

"You'd think they'd have more light in a place where hardened criminals dwell. I could have a gun or anything hidden in here."

Madison wasn't sure but she could have sworn she also heard a scraping sound coming from the figure. Madison had to check herself to realize what the deputy was doing.

"If you're doing what I think you're doing ..." she said, lowering the tone of her voice as she breathed slowly, "you're in more trouble than you can handle." She maintained her composure, her de-escalation training kicking in by instinct.

The figure staggered forward, mumbling and trying to slow his breathing. He emerged from the shadows, rolling up a leather-sharpening strap, the type used more commonly in old barbershops.

Madison squinted in disbelief. It was the guy from the car that had pulled up behind her the day she went to Jane's.

"I've got something for you," he murmured in a cold voice. He raised a blood-stained hand that contained a fearful blade. "Relax, it's a zoological scalpel for cutting open rhinoceroses and elephants ..." he whispered, having an infantile difficulty in pronouncing the words, "and other thick-skinned animals."

Madison still fixed her expression in disbelief. He pulled out the jail keys from his pants pocket. Strangely, the only thing that occupied Madison's mind was that she somehow wanted a sample of his DNA so that she would have some evidence that might clear her name.

She caught sight of his bloated, disfigured face that strangely portrayed a hint of vulnerability. Madison wasn't going to give up without a fight. "That's just my luck, stalked and killed by the village idiot. Why couldn't my killer be someone a little higher profile?"

This statement caused the killer to develop a twitch, making him lose his grip on the keys. He caught them before they had fallen a short way from the keyhole of the long iron-barred door.

"Christ, you must be kidding. Are you sure you're mentally proficient enough to go through with this?"

He stopped moving. He shook with anger. He dropped the keys again. They fell to the jailhouse floor this time. He gripped the flat, strengthening bar that all the other bars passed through at his waist's height. He continued to suffer from some kind of furious seizure, rattling the holding cell bars and practically growling.

"Oh, I'm going to shred you up," he gargled.

"'Impulsive Murdering Blanco Trash Kills Santa Monica Forensic Author.' I can sell the embarrassing headline now. Darn, you're ugly," Madison screamed out, more scared than she had ever been in her whole life.

Her nostrils filled with a tingling, primitive anger that refused to let her be killed. She leaped from the cell bed toward him, uncertain who was contained in this situation. In one move, she scuffled back the set of jailhouse keys with her training shoe, sending them sliding under the gap of the bars into the cell. Her arms went through the bars. If she wasn't fortunate, careful, or insane, or all three at once, she would die. Her fingers locked behind his head, toppling the peaked sheriff's cap he wore. She jerked his bald head toward her with all the strength she could muster, wedging her feet on the horizontal, flat supporting bar at the base of the spaced, vertical ones.

His face smashed into the bars, causing him to eject a tooth in a jettison of blood. Despite her efforts, his arms pushed through the bars frantically to embrace her. He lost his grip on the huge scalpel. In the commotion, it clattered to the cell floor behind her.

In the scuffle, his panting non-sensical remarks filled her thoughts as his fist clenched his opposite wrist, squeezing her in a bear hug against the bars. She struggled to catch her breath, but his sheer strength crushed her. Lightheaded, slipping into unconsciousness, she heard shouting from the end of the corridor.

"Don't shoot. He's got her. Back off!" someone far off called out.

Her hands fell back through the bars. She willed her loose arm to the gap in the bars between them. She found the pepper spray in his textured leather utility belt that he'd obviously taken from the officer he had killed to gain entry. She maneuvered it in her hand, lifted it, and depressed the canister plunger, sending a jet of pepper spray into her own face. Realizing her error, she used her fingers to twirl the canister the right amount of times to fire another squirt into his face. He dropped her. Her eyes were on fire.

She fell to the floor, still lifting her head, although she could only see everything blurred through a cluster of tears. He had pulled out a gun from somewhere. She regretted she hadn't found that, but then she decided the non-lethal was better after what she had just done. With terrific endurance, she pulled herself back up using the bars. The flashes of his gun glistened on her face. Receiving no retaliation from the other end of the corridor, she feared her rescuers had missed their target but he had hit his.

She reached out through the bars again, distracted, caught off guard, pressed sideways into the bars. Madison successfully slammed his head into the bars once more. She held him there with all she was worth. She strained to push her mouth against his. She could smell his stale breath, taste the stinging pepper spray.

Pulling his head more to the side, she pushed his lips apart with hers. She could taste his blood. His tongue moved forward in an automatic reaction to repel her through his broken teeth. She sucked the tip of his tongue into her mouth and bit it as hard as she could, taking it clean off. She let go of his head.

He stepped back from the bars, putting a hand to his mouth. His eyes registered his painful surprise.

"Got ya!" Madison mumbled like someone politely talking with their mouth full. She wasn't letting go of this evidence until it was safe to do so.

He lifted the gun in his hand, pointing it at Madison. It fired, hitting one of the cell bars. It ricocheted, blasting a hole in the wall behind him. He didn't flinch, entranced by his murderous intent. He pulled the trigger again, but it clicked out of ammo. He threw down the gun to run.

A shotgun blasted outside, followed by sirens. An incredible urge to throw up overwhelmed her, but she wanted to make sure that he was caught or dead before she could let go of the tip of his tongue in her mouth.

Eddie ran in with his gun drawn. He looked through the bars at her. She spat at him. "There's your evidence. I didn't do it, okay?" she screamed, her teeth red with blood. Then, she turned to run to the sink in the corner of the cell to succumb to overdue nauseousness.

Chapter 13

Anton laid the last packed items in the back of his hatchback. He turned to go back into his rented house when he caught site of Madison's car slowing down next to the curb to park. He blinked. A fear of betrayal, if she found out, rose inside of him. Guilt twisted his innards through thick screens of love and power wound so tightly his chest could snap with conflict. He wasn't in the mood to have to explain anything. He went back to the car to skillfully hide his walkie-talkie wavelength scanner under a rug in the hatchback.

At terrific speed, events from the previous day impulsed around his brain, as if they were digital information being fired through optic fibers ... Jane complaining at his front door that she couldn't possibly help him because she had a doctor's appointment that afternoon, but he had determined he would work on her. He hadn't given in.

"Thanks, Jane. I really appreciate this," he had said, sitting in her car beside her when she had closed the conversation on her cellular to reschedule her appointment for the day after tomorrow.

"Where is your car exactly?" she had asked, unsuccessfully masking her disinterest.

"Up on the road, near Point Conception."

"Wow, all the way up there ... You'll owe me a biggy for this."

It had occurred to him that it was a real sacrifice for someone so self-centered to help anyone. When they got to the narrowest curves, closest to the cliff edge, Jane's tires on her S.U.V squealed. He pictured the lug nuts he had loosened on the car's front wheels the night before. He imagined them twirling, vibrating off their thread posts, and rattling in the deep alloy wheel rims, like steel balls in a roulette wheel, before they fell into the road. He debated whether he was more petrified with fear or more fortified with the danger of his risk-taking.

They flew over a hill crest on the last third of a mile to his car that he could see in the distance. Jane pulled up beside his car in the observation spot, creating a fleeting dust cloud that dissipated toward the ocean below.

Anton climbed out. "Jane, you're a saint."

"Don't people have to be dead before they're ordained?"

"Yes," Anton chuckled, visibly relieved to be out of her car.

"Follow me home. I'm going to treat you to lobster at Waldo's for this," Jane said as she was licking her fingertip and rubbing it on a stain she had noticed on her blouse. "I have something to celebrate," Jane continued.

"Celebrate what?" Anton asked.

"Have you seen or heard from Madison lately? I keep calling, but she's never home."

"Jane, don't change the subject. You're killing me. What are we celebrating?" Anton asked, smug, applying a blank stare.

"Well, it looks like I'm going to be a mum at last. We've been trying for months, and it looks like our treatments have finally worked, just when we were about to give up."

"That's why you were going to see your doctor today," Anton replied, feeling a shift in his chemical imbalance.

"ER! Hello, you're supposed to be happy when receiving such information."

"I am, but—"

"Come on! Let's get going," Jane called out before Anton could finish.

She revved the engine, pulling away fast, giving Anton just enough time to slam the passenger door shut on the moving vehicle.

"No, Jane. Stop!" he called after her.

He ran to his car, cursing the day he was born, coming back to some humane resemblance. "What the fuck was I thinking!" he screamed, slamming his palms on his car's steering wheel.

The supposedly broken-down engine started immediately. Madison's voice in his consciousness from the week before told him how she dreaded the day Jane would announce she was with child. She had doubted it would ever happen, but if it did, Madison had hoped it would turn Jane's life around and she would have someone else to think about, apart from herself.

He caught up with Jane who had just begun to turn into a tight curve made by the road builders who had blasted away the rock face to continue around, instead of expensively going through the risen cliff mass. From the angle he was at behind her, her front left wheel, abnormally, wobbled.

"Oh, shit! Hold on another few miles please," Anton prayed out loud, then he swerved, breaking hard with lightning reflexes when Jane's S.U.V flipped on the road ahead of him. It happened so fast, an action replay went on in his head—slow, continuous, slamming, rolling, and disintegrating over the cliff edge to the low-tide rocks below.

He drove home as quickly as possible, the accident tearing through his mind. He pulled up, parked in the driveway, and sat on his front step. As Madison walked up his driveway toward him, how a person who has been robbed of their soul does, the EMT's voice that he had heard on the scanner further on down the road churned through his mind: "the driver was thrown clear from the wreckage." Everything else the EMT said became a garble as he recoiled at the sight of Madison. Anton had hoped Jane might have survived, but then, the static-produced dispatch had described with a macabre fascination how her head had exploded like an overripe watermelon when it had been dashed on the rocks.

"Anton, why didn't you come forward? Why did you let me sit it out? What have you got to hide?" Madison asked, still shaking from her ordeal.

"I've got nothing to hide. Oh, Madison, you haven't heard yet!"

"Heard what?"

"Jane, she ... there was an accident."

"Next, you'll be telling me all kinds of bullshit about Jane dying to deflect your responsibility for not coming to bail me out."

Anton convincingly deflated his stance. "It would be pretty easy to prove me wrong, wouldn't it? She's dead, Madison. It's the truth."

Madison stood still, confusion covering her face and silencing her. "You possibly couldn't begin to hazard a guess as to the last couple of days I have just had. Now this ... is ... the final ..." She moved forward, grappling to find the comfort of Anton's embrace.

He hugged her close to him. Their heads were side by side. Madison moaned in agony, relaying to him the reference points of damage on her heart that she knew would only begin to heal now because he held her. But he wasn't listening. He was planning to get her into the house for a more physically rigorous form of comforting. Her sobs released the pressurized tension in her chest.

Anton was tempted to yawn.

She reached a climax in her grief just as Anton cast his gaze across the grass in the house's front yard. He made a mental note to remember to cut the lawn the following weekend.

Chapter 14

Blown-out debris of composite target board took time to land while more heavy-grain shell tips punched through the scoring zoned outline of an assailant seen from the other side through a neat bullet hole. Madison's extended locked arms streamlined to a point level with her line of vision where she stabilized her handgun for each carefully aimed shot. Her intense squint remained fixed through protective eyewear.

She stopped firing to reload.

"Ouch! Good grouping ... Looks like five or six in the groin and one between the eyes," Eddie praised.

She hadn't seen him approach. She turned the pistol skyward. A slight movement of her little finger on the grip catch dropped the firearm's empty clip. She held up her forearm encircled in a Velcro cuff. She bent back her wrist, causing a sprung spindle to raise a full clip, ready for insertion. Madison smacked the gun's handle against her arm, snapping the full clip into position.

Eddie broke a smile while looking down at the speed with which she had reloaded.

She hesitated. "I don't want any distractions right now." Madison followed his line of vision to her gun. "I ordered it from Gunsgalore.com, with free delivery," she called out to her side, against the kick and noise of her shots, knowing full well Eddie was bound to ask.

"I've got to admit this seems way out of character," Eddie shouted, his fingertips embedded in his ears.

Madison lowered the pistol from the target. "The entire Law Enforcement Agencies of Santa Monica combined had him trapped in the detention center, but miraculously, he escaped. Now, call me old-fashioned, but for some weird reason, probably only known to his own deranged sense of understanding, he's got a personal vendetta against me. If there's a next time, I'll be ready. I now accept I can only rely on myself."

"But, Madison, it's only fair to tell you everyone is talking. You're a part-time consultant, basically a civilian. Don't you think twenty hours a week on the range is a bit vigilante-excessive?"

Madison lowered her pistol to face Eddie. "What I do in my own time with my own gun—"

"That's not a gun, Maddie. That's a cannon," Eddie interrupted, motioning with his eyes to guide Madison's attention back to the target that she hadn't noticed had splintered to collapse in half from the last shot she had fired.

"If that's all, Detective Manfred, you're disturbing my workout schedule."

"No, that's not all." Eddie took a deep breath to lean back on the marksman rail. "I wanted to wait until we buried Martin. It's been ten days."

"A whole ten days!" Madison interrupted, dropping her posture.

She bowed her head to remove the protective goggles she wore, then wiggled the foam plugs out of her ears, placed them into a small case, and slipped them into her top pocket.

"They come in useful for Anton's snoring as well."

"I'm sure you're strong enough to take what I've got to tell you."

Madison stockpiled some strength from the site of the wrecked target, deflecting the purpose of the look for Eddie so she wouldn't seem insulted by his sexist remark about her being strong enough. She transformed the look so he would assume it was arrogant pride on her part. "I would say so," she said wryly.

"Firstly, I spoke with Martin's wife last week. Now, she tells me, Martin's doctors had diagnosed him with some serious disease. They had given him a year, max."

"What?" Madison expelled, letting her guard down completely. "So, why didn't he tell anyone?"

"She told me he apparently tried to tell you more than once. If he were going to tell anyone, I would have thought it was going to be me. I was his partner after all."

Madison closed her eyes to bow her head fully.

"Secondly ..." Eddie hesitated, "we found a rogue print in the alloy that came off of Jane Mitchell's vehicle."

"A rogue print?"

"A print that came from your friend Anton Winter." Eddie waited for her to respond.

"Anton!" Madison yelled with her eyes still closed.

"Well, when I interviewed Mitchell's husband a few days after the accident, he was standing in front of their fridge ..."

"Wowee! That's amazing police work," Madison called out, cutting across his flow and furious that it was being implied that the only decent aspect of her life might be corrupt and was being questioned at all.

"If you'll let me finish. On the fridge behind him, I noticed something he hadn't. A magnetized memo pad page," Eddie continued.

He bent down to pick up a briefcase he'd brought along. He rested it against his thigh and the marksman rail, flipped the catches, lifted the lid, and produced a clear plastic evidence bag.

Inside it, Madison could see a yellow, faintly ruled notelet page with Jane's handwriting on it. Her eyes narrowed to read the scrawl aloud. "'Take the dress back. Garage-oil change. Doctor's appointment. Anton?'"

"How old is the note?" Madison inquired a bit too triumphantly.

"That's what I had to determine ... So I checked with the local practice she was registered with. They told me, she was booked in that day, the day of the accident to see her usual doctor but canceled to do something else."

"So, you think she canceled to do the recipient of my private life?"

"No, I didn't say that …When I interviewed your Mr. Winter, he said Jane had declined to help him out, had felt bad not doing so, and had gone up to the cliffs on the coast road to try and catch him."

"I think the only person who's trying to catch Anton is you."

"We found his print on her cab audio system controls as well."

"Eddie, this is going to come as a shock, but Anton and Jane were friends long before I came along. They knew each other. If they didn't, it might be weirdly suspicious that his prints were everywhere, capeesh?"

Eddie coughed, a riled look overshadowing his face. "So how come he initiated the 911 call about her crash from his cell phone?" He dressed her down with his eyes. "I admit that maybe your guy can run fast, but he cannot keep up with an SUV for three miles, or did she conveniently drop him off just before she crashed? In his statement, his car was still not working at the time of the crash. He called the tourist information board in Santa Monica for some outlandish reason and told them a car had just gone off the cliffs. He gave the exact location. They called 911. By a sheer fluke, we pinpointed his call by checking all calls made in Santa Monica within minutes of when the car left the road and flew off the cliff, which puts him at the crime scene when it happened. So your choices are: he is either superhumanly athletic, or his eyesight is guided by some experimental, high-tech military system no one in the world knows about, or more bizarrely, he lied in his statement. To make matters worse, the coroner's report says Jane Mitchell was pregnant. That's maybe why he wanted her dead," Eddie yelled, hammering home the facts to Madison's disbelieving sense of reality. "So, which one is it going to be?"

"Oh! Anton, you idiot," Madison exhaled, letting the repercussions of the information she had just received wind her to tears. "Eddie, please don't move on this yet. I'm sure there's an explanation. Let me work on it. If it looks indisputable, technically speaking, I will help push for a prosecution date. But please, let me try to see if he's innocent. "

"I don't know, Madison. It looks pretty indisputable, to me, already. Your judgment seems to be pretty clouded by this guy. Can I trust you to uphold your responsibilities?" Eddie asked, pausing with an 'are you serious' expression. "I mean, if anyone in the top brass knew, I'd be gone like that." Eddie snapped his fingers. "What, with your relationship to the suspect and all ..." Eddie added as Madison's body and face conveyed how mortified she felt.

Eddie broke the silence. "Okay, we haven't spoken today, and you've got exactly the life expectancy of a mayfly to prove us all wrong," Eddie announced, clearing away the suitcase to leave. He got two steps away from Madison.

"Does your personal crusade on criminality extend to the disturbed lobotomy-lottery contestant who wants my guts for garters?"

Eddie stopped in his tracks to turn back to Madison. He pulled out another evidence bag, containing the scalpel. Its blade in a grooved plastic strip guard, left behind by the killer who tried to attack Madison in the detention center. "That's on the top of my priority list."

"What is that thing?" Madison asked, regretting the brattish remark she had made.

"I'm told it's a pachydermal scalpel. A tool used in zoological surgery."

"There cannot be too many people with access or knowledge of those. I would have thought it under the specialized category."

"We've got a lot of people chasing that up, don't worry. When I get a 'for sure,' you'll be informed immediately."

"That's what I'm afraid of."

Eddie took two more steps back toward Madison. "You shouldn't be afraid of this fruitcake."

"It's not him I'm afraid of. There are hidden forces at work in all of this. Hidden loose ends I'm incapable of seeing. It's all too personal. I'm afraid of myself. I'm afraid by piecing this together I might discover dormant secrets to do with my past, sealed off by those around me for my own protection."

Madison altered her attention from the intangible she was grasping for back to Eddie. "Thanks," she exclaimed as enthusiastically as she could under the circumstances. It was all she could do when she saw that Eddie's expression communicated that he had no idea what she was talking about before a look of worry crossed through his eyes.

"Don't worry, Eddie. I'm glad you're on top of everything. I can see why Martin considered you a symmetrical equal," Madison threw in, cringing at her own sham style of praise. She could practically see Eddie waving his hand to clear away the annoying stench of bullshit.

"Okay, play it where your instincts take you, but keep your insoles planted firmly on the ground. I'll be seeing you ..." Eddie offered without conviction. Eddie crossed to the entrance-exit. "I know Martin never said that about me, though I'd like to think he thought it once or twice," Eddie called out with an emotional obstruction in his voice.

He had his back to Madison in the doorway of the outdoor firing range. She glanced over to the door with some compassion, but Eddie was gone. She wanted to hide her face in shame for selfishly trying to inflict a wound on someone whose dignified decision it was to successfully disguise his pain.

Chapter 15

Madison tidied her apartment, awaiting Anton's arrival. She moved two armchairs in the lounge so they faced each other. To avoid a staged interrogation vibe, she altered the standard lamp's direction she had just moved away from the armchair she had assigned for him. A box of tissues on the coffee table between the two positioned armchairs might come in handy for her since she'd never seen him get too upset.

He buzzed on the intercom, so she quickly searched for the enlarged photo she had gotten from Jane's husband that morning. She snapped it into the silver-colored frame she had brought specifically for that purpose in Jane's favorite color, placing it by the tissues on the coffee table so Jane's face sat before him. She pressed the recording button on her Handycam, then hid it between a couple of books beside the gargoyle bookend that sat on her set of shelves against the back wall of the lounge. The three-hour tape would be enough to capture his innocence or guilt.

She rushed over to the intercom. "Who is it?"

"Someone who wouldn't mind getting naked with you," Anton called back.

"Oh, hi, Sebastian," Madison joked, feeling a dark mood pull her down when she thought of the unformed embryo in Jane's womb. She wiped some tears from her eyes.

"Oh! It's me, Anton. Who is Sebastian?" he called back, playing along with the act.

Madison hit the in button. While she waited for him to reach her door, she assessed the events that had urged her to deviously construct a confrontation with the man she thought warranted a preliminary living room trial to establish if he deserved being given the benefit of the doubt. Her thoughts stretched to evaluate the day before. She heard a tap at the door and went to answer it.

Anton strolled into the apartment. He scanned the key holder. He paused as he scanned the room then resumed strolling inside toward Madison and planted a kiss on her lips.

Madison went into the open-plan kitchen area to pour them both a glass of Sonoma Merlot. She looked up from monitoring the steadiness of the liquid contained in each glass in conjunction with her paces to see Anton had opened the sliding door balcony. Madison stopped at the threshold.

"Hey, spring evenings in Santa Monica are not renowned for their cotton-blouse temperatures," Madison said with an inflection of humor.

"There's something exciting going on out here. I heard sirens all over the city."

"Well, take this, and I will put a jacket on." Madison giggled, hiding her disappointment that the moment was not right for her questions to Anton.

The distraction softened the moment. Above, the throb of a stationary engine over the apartment complex's roof intensified, but she thought nothing of it at first. Hollywood studios filmed over Santa Monica regularly, or it was another of L.A.'s phenomenal amount of police chases going on. She came out of her bedroom, doing up buttons on a thick, woolen jacket.

She snatched up her glass to join Anton who sipped his wine on the balcony. She leaned forward, resting on her elbows beside him. Multiple sirens grew louder. Madison gaped up to the rapidly sporadic lights of a helicopter above them.

"That's either a police chopper or it's a news crew ... Something big is going down somewhere—" Anton replied, tensing his face.

They both stared up, intent to watch a second helicopter dash across the view of the sky, allowed by the rectangular confines of the apartment complex's walled-in structure.

"That was close. They almost hit this place."

No sooner had Madison got the eight words of the sentence out than the recklessly flown helicopter swooped back toward the stationary aircraft. The night's sky emitted a loud fiberglass shattering sound.

Anton and Madison stood upright to move back, uncertain of what had just happened. The sequentially pulsating aviation lights a hundred and forty-five feet overhead transfixed them. They stared in horror as three people appeared, tumbling downward from the black sky above them.

Two of the bailing crew splash-landed into the pool at the center of the complex. The other hit the pool's edge in a sitting position. His legs slammed into the water. The squelching, bone-crunching sound his body made on impact compelled Anton and Madison to moan out loud.

Before they could react further, the helicopter's tail rotor spun down to the pool, going from darkness into light. It achieved some leverage on the pool's surface, flipping to catch the tiled pool's side, then shot off like an arrow to the left-hand side of Madison's apartment. Traumatized by the overall accident's sheer speed, Anton and Madison followed the progress of the tail rotor blade's journey across the apartment complex's recreation area. It pierced the blank cinder-block, rough-plaster-covered stretch of wall beside Madison's bedroom window where it quivered off the rest of its unexpended energy. The downed chopper's fuselage fell sideways onto a row of white sun loungers. Its main top rotor blade thrashed in the water, fragmenting its blades on contact with the dolphin-mosaic bottom.

Madison still stared at the tail rotor blade stuck in the wall beside her home. As Anton pulled her back to lay flat to protect her from flying glass, they fell to her apartment's floor through the open balcony door. Then it came ... a rumble compatible to thunder. An incandescent glow filled the room, rolling up to the sky, until the apartment grew dark again.

A shower of glass expanded to fill the room, pelting Anton's back, covering Madison, and becoming a heavy, sharply dangerous version of confetti in a brutal, parallel universe.

She pushed him off of her to stand up with her fists clenched in desperation.

"It's him!" she yelled.

"Get down, get down," Anton called out, trembling.

Madison ran to the kitchen counter. She grabbed her car keys to run for the door. She ran out to the stairs that led down to the tenants' underground parking lot. She stopped on top of the stairs to catch her breath so she could continue sobbing. When she threw open the door to the parking lot, she squeezed the button on her key ring remote to disarm the alarm and disengage the central locking. A fizzling noise discharged from under her car hood followed by an electrical pop. A lick of flame on the dashboard blackened the windshield's low-middle glass.

Anton's back was numb. Madison had convulsed with fear beneath him before she had run off. Standing up, he gently made his way through the open door to Madison's bedroom to the full-length mirror. The shock wave of the fuel flare-up had exploded all the light bulbs. Cautiously, Anton crossed his forearms over the back of his neck to lift his shirt. He tugged at the cotton of his clothing, but it was caught on resistance. Darting pain accompanied the loosening of his shirt's tightness.

Madison burst back into the apartment. "Anton, where are the fire extinguisher and your car keys?"

"The extinguisher is in the trunk. My keys are in my pocket."

Madison ran over to him.

"Anton, don't move."

"Madison, help. I'm gonna pass out."

Madison rushed forward to assist him in the gentle transition from standing to sitting on the edge of her bed.

"I don't feel a thing," he cried.

Madison didn't want to tell him that his back was bleeding worrying amounts. She reached out, alarmed to feel some nasty-edged glass slithers protruding from his torn shirt that were definitely lodged in his back's more muscular parts. She ran the side of her flat hand down his backbone to perform a quick examination to establish his spine was uninjured. It concerned her that he was numb to the pain. She pinched the widest piece of glass she could fathom by touch because the amount of light in the room did not permit her to see Anton's face, which was right next to hers. She wiggled the triangular-shaped shard.

"Can you feel that?" she asked.

"What?" Anton replied. "Ouch!" he screamed when she extracted it from his body. "Please don't touch me!" he yelled. "I'm going to faint."

Anton fell to his side, silenced by his resistance's cutoff point.

Another helicopter outside circled above the apartment complex, bringing Madison back to the job at hand. She tapped on his exposed thigh to find which pocket his keys were in. A restrained jingle of metal on metal enabled her to acknowledge that perhaps, in a phase in her life when luck was at a premium, she could at last take comfort from the odds that he wasn't lying on his keys. Madison felt around his belt loops to the entrance of his pocket when something sliced into her knuckle a little way in. She hastily transferred her hand from his pocket to her mouth, expressing some distress. With the other hand, Madison carefully felt around the fabric of his pants outside his pocket until she located the sharp obstacle.

Madison stood up to go out to the kitchen to search for a flashlight in one of the drawers. She found it and twisted the lens head. It blinked on. She went back into the bedroom, ignoring the urge to go to the balcony to check on the crash site at the pool. Madison shone the flashlight onto the carpet to identify what had cut her knuckle. The flashlight beamed on the elliptical focal ring that slipped up Anton's leg to his pocket. She shrieked. A wide, triangular slither of flying glass had stuck a long way into his thigh. She wiggled it also.

"Does that hurt?" she asked.

"How long have you wanted me to be a voodoo doll?" Anton groaned, lost in unconsciousness.

Madison pinched the piece of glass, withdrawing it fast. Anton attempted to do a sit-up with both his hands on the hole left by the glass. He moaned, then promptly fell back, quiet. Madison felt his pulse before she called for an ambulance on the landline.

While she sat waiting for them, she tried to figure out what was going on. Her cellular rang out for attention, charging its battery on the kitchen work surface.

"Madison Paige," she said, her voice trembling beyond recognition. "You don't say, Eddie. You're currently running twenty minutes behind the rest of us ..."

She inhaled, then exhaled, not concealing a sob.

"Well, the stolen police helicopter was used to ram the tail of an airborne news crew ..."—she ran a tissue under her eye—"who with their chopper crash-landed in our pool ... at my place, yes ... I suggest you get back on duty. I suspect the same thing. I can't bring myself to call him a person. He unsuccessfully rigged explosives in my car ... It malfunctioned, I guess ... Upset, Eddie? Consider how much planning it took just to get the news chopper in the right position. He's been watching me for months. He's been in my apartment when I'm not here. Now, if we don't get a few steps ahead of him, you'll be sending out invitations for my funeral," Madison rationally submitted to the cellular phone's receiver by which time she had reached Anton's car to get in. "I've called an ambulance, but there's no sign of them. Ant's hurt pretty badly. Can you get up here?"

Madison rotated the car to the exit ramp while the gate lifted upward. She stopped talking to check her car was not ablaze, but the fire had gone out of its own accord. She grew tired of listening to advice. "No, Eddie, something has to be done tonight. Bye," she added, closing the call.

The car climbed out of the underground parking lot for Madison to find several randomly parked ambulances blocking her way. She let down the car window.

"There's a guy bleeding to death in apartment A-306. Get someone up there immediately."

The technician talking into a lapel-fixed radio microphone didn't ask who she was but headed for the gate that Madison had already initiated to reopen with her remote key transmitter.

She pushed the accelerator, pleasantly surprised how in control of the situation she was, how utterly churned up her insides were by the fact that her nerves had switched themselves off to be untangled at a later date and how rapidly Anton's car went from naught to sixty in a matter of seconds.

She made a right turn below a street lamp and noticed the 911 scanner in the passenger seat next to her. She satisfied her doubts that its existence explained how Anton had intercepted a cellular call about Jane's accident and that he could not get through to 911 for some reason, either, so he had called the tourist information board to make sure one of the rerouted calls got someone out there. Pleased with herself, she nudged the switch to turn the scanner on, keeping a visual on the road. She skipped across the emergency airways that communicated in their own robotically numerical colloquialisms. Carefully, she monitored each coded dispatch until she came across a conversation between a police pilot and a highway patrol car.

"That's a roger, 249. Suspect bearing west back to Santa Monica. Over." The chopper blades whisked the base of the clouds in the background.

"Roger that, Sierra Bravo 4410, give locale of bearings. Over."

"Sector 31. Repeat Sector 31. Over and Out."

The A.B.S. system on Anton's car allowed Madison to do a U-turn without stopping, much to the horn-honking protest jitters of extremely close, oncoming traffic going in the opposite direction.

Soon, Madison headed out of the concentration of streetlamps in downtown toward a collection of flying, sequential strobe lights, busy overhead. The legitimate police helicopter, chasing the stolen one from the airborne division, closed in. It sped beneath the front of the suspect's aircraft, banking in a sideways maneuver, to rise in a swift ascent and then down again, threatening to block its path. Unfortunately for the brave police pilot, he didn't realize he was dealing with a desperately unstable criminal who couldn't have pulled back on the joystick in time anyway.

From inside the stolen chopper, the smash of the pilot cockpit canopy against the undercarriage section of the police helicopter's viewing bubble rammed both chopper blades' top rotors so close to collision they chaffed. The glancing collision, instantaneously, created far-reaching fractures that appeared forked stretching along and around each aircraft's bulbous transparent observation casings.

Madison slowed down to pull over by the side of the road. Both pilots were now flying in potentially flawed eggshells that could come apart at any minute, throwing off canopy fragments into the blades keeping them aloft. Madison lost track of which police helicopter was stolen and which one was in pursuit.

Splitting up, one chopper spun around its own point of axis and went down into a clearing in some trees. The second hovered, observing, but dropped in altitude gradually close by.

Madison shifted the transmission into gear to go cross-country. She turned off the headlights and decreased her speed. She looked in the rearview mirror, curious why no patrol cars followed her. Madison pulled up to stop her vehicle close to the clearing. She moved from tree to tree until she was close to the legitimate police-piloted chopper.

The police pilot swung open his chopper door to get out. Madison was close enough to hear his radio dispatch over the roar of the damaged aircraft that stammered to close down its engine. She sank back into the shadows.

He scoped the chopper in the clearing on his tiptoes. Its blade still turned on a malfunctioning whisper mode. He leaned back into his chopper's cockpit to engage his radio. "This is Sierra Bravo 1104. I'm on the ground. Situation is still ongoing. Advise. Over."

A crackling fed response made him put the radio mouthpiece, attached to a curling, coated wire from the control panel, to his chest. He looked past the forking splits in the downed helicopter's cockpit plexiglass. "If I wait for backup, he'll be gone," the pilot told himself. Her moving reflection in the chopper cockpit plexiglass must have gotten his attention because he put his hand on his gun handle, hugging his hip in its holster. He whipped around in the instant it took to withdraw his pistol.

"Put it down," he called out to Madison who was aiming a high caliber weapon at him just steps away.

She waved the gun, staring past him. "Move, you don't understand what you're dealing with. I'm Madison Paige. I work with … I worked with Detective Martin Thompson. Radio Detective Eddie Manfred for the all clear. He's with the Santa Monica Homicide Division."

"Do you have a badge to back that up?" he asked.

"No, but if you don't take my word for it, you will lose him. You must have heard about the recent detention center incident. I'm the woman who was mistakenly locked up."

The pilot looked back over his shoulder at the downed chopper. "What, and you think that's the animal who killed six officers just to get to you?"

"Without a doubt," Madison answered.

The pilot lowered his gun to crouch down for Madison to get next to him. She did so.

"Why did you take my word for it?"

"Because you could have shot me long before I turned around if you weren't who you said you were."

"Good point ... Any movement from in there yet?" she asked.

"None as yet. Do you think he's got full body armor on? Like the day he went after you? It's real tough downing a suspect in that getup," the pilot replied, staring at the kind of gun Madison was holding. "Mind you, that should cause him some trouble."

Madison surveyed the pilot's face beside her. He was a lot younger than her, nervous but brave enough to stand up for what he believed was right.

"What's taking them so long?" the pilot complained, referring to his backup.

"What's your name?" Madison asked, struggling to move her head over to read the name badge on his breast pocket, but it was only an initial followed by his surname.

"Bennett," the pilot answered, giving his surname.

"How long have you been a cop?"

"I'm a veteran, entering week two of active service, hence the incorrect sector number I gave for backup."

"And they put you up there alone?"

"Not normally. I just saw 091 go up, heard on the radio it was unauthorized, and gave chase."

"Well, Police Pilot Bennett, we can't wait any longer for the cavalry to arrive. Make sure you keep a good aim on that cockpit. If you see anything move before I get there, blast it. Whether I'm in the way or not."

"Will do, ma'am," Bennett answered, pulling back his pistol's outer casing to move a bullet into the firing chamber.

Madison stooped down to run with her gun, angled to the ground. She came to an abrupt halt. She pressed her body flat behind a tree. Some fifteen feet from the chopper, she monitored Bennett to make sure he was still holding down the potentially dangerous cockpit. Through the darkness, Bennett could be seen waving an arm in the air that was quickly brought under control. Madison could just make out a patch of beige clasped over his mouth. He was being used as a human shield while the other hand holding his gun was being smashed against his chopper's outer cockpit window to make him relinquish his grip on it.

"Come out, come out, wherever you are! I promise I'll let him go!" a voice called out, sounding more phonetically demented for not having the required length of tongue necessary to speak.

"You'd better. Backup will be here any minute," Madison called out, still hidden behind the tree.

A gunshot rang out. The bullet grazed the bark on the tree Madison hid behind. It thudded into another tree's timber, much further back. The faint wailing meant backup was at last moving in the right direction. A series of muffled shots followed. Madison put one eye past the line of the tree trunk just as Bennett fell to his knees, exposing his killer behind him. The killer held the gun in the same position it had been fired in. He had shot Bennett at point-blank range in the scapula to exit through his name badge. Bennett died before he hit the ground, face first from his kneeling position.

Madison stepped from behind the tree, running toward the killer without a care for her own safety. She squeezed off a volley of shots, one of which struck its target, passing through the killer's pelvis to cut out from the other side. The powerful round threw him back, taking him off his feet. He lifted his gun to return fire, put off by a spotlight that had swung into the clearing on another police helicopter's thumping beat. Madison used her forearm to protect her sight from the overbearing searchlight.

"Put down your weapons!" the chopper hailing system commanded.

Madison ignored the order, still trying to take aim while warding off the spotlight's glare. Noisy patrol cars, their lights blinding in the blackness of the clearing's acreage, appeared from every conceivable point of the compass. Madison made a final attempt to search beyond the commotion to where she had seen him go down.

They searched all night, but he had only left behind traces of blood from his gunshot wound.

Lack of sleep made Madison irritable, so she had a hard time focusing on the next task at hand—getting to the hospital. A headache that would make a woodpecker want to lie down with some Ibuprofen closed in on her overactive thought processes how a high tide rushes into a bay shaped like a horseshoe. By the time she finally got to the hospital, Anton was in stable condition and a nurse was checking his stitches. Madison waited outside the walk-in emergency room's cordoned-off ward. She needed to get home to sleep, but the thought she'd almost got the tongueless bastard harassing her persisted. She chased up Eddie by way of his pager and satellite phone for the sixth time that morning but couldn't get a hold of him. She wondered if he'd switched off his devices.

Chapter 16

His fist was double the width of an average man's, with nails that could accommodate a quarter being rested on them that would leave a perimeter around the edges that showed pink, linear formed nails underneath. Across the bottom section of his substantial digits, D.I.Y, indelible ink letters spelled out 'FATE' for reading outward. He sank the finger, marked 'E' as far as it would go into the byway Madison had commissioned through his pelvis. He removed his finger, producing a noise connected with the subsidence of suction.

Feeling around to the space above his buttock, he writhed the same blood-lubricated forefinger into the larger opening, acknowledging the bullet had passed through at great velocity, piercing the bone instead of smashing it. Long lit coals in a domed barbecue unit shimmered red with heat in the grill, a treasure trove of miniature suns. He used tongs to pick an orb of glowing coal while his blood-soaked grasp picked up layers of meat lying on a cutting board. He prodded a portion of the raw meat into the gaping hole beside his hip. He packed the hot coal down into the wound, similar to the loading of an old-fashion musket.

He savored the aroma of sizzling flesh. A true connoisseur of torment, he'd extended his barriers by a lifetime of inflictions. To him, torture had become a pleasure, in both its receiving and giving. When the coal had cooled down from fusing the graft, he pulled it out of the smoldering indentation it left to smell it closer to his nostrils. A thought occurred to him. He pushed out his stunted tongue, and with the coal's residual heat, he spawned another notion to melt together the untidy seam that the natural healing process had closed. His mouth's neuralgia proved familiar, but this time, from the proximity to the coal and the severed tongue, it made his mouth water. The lack of any sensation in his charred tongue made him welcome the numbness, but it wouldn't hold him up for long as his adrenaline rushed through him. He'd survived.

When Eddie had been satisfied all criteria set by the Santa Monica chief of police had been met to resolve recent developments, he had gone down to the morgue to view what he had trouble believing. Police Pilot Bennett's naked body lay on an autopsy slab.

"Ah, Eddie, I'm glad you could come down."

"I'm not, Luke ... So this is the poor bastard?"

"That's him ... Tell me what you see."

"A murdered cop, Luke. What is this? Who wants to be a sad bastard instead of a millionaire?"

"Now, bear with me. Keep in mind Paige said he was shot last night." Luke pulled out a telescopic indicator that looked a lot like the aerial Eddie had snapped off his Buick a year ago in the parking lot of police headquarters. "Testimony supported by the evidence of a blown-open ribcage, here." Luke pointed at Bennett's fatal injuries.

"So, the mystery here is?" Eddie asked through clenched teeth, mentally berating Luke for wasting his time.

"The mystery here is, Edward, where on earth did this young man's arm go?"

"It got shot off, I would imagine."

"No, it was hacked off by this assailant who had just been shot while a comprehensive show of force closed in around him, and he still got away."

Eddie's hands dropped to his sides. He moved back a little, his gaze unfocused. A light-headedness drowned out the room momentarily as he restricted his breathing. Focused again, he scrambled to understand. "You see, Luke. You told me this this morning. A body part was missing. I'm here, looking at it, but I still cannot bring myself to believe it."

"Well, no one would accept this butcher's methods, and frankly, I've seen a lot of shit in my life." Luke flexed his fingers repeatedly, jamming a few instruments away on his counter without care. Eddie found Luke's agitation took him over the edge as his blood boiled. He wouldn't stand for this sick fuck being out on the loose.

"Luke, ever seen a guy with his tongue half-bitten off? That's our guy. Hopefully, he'll be in that drawer soon," Eddie vented, pointing to a steel drawer beside Bennett's dead body.

Luke didn't look convinced. "I think he's going to give Santa Monica officers a hell of a time, and I'm not saying I'm totally disillusioned, but I do have to say ..."—Luke pressed his lips into a fine line wrinkling his nose like there was a bad smell—"I'm a little—"

"Don't say it, Luke. Yes, this guy's got us worked up, but better yet, I suspect it won't be long before his blood paintings convince him he can hesitate and got us beat."

Luke scanned the drawers, seemingly choosing his words carefully as his eyes narrowed in on the drawer Eddie had pointed to. He pointed to it and said, "Let's hope so, Eddie. Remember the Grendel case?"

Eddie thought for a moment, then bristled. "I resent that, Luke. We don't need to reference that one. This will pan out." An unsettling heaviness settled into his chest.

Madison proceeded to assist the computer Photofit compiler in filling out a questionnaire. The ordeal of having to identify the young police pilot's body for the coroner's report to bring the previous night's activities to closure had burned her out. As the solitary witness to the shooting, she was obligated to fulfill this duty. She leaned forward to pull another Kleenex out of a grandly designed pastel cube box. Her exchange with Bennett from the night before crossed her mind. The stiff, waxy-skinned remains of a person she had seen in the morgue that morning looked nothing like the pilot.

"Are you sure you want to go on?"

"Yeah! I'm okay. I'm just in shock at the waste of life going on around me."

"I don't think anybody could ever get used to that. Not even god herself," the Photofit compiler sympathized, reaching out to Madison's clenched hand to commiserate.

She retrieved a sheet of paper from her pocketbook on her desk and went over to a photocopying machine. She placed the sheet of paper onto the copier's glass panel, closing the lid. A line of brilliance moved through the machine, which spilled out of its gaps, to eventually eject a blotchy twin of what she had put there. She picked it up, reclaiming the original to cross the room back to Madison.

"Here, my mother gave me this before she passed away," the compiler said in a soothing voice.

Madison took the copy from her.

The compiler squeezed her other hand and let it go. "Whenever I feel I cannot take it anymore, this puts me right back in the saddle."

Madison looked down at the text on the sheet of paper.

The Photofit compiler smiled, removing the sheet of paper she had just given Madison. "Here, take the original. It's not much, but this page has absorbed a lot of love in recent years."

This simple act of kindness overwhelmed Madison. "Thank you," she said, beginning to cry again.

"Hush, read it. The storm will pass," the compiler added, pressing her palm to her heart.

"Though critics slate with vengeful hate, we still create to challenge fate. Wisdom can appreciate. It's not too late to change our date with the twisted rhymes of fate. Once mocked, hazy names, now you may laugh, passerby, with flowers bunched with life so plenty, you will be here," Madison read, thinking the unusual verse was a tongue twister.

"I know, what you're thinking," the compiler said. "I thought the same. But over time, this came to be a song of strength for me. Use it wisely, and it will get you through anything ... It's almost like an incantation." She grinned.

Madison folded it up, not saying a word, feeling remarkably better. She stood up to bend forward, landing a kiss on the compiler's cheek. "You don't know how much this means to me."

"I do, probably as much as this means to the both of us," the compiler answered, steadily completing her task and activating the computer program. The monitor screen displayed the loading icon, which grew in length, gaining blocked-in color and increasing its percentage downloaded.

It went blank to return the face Madison feared the most. "That's him. You're a genius," she complimented.

"It's the program, not me."

While the ink jet printer produced Madison's nightmare into a reality repeatedly, Eddie knocked on the frame of the open door. "Coffee machine. Five minutes," he directed at Madison. "There's been some hard-line decisions made upstairs," Eddie added, meaning decisions made by the pay bracket above his.

"Okay, quit bugging her. She'll be out in five minutes. Now, get off my property," the compiler answered for her, scolding Eddie in a lightheartedly serious fashion.

Eddie pulled a face like a schoolboy who had been verbally rebuked by a tutor. He disappeared from the doorway.

"What do you think of that rude, arrogant man?" the compiler asked Madison.

"Who, Eddie? He's clever, kind, courageous, and about the best cop any police force could come across," Madison strung together eloquently in Eddie's defense, suggesting she was opposed to the compiler's disrespectful view of him.

"Well, it's a good job I gave in and married the cheesy, old critter once upon a time, I suppose," the compiler confessed, giggling. She followed up with a wink and contorted her face as she repeated in a low, gruff voice, "There's been some hard-line decisions made upstairs!" she whimpered, clutching at Madison for support. "What kind of way is that to say, 'Um, shit just got real, and I got no say!?'"

Madison chuckled. "You're Eddie's wife?" Madison voiced, astounded and pleased she hadn't voiced a negative opinion of him.

"Vegas, 1979, I remember like it was just yesterday. Oh, it was. He's nothing like he is here at home. I still get off a different shift than him to find a red rose next to a perfectly prepared dish. He loves to cook. If you can keep it confidential, he enjoys cooking more than I do. But don't just take my word for it. You should come over to our place next Tuesday night. Don't forget. Now, go and see what that old snoop wants," she said. "I'm Carolyn by the way ... and you are Madison. I've heard all about you."

Madison shook Carolyn's slender, ivory-colored hand, thanked her again, and went out to find Eddie who she found skimming blobs of undissolved instant coffee off of his vending machine choice.

"You know about the fly boy's arm missing, then?"

"Yeah, I pointed it out to the officer in charge of the investigation at the scene."

"Weird or what? This guy is supernatural. He seems to be able to walk through walls. Are you sure nobody saw him get away last night?"

"Positive! He looks human enough though," she answered, holding up the computer photo fit.

"Is it a good likeness?"

"That's him," Madison called out.

"I'll make sure this gets scanned into the national surveillance data bank. I hope you realize your reluctance to commit to the Photofit investigation procedure, earlier, after the jail incident, for example, could have contributed to a delay in this animal's capture."

A pained expression covered Madison's face. She'd relived the moment so many times, regretting she hadn't been able to shoot and take decent photos at the same time. "I could kick myself that I could barely see his face the day he stalked me on the low mountain roads to Jane's ..."—she briefly gave Eddie a flat stare—"but I could see what he was doing, and it sent me right into self-defense mode. The light was too dim in the jailhouse. I could do this today because when I ran at him, the spotlight lit him up like a Christmas tree."

"Okay," Eddie said. He shifted his weight from one foot to another, then looked around him, accepting her explanation. He wrote something down on a note pad he held. "They'll insert this in the national data bank to be part of the instant recognition program. This guy had better not travel, shop, go and watch a movie, or even walk in a built-up area where there are cameras. Now, regarding all these shenanigans in the past few days, I need you to put your association with Anton Winter on hold. We didn't get a chance to determine his exact role in Mitchell's death yet."

Madison took a couple of steps back from Eddie. She recalled the conversation they had had at the shooting range. Him saying 'That's not a gun, Maddie. That's a cannon.' played through her mind on replay. She had told Eddie that she would see if Anton was innocent, but everything had changed, and the killer's actions at her apartment and Anton getting diced by glass buried the opportunity.

"Right, Eddie. About that, I never had a chance given helicopter parts and people were falling out of the sky." She swayed slightly as tears welled up in her eyes. Her emotional numbness set in, momentarily forgetting that she'd managed to give enough details to recreate her worst nightmare's facial features over the past few weeks.

Eddie continued as if her shock didn't register, but she recognized a slight indicator light had gone off in his eyes that told him he'd touched the right nerve. "He is a prime suspect in our investigation of Jane Mitchell's made-to-look-like-an-accident murder. It's been decided we will hold him for extensive questioning for as long as we can. It might turn out we get a conviction. So,

I would advise you to end it," he continued. He leaned closer to Madison to emphasize the gravity of the advice he had just given.

"End it? Who the hell do you think you are?"

"A friend who doesn't want to see a lot of hurt, which could possibly end in a spotlessly maverick career getting trashed."

Madison stared at Eddie, unable to find any more fuel for her outrage.

"He is being brought down any minute now for a polygraph examination."

"How did you get permission for that?"

"Tony Mitchell, Jane's husband, plays golf with the district attorney. One palm greases another in this town," Eddie explained, looking from side to side.

She looked around herself, simply out of habit, to also ensure no one was eavesdropping at the vending machines.

"You've got nothing to lose. If he is morally sanitized, he'll understand and take you back in a flash. If he's a germ-ridden, murdering son of a bitch, you've said farewell to the dark ages. The last thing anyone wants around here is the local news asking if you're implicated in any way."

"I see, but it's hard if you're attached," Madison said, preparing herself. She found it hard to stop the rippling cartilage in her throat from making her swallow this defeat while her tear ducts began to adequately express her disappointment.

Eddie put his hand on her shoulder. "I know it's hard to say goodbye to someone you care about. That's why none of us here want him to get a chance to drag you down with him."

Madison looked up at Eddie, not understanding what he had just implied.

"So we don't have to say goodbye to you, should the worst come to the worst. This is not a job, Madison. It's a way of life."

Madison drew in a deep breath to reinforce herself. "I know. Thanks for reminding me who I am, though I complain about what I feel I was born to do."

"Don't mention it. If I were a crooked cop, I would hope someone loyal to the fraternity of good cops would advise my Caroline to start divorce proceedings before my first court appearance had been set ... in a profession filled with temptation, my love for her has kept me on the straight and narrow." Eddie glanced at his watch. "He'll be down in interrogation room six, to the left, second on the right, when you're ready. Show your driver's license to the crew down there for I.D. They know you're coming."

Madison took a while to compose herself before she followed Eddie's directions to the interrogation room. Once there, she didn't engage anyone. She showed her driver's license but kept her eyes on Anton through the observation, mirrored window while a member of the team conducting the cross examination showed her around to the interview room door.

Inside the room, Anton was receiving a cup of coffee from a shapely female police officer in tight uniform pants who held his attention.

He longingly took in the female officer's well-exercised rear and rounded hips, bending over in front of him to pick up a stack of statement sheets she had knocked off the table by mistake while she was making space for his coffee.

Before she was allowed to approach Anton, the officer in charge held Madison's arm to speak into her ear. "I'm taking everyone out of there. And I'm switching everything off."

"I appreciate that. Some privacy is relevant to this," Madison replied.

Anton followed the progress of the female officer's behind across the room to Madison. He noticed her as Madison walked over to him.

"That's the indefinable difference between men and woman," Madison said, propositioning Anton's look of surprise.

"There's no harm in looking at the menu when you're on a diet," Anton replied.

"The problem is men can only think up to when they hurriedly fire their seed, while a woman can only think what might happen afterwards. That's why we are experiencing the universe so differently. You see yourself hooked up to a lie detector machine, whereas I see you hooked up to a lethal injection machine. I was at a stage of my life, almost ready to confront the subject of whether or not I'm in love with you, Anton. Get out of this without a glitch, and you might make up my mind for me ... You think caffeine is a good idea at a time like this?" Madison proclaimed.

She turned in silence and left the room. She took a seat next to the polygraph analyst in the observation room. She had met the analyst on numerous occasions in the past, working on investigations with Martin Thompson. The analyst adjusted the sensitivity sliders on the command panel. Madison looked down to her left at the etching needles, tipped with ink jets, anticipating her own personal earthquake that would soon be measured on the Richter scale of truth. This type of new technology allowed the machine's main workings to remain hidden in the observation room.

All Anton wore was a small headset. He had skin glue sensors on his pulse and tip clamps on each index finger. Development of this device meant that a remote unit, which relayed signals to the observation room, replaced the spaghetti of wire and cables from previous models.

Two officers trained in interrogation took their seats before Anton. Madison was so tired she caught herself nodding off. She pulled her head up, quickly shaking it, to try and wake up.

"Did you take direct action by making the vehicle faulty in some way? Or by placing an obstacle in harm's way, thus causing Jane

Mitchell's car to leave the road over cliffs on P.C.H?" the interrogation officer asked.

"No!" Anton replied, bursting her awake. The erratic sound of the etchers on the graph paper followed that would decide how Anton would spend the rest of his life.

Madison entered the interrogation room with two coffees.

"It's over," the analyst told her.

She handed him a cup. "Already? How does it look?"

"So far, it doesn't look good, but I have to examine it in more detail to determine its accuracy."

Madison moved forward to the observation window that she could see through but Anton could not. He was nervous. His smiles to the officers who were peeling off the sensors were fake. Madison caught an uncertain expression in Anton's eyes when he looked at the room and at himself being released from the polygraph machine in reverse in the mirror.

Did he suspect Madison was on the other side? She held the expression in his eyes in freeze frame in her mind. "Goodbye, Anton. I really did love you," she said quietly, turning to leave the room.

"Aren't you going to wait for the results?" the analyst asked her as she passed him.

"No, I know the answer already," Madison replied, leaving the room.

Eddie got the results from Anton Winter's polygraph interrogation. "Okay! It's conclusive," he said, reading the report. "I'll do it now," he added, removing his jacket.

He rushed down to the interrogation room, stopping at the observation room's open door.

"Switch the camera on," Eddie ordered. On the monitor, Eddie entered the interrogation room.

Anton looked up at him, coming to the table he sat at.

Eddie stared at Anton. "Anton Winter, you are under arrest for as yet undetermined involvement in the death of Jane Mitchell. You have the right—"

"Blah, blah, whatever. You really don't know what a good favor you're doing for me, making me a detainee. Just beef up security on my cell. I don't want him to get the better of you again and give him a chance to get me."

Chapter 17

The gate was unlocked, so Madison climbed up the path to the house's door. She pressed the doorbell, but nobody came to answer it. She slowly and cautiously twisted the handle and let herself in. She closed the door behind her, pressing it with her back. Her probing gaze fixed on the blueing-finger-hued hallway in front of her as she scanned into the drain-cover-blue doorways and bluish-grey, morgue-cloth walls. The cooking smells of breakfast sausage and bacon faintly hung in the air. Madison put the back of her hand on the coffeepot plugged in by the aluminum stove next to the sink. It was still warm.

A further tiptoeing, room-to-room search of the house convinced Madison its occupants were out for the day, had gone to exercise, or perhaps were running some errands to return shortly. A supposition she deduced, due to the fact that Tony Mitchell's car keys were on the hallway table and from a line of footwear under the stairs, a space in the arrangement, next to some training shoes, left only polished dress shoes. She already had the evidence she needed. She didn't need to be caught in the house without a proper cop or a search warrant.

She stuck her foot on the bottom step of the staircase. "Hello?" she shouted, just in case.

A shout echoed from outside the house at the top of the stairs. She snuck into the bedroom where the open window edged in the sound. Down past the wide driveway, through a row of conifers, Tony Mitchell ran, tilted to return a woman's shot on the tennis court built at the edge of the house's garden. She recoiled, not hesitating a moment. Madison ran down the stairs to get outside.

She leapt into her car, drove out of the driveway, bounded down the winding lane that left the house, stopped, turned into another gateway entrance, reversed back into the road, and headed to the house. She took the fork in the driveway that led to the tennis court, pretending she had just arrived. She skittered out of the car, her arm raised to respond to Tony's wave. She zipped around the chain-link fencing to the court's entrance. Now, she felt like the judge, the jury, and the executioner.

"Hi, Tony! It's been a while."

"Hi, Madison! Glad you came at last. We all missed you at Jane's funeral."

"Too much, too soon. I can see you're coping okay, though," Madison delivered skillfully. Her facial expression referred to the woman he was playing tennis with.

"Yes," he remarked on a downward trend.

"Shall we go into the house to talk about old times?"

"Well, yeah! Why not ... Back in ten minutes," Tony called out to his tennis partner who waved in compliance.

His partner changed her stance to go over and wheel the auto server into place.

Madison followed Tony into the house. The one time they spoke was when Tony pointed to some floral bulbs that he had planted for Jane. Finally, they had broken ground. They adjourned to the kitchen.

"You've got a good thing going up here, Tony. Life is treating you okay, isn't it?" Madison said, pouring herself a coffee from the still-warm coffeepot.

"You could say that. I've got myself a substantially comfortable existence up here."

"The kind of existence a clever attorney wouldn't want to jeopardize. I hear prison can really affect your game, broken arms, no tennis courts, things like that."

"Ah! Shut up, and give me a kiss, you tease."

Madison crossed the kitchen to plant a kiss on Tony's mouth. They embraced tightly.

"Did they swallow Anton's jumpy detector test like I said they would?"

Madison laughed like a different person. She threw her head back. "Of course! If our planning were that bad, we wouldn't have gotten this far. How is the insurance company taking it?"

Tony nested his face into Madison's neck to kiss it. "They are worried. I'm going to take them to the cleaners for twice the amount because of Jane's coverage." He sighed, intoxicated by Madison's sensuality.

"That's the best news I've had today," Madison purred as she caressed his face. Tony turned his head to open one eye.

"So, how is the investigation going?" he asked. His expression hardened, getting stern. She touched him, and she detected a minor flinch that he'd masked by bringing her closer. She relaxed his furrowed brow.

"Eddie is such a jerk. He had the file, which I thankfully came across and destroyed before he could process it, linking Gonzales's employment history to Jane's checkbook stubs. If they knew she was your housekeeper, all of our plans would have turned to crap. I just don't understand who killed her or why?"

Tony didn't say anything.

"I would love to sit Eddie down and tell him how Jane and her boyfriend, Anton, planned to drive me crazy, then kill me, because they were mistaken that I had a father who murdered Jane's sister when they were kids. I mean it's so dumb. They were all so dumb, then my sleaze-in-shining-dollar-signs shows up—"

"Steady on," Tony interjected.

"To entice me with a plan to undermine them all, with a punch line about great sex and an even better fortune ... Are you sure you can keep whoever it is doing your killing under control?" Madison asked, changing the subject. "You should have seen what he did to that police pilot. He really didn't have to go that far. I think I accidentally shot him, whoever he is. And why did he kill Martin Thompson?"

"It has to look authentic, or it won't be. You'll get to meet him, don't worry," Tony said, feeling around to the base of Madison's back to squeeze her firm assets. "Something arrived this morning from the adoption tracers in New Jersey ... You're really going to freak when you read this. It turns out they were not so dumb. You really do have a father, after all." Tony leaned over, still holding Madison to get a letter out of the drawer beside them.

"You must be kidding, Tony."

"No, I'm not."

"Let me see it."

"Hang on, it's here. I'm glad that that fool Anton is behind bars. How you got him to kill Jane with your womanly ways is practically, genius. I mean, he completely defected out of the blue," he mentioned, still continuing to check to see if he had picked up the right letter.

"I didn't do anything. He did that of his own accord. All of this killing wasn't planned."

"Well, I'm grateful to Anton's brain. It saved me a job. I wish I could say I missed that bitch."

"I was more surprised than you when he did that."

"Maybe the idiot had really fallen for you and didn't want Jane to proceed with her plans to have you killed."

"That thought had crossed my mind," Madison said, concealing some sadness.

"You think you're so clever, don't you, Madison? I know the difference between a kiss and a kiss. I know Thompson was the only cop who knew what you're undercover responsibilities were. You would have told me if Eddie knew," Tony shouted furiously as Madison felt his hand find her cellular phone through her clothing, duct taped into the dip at the base of her spine. "Where is the mic?" he yelled, ripping open Madison's shirt.

"You're finished anyway. That conversation was just recorded into the main 911 switchboard answering machine down at Santa Monica headquarters. It gets diverted to four substations, so it can never get lost."

Tony struck Madison across the face, sending her falling into the breakfast bar furniture and cracking two of her ribs. "Did you honestly believe I invited you over here today to recap? No, today, I got you over here for you to collect your severance pay. I never trusted you one iota. You want to meet the guy who's been doing all the killing? Foster!" Tony yelled upstairs. He ran over to the intercom that went up to the attic room and leaned on the button. "She's down here, if you want to show her how much you enjoyed what she did to you. Come down! She's all yours!"

He quickly swung around to kick Madison in the stomach, bending her in half and causing her to shrill. "He has been trying to kill you from the word go, but you always got out of it. I knew you would never have agreed to come in on it all the way with me. We wanted you dead a week after I approached you, but you wanted to go it alone, without Thompson. I only needed someone with access to police files to cover things up for me. You should have been dead in that detention center. The rest has been completely out of control," Tony screamed, visibly trying to calm himself down at the same time. "Here it is, you poor lonely orphan!" He opened the letter to read it to her, barking every word, the edginess hysterical and suggested that every word confirmed his take on reality—she had always been living in her own world. "'Dear Mr. Mitchell, we are glad to inform you that our extensive search, on your behalf for your client, has located a genetic father.'"

He shifted his temperament, his voice cracking with joy, falling to his knees in front of her as she twisted on the water-hose-blue carpet. "They were right all along. It just fit in with my plans. This piece of paper cost me 2,000 bucks. Here!" Tony screwed up the letter to throw it at Madison. "The things I had to do to keep up the pretense."

Madison could hear a door closing upstairs, followed by creaking rungs coming down a ladder. She rolled over in agony, trying to crawl across the wreckage of a broken stool.

"Don't bother trying to move. He's been wanting to do some pretty nasty things to you since your dad killed his youngest back in the seventies. Oh! He wants the Anton guy pretty bad too. I get the impression he intends to do to your father what he did to him."

"I don't have a father."

"Well, it looks like you're wrong, again." Tony tapped his tennis racket against his five spread fingertips, doglegging it back to crack Madison in the jaw while she was still straining to crawl away across the kitchen floor.

The sound of someone coming down from upstairs echoed through the house. Madison rolled over, reeling from the blow Tony had delivered with the bar stool sliver cutting into her leg. She saw her orange bag on the counter, by the coffeepot, and sat up, going into a concussion. She wanted to blackout, but her hatred for Tony kept her from doing so.

"Stop! I'm warning you!" Madison called out, incomprehensibly, with her fractured jaw closed, causing her the worst pain she had ever felt. She fell to her side, catching the dangling sherbert handle strap of her shoulder bag. It fell to the kitchen floor, throwing out her pistol that slid across the tiles toward her. "Stop!"

Tony stopped before the doorway. He didn't turn around. "You're dead. Accept it!"

As Tony's tennis partner strolled up to the side door in front of Tony, the white lacy drapes on the side door went from white to spattered red instantly. His partner fell to the gravel path between two lawns. More shots cracked from the house, destroying the door further, sending Tony staggering through its weakened structure.

He fell horribly disfigured by Madison's skillful grouping of shots. He gasped to hold on to life. Then, he promptly let go of it.

Madison lay still, looking down the gun's site, breathing hard. The clean positioning of the warning shot she put through the ceiling was the final in the gun. Who was to know when the first or last shot was fired? Its existence would certainly help her case in court when she pleaded self-defense. She reached out, trying to get to her bag to reload. She heard voices in her head, memories of how it had begun, how Tony had come to see her at her apartment and Madison had thought he wanted details about Jane's infidelities. It was when she had started to date Anton. One day, Tony had arrived to tell her Jane had plans she had been working on for a year to drive Madison insane, discredit her, and then kill her. He told her how he had found out about Anton's past in New York and how Jane had blackmailed him into helping her.

Madison had told Martin about how she had intended to go in as a civilian, undercover, under his jurisdiction, not only to find out who Suzanne Gonzales's killer was but also how the entire episode demonstrated to her that fate had other plans.

Her feeble attempts to reach her bag were hindered by the rust-red gloved hands that lifted the strap before it dropped in the jerkiness of hoisting her body off the kitchen floor.

"You're definitely the scum bag's daughter. Look at the mess you made of him," he screamed out between jerky head movements, legs planted wide.

He slammed Madison in a sitting position into the kitchen sink, which broke the faucet, sending a fountain of water up her back. The pistol had slid from her hand. The huge man circled the kitchen, bulging his eyes and rolling up his sleeves. He stopped, occasionally, to stare at Tony's bloody remains outside the door, not being able to accept what she had done.

"He betrayed you all. He told me everything. I don't know who my father is. You've got to believe me!" Madison called out from between her closed teeth. Each syllable caused her unimaginable agony. "I don't have a father."

These words made his muscles and veins strain against his skin as he cracked his neck side to side. He grabbed her by the neck to lift her out of the sink. Madison brought her hand up to insert the kitchen knife her hand had fallen onto on the draining board earlier, into his cheek, missing the side of his head.

"Martin says 'Hi,'" she mumbled.

He let go of her to pull at the knife handle sticking out of his cheek that lanced the remainder of his tongue. He flew toward the counter, beside the sink, to brace himself with both hands. He withdrew the knife from his face.

"Ha, ha. You don't give up. I like that. He said you wouldn't," he gargled, sounding oddly amused.

Her eyes widened at the thought of this beast spending Martin's last moments with him. *Had he?* She didn't have time to think.

He brought his fist down hard on the coffeepot, breaking open the casing around the plug port's electrics. In reaction to the pain of the knife kicking in, he gripped Madison's neck with all his might.

Madison kicked, fighting with her last ounce of resistance. Her eyes rolled back in their sockets as if she were on the verge of ecstasy. The water started to overflow from the sink from Madison's Archimedes effect, flooding the sunken kitchen floor.

He picked up the knife that had gone through his cheek and slashed Madison's chin. She didn't react. The killer shook her violently as her body went limp while hitting the ground.

He enjoyed watching her fall back onto the wide windowsill. Her head crushed a houseplant. The soil container lifted her head enough to alter the line of her back. The water's buoyancy made her rise slightly in the continually filling sink until her legs were the counterbalance. She began, slowly at first, to slide out of the sink unit. Her arm dragged the coffeepot off of the counter as she began to slide to the floor in a rush of water. She hit the floor with the coffeepot. As the exposed electrics around the plug port contacted the water on the kitchen floor, her barefoot killer leaped without moving. The electric shock he received from the coffeepot threw him horizontally through the air to land on an upturned, broken breakfast stool Madison had smashed previously. His full weight hit the broken pieces. A broken leg of the stool impaled his chest, causing his lungs to fill with blood.

The electric shock also acted as a crude, primitive defibrillator that fired a current up the sinews and archeries of Madison's body, kickstarting her heart with a single jolt. She gasped, coughing, starved of air, feeling like she had woken up from a terrible dream. She rolled over onto her side, her mind blank. Somehow, she was alive when she shouldn't be. She managed a smile when she noticed the dead killer smoldering on the kitchen floor.

Tony's tennis partner must have dialed 911. By the time Eddie arrived, Madison was crying at the front gate describing what she had witnessed.

Eddie wandered around until a uniformed officer directed him into the house. He pulled faces while looking at the mess all over the kitchen floor. Jump-suited forensic-evidence gatherers crawled around the two bodies like drama students pretending they were crabs in a red tide's wash. Eddie skirted them to get a closer look out of the house's side door at Tony's corpse. He turned, noticing Madison sitting at the base of the stairs, wrapped in a blanket, being attended to by paramedics who told her she mustn't talk until she had an x-ray.

"Wow! Paige, you look like death warmed up. What happened here?"

"We've got to talk, Eddie," Madison said distantly. Her jaw still closed with pain.

"Let's go out," Eddie mumbled, pointing past Tony's contorted body.

"If we can go out the other door," Madison suggested, not wanting to look over at Tony's blown-apart corpse with its feet still in the kitchen.

"Yeah! Sure! I'll help you up."

"Oh! My stomach," Madison cried, wrapping her arm across her middle.

Eddie helped her to her feet. Sadness flickered across his face as he focused on her chin. She lifted her fingers to her chin, the blood on the gauze seeping through to her skin. They got past everyone present at the crime scene, much to the protest of the medical team out on one of the spacious lawns by the tennis court.

Madison filled Eddie in as they walked.

"So you were undercover, but you never told me. You should have. That was reckless," Eddie moaned.

"Jane and Anton's plan backfired. Suzanne Gonzales had cooked and cleaned for the Mitchells. She had overheard them talking and planning how they would drive someone crazy and then kill them because they were lovers. Suzanne had assumed they intended to do away with Tony Mitchell," Madison forced herself to say through her closed jaw while Eddie leaned closer to her mouth to try to understand what she was saying. "Now, it gets sordid. Tony Mitchell was servicing the help, when Jane was not in the house, and they were alone together. So when Suzanne told him what she'd heard with her ear to the bedroom door, he got her to go through Jane's papers, eavesdropping and so on ..." She clenched her jaw from the pain as it increased the more she used it, though she had to fill

Eddie in before she went to the hospital or fainted. "Until Tony found out it was me they were after, which was substantiated by the arrival of Jane's father who came to stay. Jane started to suspect Suzanne was conducting her own mop-and-bucket investigation, so she confronted her. Suzanne completely blew her cover and demanded a hundred thousand dollars to kindly keep it all a secret. A week later, we assume, a serial rapist-killer was on the loose, but we know it was staged."

"God damn, amateurs ...! Where does Jane's dad fit into this?"

"The big, nasty, bald old guy dead in the kitchen, that's him. All I know is, if what Jane told me is true, that he was a recently retired instructor in the Marines. Now, what Tony Mitchell told me is, they think my father, who I don't have, killed Jane's younger sister, and her dad wanted revenge. The really odd thing is there's a letter in there from an adoption-tracing agency that clearly states I do have a father."

"We will check it all through and sort it all out. You don't look so good, Madison."

"No, I have to get up to the hospital."

"Okay ... Oh! Wait a minute. Did you kill any of them? Or did they kill each other?"

"Only these two, Eddie." Madison appeared confused with shocked exhaustion.

"Oh, jeez! I'll sort it out. You should think before you get trigger-happy ..."

"I only shot one."

"But you're a civilian, for chrissakes. That's first-degree murder. You shot him in the back."

"There's a warning shot in the ceiling."

"Self-defense. You shot him in the back. Okay! I'll work it out."

"I'll be at the hospital ..."

All she heard Eddie say before collapsing to the lawn was "OK, heal up, in the meantime ..."

Chapter 18

Madison sat up in her hospital bed, flicking through a magazine and half-watching TV. She threw down the glossy, giving herself a self-talk to calm down and get her mind off replaying the sight of her doing nothing but healing. She had wire curving around her chin going into the bone on either side. She had difficulty talking, but she was glad she still could. A light tap on the door pulled her out of her fixating on the tightness in her chest, and a man Madison didn't know appeared.

"Can I come in, Madison?" he asked.

"And you are?"

"Eddie sent me. I'm Ben Kacey from the District Attorney's office. I'm here about your defense when you end up in Santa Monica Court."

"Can you tell them to let me go home? Being under observation is very uneventful."

He paused for an uncomfortably long time before he shrugged half-heartedly. Madison wondered if he would pointedly ignore her request.

"Ah, no, unfortunately I can't. Now down to business! What you might not know is that several agencies were interested in other activities Tony Mitchell was involved in ... Sign this, please," he ordered, spinning a sheet of computer-generated text on the table that bridged Madison's legs on the hospital bed.

"What is it?"

"It's your enrollment into the Santa Monica Homicide Division. You will be filling the position left open by Martin Thompson. He was assessing you in training hour documentation. You completed the required amount of filled hours with him to qualify for basic training, which can be attributed to your number of hours served in total on the division's payroll."

Madison pulled herself upright. She coughed. "What does that mean exactly?"

His gaze wandered. "It means Martin Thompson put you forward to his superiors as a replacement for him at a later date, and he was assessing you for that purpose, which has now been approved. You have served enough hours of training to forgo basic training. When you sign this piece of paper, you will be sworn in to be a fully-fledged detective in the Santa Monica Homicide Division."

What, Martin? Madison stared toward the window for a long time. "Why would I want to do that? I never asked for this."

"Because, if we can convince the judge that you were in training, in transition to becoming a detective, it will be a law-enforcement issue in court, a self- defense case. The likelihood of you making it out scot-free without repercussions is around ninety percent."

"So, you call this scot-free?" Madison said, referring to the fact that she was lying in a hospital bed. "So, I take a job I don't want, and I get to avoid punishment."

"Yes, something like that. What are the alternatives?"

Madison remained silent for a very long time, reading the document on the table in front of her.

"Thompson was an annoying, meticulous guy, but he really cared about you. He really protected you. We care about our own, and he considered you one of us," Ben said with diplomatic emotional courtesy. He swallowed like he was negating some real sadness.

Tears filled Madison's eyes, then splashed heavily into the documentation before her.

"What kind of maternity leave can I expect?"

"That I don't know, but I can get the details for you," Ben replied, making a note of her request. "Congratulations, nothing here said you were—"

"No, I only found out myself yesterday. I'm deciding if I want to keep it. I'm being punished for forgetting my pill for a day as well."

"Oh!" Ben remarked, shifting around uncomfortably.

Eventually, Madison reluctantly picked up the pen to put her signature on the line, marked with an x.

"Eddie also wanted me to give you this," Ben added. He passed Madison an envelope marked 'private.'

She thanked Ben and shook his hand even though she was not entirely convinced she wanted to be a detective to avoid going through a court case. After he left, she picked up the light brown, six-by-nine envelope and tore it open. Inside was the blood-stained letter Tony Mitchell had read to her in the Mitchell's kitchen. Enclosed was a photograph of an elderly malnourished man attached to some kind of medical equipment.

Eddie had scribbled a note that was held onto the back of the photograph with a paper clip. "Dear Madison, I did some extracurricular research on this letter for you. I found out that the guy, Tony Mitchell, received this letter about a serial killer from New Jersey. It is mentioned that this guy is supposedly your biological father. This, I find highly unlikely. This particular killer's crimes were so gruesome, the wealthier families of his victims pitched in together to overturn court orders to allow him to be connected to a life-support machine to ensure he served all of the life sentences he was convicted of. You should check it out for your own peace of mind, anyway. I decided this was not relevant to the investigation, so I took it. Nobody else knows about this letter. No wonder you wanted to talk to me before you went to the hospital. I hope this is helpful to you. Get well soon. Your friend, Eddie. P.S. Ben Kacey is a good guy. Just follow his lead, and he will take you through the legal minefield ahead of you ..."

Madison didn't bother reading on. She had to gasp for air, the hospital room's cleaning-glove yellow walls blaring at her giving her an instant, irritating headache. She pushed the sheets off of her trying to cool down since she was overheating second by second.

She sat on the bed's edge, trying to avoid holding her breath but desperately aware that she was seeing stars. She closed her eyes, focused on deepening her breaths. She opened her eyes and stared at her dangling feet, tapping her toe on the dark olive green floor to feel something, anything. When the sensation of the floor's coldness went up through her feet, she went back to the photo of the serial killer who was supposedly her father attached to a life-support machine because the notion she had just absorbed began to sink in. The thought that her father, if she really had one who was still alive, was a killer—the kind of criminal she despised the most—who maybe she came from, made her look up to the ceiling and burst into tears. She decided to pursue the matter of her newfound genealogy with thoroughly methodical research until she was certain there was no connection.

The hospital's bustle outside her door reminded her of the life she wanted back so desperately. She itched to get out of there, but instead thought about texting Eddie to bring her her laptop so she could disprove this nonsense that Tony had stirred up. She wanted her feelings about killing Tony to last indefinitely. She sighed in satisfaction, but her smile wavered as she wondered how Tony had even lived as long as he had.

Chapter 19

Released from the hospital with a clean bill of health and a jaw that ached instead of hurting when she used it, Madison drove straight to work. *Where is he?* she thought as she tensed her shoulders and neck. She clenched her teeth. *Come on, asshole, get out of the way,* she thought as she sped around a slow driver. As soon as she got to work, she contacted Ben Kacey to establish Anton's alternatives. The reoccurring comment Ben kept finishing each sentence with was "It doesn't look good." This made Madison find out where Anton was being held. When she found out where he was, she called the prison's automated switchboard. She jotted down the visiting times.

The next day, when she arrived at the prison, she was let into a stark, bare room with a row of partitioned cubicles built into it. She sat down, and after a long wait, Anton tromped in to sit down on the opposite side of the toughened glass screen between them. They stared at each other. Both reached for telephones, affixed to the partition beside them.

"Who would have thought it would be so hard just getting to hell?" Anton shouted into the phone, his speech stilted, stiffening as he looked into her eyes and scrunching up his face then relaxing it on repeat.

"What a mess. How did we end up in this mess, Anton?" Madison whimpered, closing her eyes.

"Because I couldn't go through with what I started ... and looking at you now, I don't regret anything."

"How do you know I knew?" Madison asked.

"I was questioned for hours about Jane, Tony, and you. It's obvious they knew the whole catastrophe."

"Well, I can understand why you didn't tell me before about your involvement in the killings in New York."

Anton stared at Madison with the eyes of a man who had been given a matter of months left to live by a specialist. "Who told you? How did you get …?" Anton stammered, mystified.

"The police department in New York knew you had something to do with it, but they have no proof to pursue it. They are of the opinion, the sweet old man, your ex-boss, took the wrap for it, which he got off of because of lack of evidence. They don't want to hunt someone down who was protecting a senior citizen from a protection racket, but Jane, that's a problem. They are going to go for a manslaughter charge if you don't cooperate and plead guilty at the end of the day so—"

"So, that's why you're here?" Anton snapped. He stood up to punch the screen between them. "You came to get me to confess so they can get an easy conviction? I only wanted to stop her from carrying out her hair-brained plot to kill you." Anton's lip curled as he swept his arms and pointed at her.

Madison could only see his anger. He had dropped the phone to stand up and move back as he shouted.

"Prisoner 1222, calm down, or you'll go back early," a prison guard announced over a loudspeaker from a surveillance room.

Anton settled down and went back to the phone. "Anton, listen to me," Madison pleaded. "I came here today to tell you something important to us both. We made a terrible mistake. Somehow, I missed the sequence of the pill when I came to you that day from my jail stay."

"Just tell me," Anton ranted.

"I'm carrying our mistake, and I want to get rid of it."

Anton still held the phone to his ears but had put his head on his parallel arms on the table, devastated. "Murder, murder, and more unborn murder," he groaned, crying. His face was a mask of torment. He had dropped the phone, but she could hear his screams through the dividing glass screen. "You, how could you? You're evil, evil," he screamed perpetually.

Two guards hurried in from a nearby door to restrain him. Tears trickled down Madison's cheeks. They dragged Anton away still screaming and struggling. Madison's head dropped for her shoulders to convulse in spasms of sorrow.

Chapter 20

Madison's editor, friend, and literary agent finished reading the last pages of the manuscript. Her only reaction was determining that she not only knew that the author she had just read was incapable of writing pure fiction, a view enforced by the extended swelling of the author's maternity dress, but also by the use of her own name and the way all 95,000 words of it felt fictitious but to an editor's intuition was entirely autobiographical. The first draft of Madison's novel needed some changes. But the editor's confidence in the knowledge that the author's writing was based on a subject that she took from experience made her scribble a note on the author's fly sheet biography, destined for the book's back cover. "It should be rewritten with more detail and lengthened to include Madison's professional credentials, highlighting her consultancy work with Law Enforcement Agencies, and should also include all of Madison's past works ..."

When it came to classifying what section the book should be labeled under, so shelf fillers in bookstores would know where to put the book, the temptation for the editor to establish her role in the book's integrity compelled her to slip the word 'other' into the line.

"A list of non-fiction by Madison Page ..." But she resisted the urge.

The deadline loomed. Madison's bulging belly meant she could no longer reach the laptop on her desk. Now, she would adjust to her editor's suggestions lying on her side on her bed while she enjoyed the fresh flowers' scent that filled the room from the open balcony doors. Madison's ability to write about murderers and their crimes had gained her quite a reputation in that genre. She calculated how long it would be until her baby would be born.

Something made her scribble some notes on a piece of paper. She decided to write a novel about an idea she had had for a long time. The female detective-author outlined a very brief synopsis in an email to her literary agent. The response to Madison's email was "I fully advise you to pursue a novel along the synopsis that you sent me. I will wait for the first draft by spring at which time you should have the patter of tiny feet and a brilliant new novel."

As the weeks passed, Madison worked on altering her current novel and spent three hours an evening working on her new novel about an experimental prison that she had envisaged in a dream. It dawned on her that her current novel was fading into obscurity for her and that the new novel she was writing back to back was taking over to be the most interesting thing to her she had ever written.

Chapter 21

The morning roll call room of the Santa Monica Police Department had a smell. Madison's analytical mind had briefly gone over the odor's possibilities on her first visit when she had put on her uniform and accepted she was a female police officer in training to become a detective.

Vomit? She knew that smell well enough. Morning sickness had become as routine as regular bathroom visits, except she sometimes had to swing open the patrol car door in traffic on the freeway and try to discreetly puke into a grocery bag, if that was possible.

No, the roll call room smell, though sweet and sickly, was not puke. Chemical, then. Was it coming from the marker pens the captain wrote his goal of the day with on a wipeable white board? Mothballs, floor polish, dry cleaning fluid still left on uniforms? The possibilities were endless until Madison's mind switched to writer mode when her brain's detective zones switched off. Fear, uncertainty, were something intangible that everyone could smell in their own different ways but never mentioned.

Madison put a few items that looked nutritious or remotely edible on the tray she carried. She took a seat at the cafeteria table, surrounded by eating law enforcement restrictively trapped to behave in a manner twisted by frat boy informality.

"Does anyone know what that smell is ...?" Madison asked out of context to the silent members gathered at the table.

Officer Tomes put down his deep-fried chicken leg when no one else was going to address Madison's question. He wiped his mouth with a paper napkin. "What smell?" Tomes mumbled.

"In the roll call room."

"That's the janitor's secret cleaning agent that he mixes up out of paraffin and all sorts of crazy shit," Officer Muller replied for Tomes with his mouth full of food.

The table burst alive with a speculative conversation on what exactly the strange smell was and where it came from, like Madison had pressed a button for the close-knit people to begin interacting with each other.

"Cop lockers," Sergeant Coombs growled above the mix of crisscrossing conversation. "It's not wise to desensitize that essence. When I did my service, every stat room on every Marine base I went to smelled like that. Topic closed. That's the aromatherapy of luck. Don't take the magic away. The topic is closed cause real cops don't mention it."

Madison stared across the table at the sergeant. His gaze penetrated her. Her mind quickly reenacted the chain of events from her leaving university years ago to her sitting in that cafeteria in the Santa Monica Police Division headquarters. The sergeant was the only one who knew something wasn't regular in her past that she still came into contact with. He knew Eddie and had known Martin. He knew Madison had been on a civilian freelance program. Surely, he had wondered how she was one minute writing books, then the next was sworn into service with SMPD ... after rumors circulated that she had no choice but to capitulate to certain terms.

Sergeant Coombs's journey of passage had been spattered with the blood of friends from his military service to him receiving the three stripes on his upper arm. Madison's guilt trip ran out of gas. She pulled herself together. Her journey of passage had been equally arduous—colleagues and friends had perished. Not just family but close loved ones had died in her journey to that chair.

"I guess all I'm trying to say is a cop shouldn't question superstition," Sergeant Coombs added, softening his intent.

"No one was directly," Madison said, shaken by her own comeback. *Did I really just blurt that out?* she thought to herself.

"Sometimes, unspokenness is all we have, and it's where truth hides," the sergeant said, staring through Madison.

The radios they all wore at the table delivered a static command after a long silence.

Madison stared at Sergeant Coombs, convinced the treachery of her being sworn in was in his mind. Replayed like a movie in the dark pools of his eyes. He blamed her secretly for Martin's death and Eddie being transferred to the LAPD. All be it through promotion. For him, Madison was a uniformed Lady McBeth character who couldn't, however hard she tried, wash away incriminating stains of herself in the glow of his UV-equipped scrutiny. Madison was lost in the chaos of her guilt. Redemption and righteousness, questioning every minute of it.

All she registered from the radio dispatch were the two words that triggered her inner self's true core. "Amber Alert." Madison was up from the table first. Her cognitive interaction with the sergeant was already in another time and in another place. All the chemistry of prenatal motherhood spiked her blood.

The forming life inside her and all it needed to be born hormonally challenged her to be the first to turn the key in the ignition so the squad car she sat in could force the tires of her vehicle led by physics to scream their rubber fury.

Something trickled down her stomach in her shirt. She wiggled her fingertips through the opening in her buttoned-up shirt to wipe the substance. She pulled out her hand to study her fingers.

"Breast milk already. This whole thing isn't going to be easy for me." Madison punched the steering wheel. "Damn, damn!" she yelled, realizing she had not waited for her partner to get into the car.

Madison picked up her cellphone and dialed. "Bevin, I apologize, I don't know what got into me. I just realized," Madison said into the phone.

"Not a problem, Madison. I ran after you, but you were oblivious. I was more concerned you had no backup. My ego is not ruffled. I've been with you long enough to know you're gonna be gone if I'm slow on a call like that. I'm not gonna write it up, if you don't," her partner reassured.

"Suspect driving a 2002 metallic-blue Dodge Neon. Child believed to be in the vehicle and in harm's way," the dispatcher announced coldly via the speaker in Madison's patrol car.

She drove until the sun went down. Her fuel light's constant flickering glow was the only deterrent in her relentless visual of all traffic in the ever-changing vicinity.

By the time Madison got home, she was exhausted. She left the radio on to monitor any new developments to do with the Amber Alert that the dispatcher might give out during the night.

The phone on her desk rang.

"Oh, hello. It's been a while. Sorry, it's been a long day," Madison aggressively said.

"I'm sorry it's late, Madison. It sounds like to me you need to channel some of that aggression into a new book! But I'm dying to see how the rewrites for the serial killer prison novel are going. How much longer than 95,000 words is it?" her agent suggested manipulatively.

"My writing career is over after this prison novel. It's almost finished. I added a lot of details, and it's a little over 140,000 words," Madison replied.

"So what do you think?" her agent asked with a throaty laugh.

"Think of what? Wait a minute ... I'm gonna take you over here to water my plants."

"Clearly, you understand the topic well. I can barely wait to see the additions! Your perfect therapy for your particular character trait and profession is novels."

"What's that?" Madison inquired.

"Pen another book. The synopsis that you recently sent! You sounded so thrilled about pursuing it when you sent it to me. Why not? A thick volume of scar-tissue oozing with educated torment and subsequent retribution. Come on, Madison, you have a natural propensity to create bestsellers. It's time to dust off the laptop and put an ink cartridge in the printer. You should be dazzling the literati, not writing traffic tickets."

"Did the phone cut off minutes ago? This will be the last book. It's over. I'll maybe pen some children's books when I'm old and gray. Look, I'm sorry. I've got some important police business to attend to."

"Bye, Madison, but remember it's time to clear the cache. When it builds up, too much for you to handle, and you've got to have a release, I'll be here to receive your next book idea. Plus, that synopsis is a thrill ride, and I bet you've got another one just as good! Give it some thought!"

"Don't worry. I'll be sure to send someone over to your office to dust the cobwebs off of you once a decade. Bye." Madison put down the phone and stood in a trance-like state to stare at it. She lifted the receiver and dialed. "Hi, I'm a police officer. Privacy means a lot to me. How would I change my phone number and become unlisted to the public? Errr ... Okay. Thanks." Madison put the receiver down again.

Always biting off more than you can chew! she disparaged herself.

She went over to her desk. Her fingers lightly touched the keyboard. Something trickled from between her legs. A sharp pain in her stomach followed. "Oh, that's not right," she said to herself. Quickly, she fell over doubled up in pain. "What's going on?"

She staggered to the table in her hallway. She snatched at her car keys but missed. The pain threw her to the floor for the second time. Madison curled up on her side, holding her stomach. "Ahhh. Shit, shit! What the ..." she cried out.

Horrific images of deformed fetuses flashed across her mind. She saw herself pushing a stroller to a playground. Hers, the only stroller covered in a blanket. She saw herself telling other mothers it was to shield her baby from the sun, but they knew it was to hide her child from the sight of the normal world.

Madison staggered into the quiet emergency room through the automatic doors, holding her lower stomach. A trail of blood dripped from the inside hem of her uniform pants into and down the sides of her shoes, smearing the blood into larger, more terrifying linear amounts behind her. Madison's body quaked, her breath too rapid as she gulped for air.

The reception nurse was talking to a woman at the main desk when she noticed Madison shuffling through the doors. "Excuse me a minute," she told the patient she spoke to so she could run to Madison's aid. "What happened to you? Are you shot?"

She massaged her throat to try to swallow and talk easier. "I don't know," Madison whimpered, every word catching in her throat. "What's happening to me?"

"Orderlies, I need a gurney now. Emergency."

Two men appeared from nowhere. They helped Madison onto a gurney, even though they seemed to have trouble positioning her to climb onto it.

"I'm pregnant. Please save my baby," Madison uttered, wrapped in agony.

"Possible gunshot wound. Complicated by pregnancy. I need a trauma room equipped and ready now. No, I don't want excuses. I want a number for chrissakes," the reception nurse yelled into the walkie-talkie. "Bear with me, honey. It's my first night out here from training," the reception nurse told Madison, patting her shoulder, which did nothing to calm her down during her pain contractions.

Within minutes, Madison was connected to tubes. Bags of fluid and sophisticated machinery monitored her vital signs.

A trauma specialist burst into the room, staring intently at Madison on the gurney while nurses forced latex gloves onto his hands. When he was sterile, he began to tear at Madison's clothing, bewildered. He looked at her bare stomach, then rolled her over slightly both ways.

"This woman has no gunshot wound," the trauma specialist said to his team. With a scalpel, he cut the pants material, pulling it back near Madison's uniform waist band. He tilted his head when he saw the blood in her underwear. "She hasn't been shot. She's losing her baby."

During the night, Madison was wheeled to three separate rooms to be treated by four different doctors. With every move, her entourage of tubes and noisy monitors went with her. Madison woke up when her body's blood volume was restored to its normal level. The first thing she saw was an ultrasound screen.

"Good. You're awake," the specialist screening her womb said.

"I'm still alive, then?" Madison groaned.

"You don't sound too interested or even happy to know the answer."

"It depends on how my baby is doing."

"Well, if you take it easy and don't wear that big, black cop belt too tight, like you have been, the baby will be fine. Sure, you don't want anyone treating you differently from anyone else on the force, but a pregnant police woman, like any other woman, will at some point start to show, no matter how tight you pull a wide belt. But we will give you the benefit of the doubt. Perhaps they make you wear it tight ... Do you want to see your boy's little fingers? They are just there ... and his little heart is beating like a drum on parade day."

Madison's eyes became a squint that poured tears on both sides of her face to fill her ears. For the first time in a long time, she cried, manifested in deep sobs.

"Oh you're gonna get me going if you keep that up, but let it all out," the specialist said, his voice hushed with emotion.

He reached over to hold Madison's hand. Although it was a simple human gesture, it took Madison by surprise in her vulnerable condition, and for some reason, Madison could not stop crying, however hard she tried. A jumbled collection of emotions surfaced from her insides, connected to all that had transpired to make her Madison Page.

"I can't stop bawling. What did they give me?" Madison sobbed.

"Oh, just something to relax you, but the side effect can put you in a kind of shock, and it brings up a lot of suppressed or dormant emotions. I've been doing this job for almost eight years, but I still crumble when a new mom cries on my table."

Madison fought the pharmaceuticals, but lost. She slept most of the next day. Madison came round in her small room. She turned her head, surprised to see a massive bunch of flowers in a vase next to her bed. She sat up quickly to look around, finding a red button on the wall and leaning on it until a nurse hurried into the room.

"I should have been on duty six hours ago," Madison exploded.

"It's okay. Relax. We backtracked. You got hit in the stomach when your baby kicked. When you stayed with us before, we didn't see anything then, but you had blood and fluid built up at the head of your womb. We found your division chief's phone number in your cell phone. I hope you don't mind. There was no password on your phone. You're excused from duty until you feel better."

"I feel better now. Can I get my radio in here so I know what's going on?" Madison asked, raising one eyebrow and door-watching.

"No, ma'am. This was a false alarm. Next time, it could be more serious. You're gonna have to content yourself with the TV," the nurse continued, repositioning Madison's pillow so she could sit up in more comfort.

Madison reluctantly settled down to use the remote to turn on the TV. A thought occurred to her, and she surfed until she found the local news channel. Madison didn't see the news item she was looking for. Soon, her attention wandered back to the flowers next to her bed. She pulled herself sideways to pluck the card out of the bunch. The card read "From the SMPD's Hospitalized Officer Foundation." The card was not signed by anyone she worked with.

The sun disappeared for the day. For Madison, this meant shift change. When the fluorescent strip in her room blinked on in its long, transparent frosted casing, Madison got up to peek out the door. The corridor was empty.

Madison crept toward the reception desk.

A nurse came behind her. "Can I help you?"

"What do you mean by help me?" Madison replied.

The nurse discretely pointed to the base of Madison's back and coughed. Madison felt behind her. She had been so sedated she had not realized that her hospital gown had no fabric around her backside.

She froze in place. "Yes, I'm looking for the restroom. I can't do bedpans anymore," Madison said as her cheeks flushed.

"It's back down the hallway. What wing are you from?" the nurse inquired.

"I'm not. I'm in a room down there."

"Well, it's probably better you rest and go back down there." The nurse's pager went off. "I've got to go. I'll be back," the nurse said, darting away in a hurry.

Madison had pulled the slack of her hospital gown around her exposed bottom. She turned her back on the nurse. "Okay, later," Madison replied. She shuffled back down the corridor toward her room, holding her gown's fabric together as best she could. Once inside, she was in time to read the tickertape running across the bottom of the TV screen. "Police pursuit taking place. Believed to be car connected to an Amber Alert issued last Monday in Santa Monica, California."

"Yes," Madison yelled out.

She hurried as quickly as she could down the corridor with a bath towel around her waist. For reasons of comfort, she ran with her legs open, which made her upper body move from side to side.

The nurse she had spoken to minutes earlier was heading her way.

Madison jumped into a doorway and tried the handle before the nurse looked up from arranging some detail on her uniform. The door opened. Madison slid around the door to close it behind her. She fumbled for the light switch in the darkness. A thought crossed her mind, making her grasp the door handle as tight as she could. Someone on the other side of the door was trying to open it. The handle in Madison's hand was forced downward. There was a pause, and then whoever it was who was trying to open the door tried again. Madison closed her eyes to press her head to the door. She placed herself into the mindset of a safe-cracker-turned-psychic. Patiently, she waited for the person on the other side of the door to let it click. Madison just didn't know if the person was checking or if they had the keys out and were trying to get into the room.

After a while, Madison let go of the door handle with a sigh of relief. Time had told her they were checking to see if it was locked. She switched on the light to busily examine the store room's contents. All she could come up with were disposable blue surgery overalls. She dressed herself, then went back to the door.

Madison counted to three, took a deep breath, then whipped it open. She marched into the corridor boldly.

Outside the hospital, she turned back, at the door she had walked out of, deep in thought and relieved to discover she had not been followed or detected. Madison felt under the wheel arch of her car in the parking lot for the magnetic box she kept with a spare key inside it. In no time, Madison was pulling onto the ramp to join the 10 Freeway. She leaned over to pull her radio scanner out of the glove box. The car swerved off the road. Madison controlled it back into the lane. She let down the window so the air could slap her sedated face. She turned on the scanner, turned up the volume, and fixed it into her dashboard.

"That's the old me back," she said to herself out loud. It wasn't long before Madison got the location of the car described in the Amber Alert.

She braked hard. Traffic behind her swerved around her or came to a complete standstill to let the crazy driver exit the freeway. Madison called her partner to meet her en route in a squad car.

"Aren't you supposed to be resting on sick leave in the hospital, Madison?" her partner inquired in a concerned voice.

"Yep, but I've got something that makes me even sicker traveling in that car up ahead. The hospital gave me the okay. The rest, they say, is just being lazy. I won't lie around for days. It's time to take the human trash out. Wow, that was lenient of me to call him human." Madison stopped to ponder her words.

"If you get me in more trouble than you have in the last few months we have been together, I am not gonna speak to you anymore."

"How can I get you into trouble? Do you work for the hospital?" Madison replied flippantly looking at traffic around her to pull out. She pushed forward in her seat to increase her vehicle's speed.

"Yeah, Madison. But when you were sworn in as a police officer, you made an oath."

"That's where you're wrong. Every child taken or put in harm's way is mine, and I will get them justice to the best of my ability. I took the Law Enforcement Oath so I could abide by my own."

"Even if it means endangering your own unborn child?"

"My kid is my business, and I was told my baby was doing fine. If it's a boy, I was kind of thinking of a name like Bevin."

"After me?"

"It's a possibility."

"Against my better judgment, where do you need me to meet you?"

"The junction where the 405 meets the 101."

"I'll be there. I knew it was a mistake to take the nightshift while you were away."

Madison threw her cellphone into the passenger seat. "You're going to hell, Madison Paige," she mumbled to herself, uncrossing her fingers.

Bevin pulled up behind Madison and blinked his roof strobes.

Madison pulled her legs out of the squad car to lift her pregnant bulge up and out of the vehicle. "Have you got a stinger?" she called out.

"Two," Bevin replied. He reached back into his squad car to pop the trunk.

Madison leaned into the open trunk to pull out the extendable cross of hollow spikes on rollers.

Bevin ran to assist her. He proceeded to sling the unit across the road's puckered blacktop surface. Madison was already back in her car as Bevin looked around for her.

"Where are you going?"

"I'll chase him your way. Put the other stinger unit down the verge of the freeway when you see him coming ... Anything followed by flashing blue strobes is him," Madison ordered, pulling away in the car.

"Gee, you really think so?" Bevin mumbled sarcastically. "At least try to put your belt across your shoulders and call this in!" he yelled after Madison. She raised her hand out of the car window in a gesture of goodbye.

It wasn't long until Madison had located the Amber vehicle pursuit. Madison swung her car in front of the line of squad cars following the suspect's vehicle. Static interactions filled police radio channels.

"Who the hell is that?"

"An unidentified vehicle just joined it."

"It's Officer Paige," Bevin, her partner, answered when a comment crackled on his radio.

"I thought she was hospitalized. She shouldn't be out here," the officer in charge barked over the radio.

Bevin stayed silent.

Madison's car swung sideways, blocking the way of the swat cars in pursuit.

Squad cars went out of control in different directions to avoid colliding with Madison's sideways car. Madison's car continued to spin in a circular skid, deterring her colleagues from following. After several full-circle skids, Madison's car stopped, still in motion in the direction the suspect's car traveled. As if uninterrupted, her vehicle continued to follow the suspect.

The chopper spotlight moved erratically above, setting its focus on Madison's speeding car.

As Madison looked up at the spotlight, she screamed. A passenger airliner was on a collision course with the chopper pilot. "Holy crap!" she hollered.

Bevin spoke over the radio, "LAX is navigating the chopper into a vertical landing on their east runway."

She was relieved, although the images of the copter and air collision at her apartment building flooded her mind. "Focus!" she screamed to herself.

Madison's car got close to the suspect's car before she could take evasive action. The suspect's car locked its wheels to slow down and swerve backwards until it moved parallel with Madison's car. The suspect edged over to push the side of his car into Madison's vehicle to force it into the freeway crash barrier. The side of Madison's car sparked on contact. Madison's 'unborn baby on board' sticker stuck on the rear window with a suction cap fell onto the back seat.

In no mood for games, she turned her steering wheel to its extent counterclockwise, pushing the suspect's car onto the outer lane. Madison spotted the sign for the off-ramp where Bevin waited with the stinger. Relieved, she saw Bevin waving a flare in the darkness beside a long line of flares directing freeway traffic away from the off-ramp.

Madison sent Bevin a text message she had already constructed in her cellphone, instructing him to activate the second stinger across the freeway. The lack of other traffic using the route made their plan much easier. Bevin's call to highway patrol meant traffic bulletin boards along the freeway alerted drivers to pull off until further notice. As Madison drove toward the off-ramp bulletin board, the lights flickered, changing the Amber Alert so it read 'Pull off at next ramp.'

She swerved to smash into the side of the suspect's car again. His compact car, hit by Madison's heavier mid-size vehicle, went straight up the off-ramp. Its tires burst when it crossed the stinger's hollow spikes.

Madison almost stood on her brakes and quickly pulled on the handbrake. The front right tire of her car pinched the stinger across the freeway. Madison put her arms around her stomach. She was sure she felt her baby kick as the vehicle tipped over to roll, roof to wheels. Glass, interior lining, and rubber window sills flew off and flopped out of the car's broken windows. She pushed her driver's side door open. Apart from cuts and bruises, Madison was hardly injured. She crawled out of her car's wreckage. She still held her stomach as she staggered up the verge of the freeway off-ramp. She picked cubes of auto glass out of her neck while she assessed the amount of bleeding associated with it by glancing at her crimson, sticky fingertips. She scanned the ramp for Bevin.

When the driver got out of the suspect's car, he steadied his aim on the roof at her partner. Bevin's uniform pants exploded above his left knee. Bevin took two paces back and fell on his butt. He rolled over in agony. As a reflex, his hand drew his own pistol, but he lowered his firearm, succumbing to the pain, and passed out.

The suspect's aim went from the downed Bevin to Madison coming up the verge. He fired and missed. He wildly fired his pistol in her direction until he ran out of ammo. He yelled something incoherent as he threw his gun at her. He reached in to pick up the kidnapped child inside the car.

Madison's eyes stared wildly, set on the cause of his destruction. His soul was now hers. Tonight, she would be judge, jury, and executioner. Nothing, and no one, was going to take that away from her. He had corrupted a child's innocence, endangered her child, shot her partner, ruined her car, and the list went on. Madison had already prepared herself for the news. She had probably lost her baby by now. She took a deep breath, wondering how single parents adoption policies favored law enforcement. All the while keeping the fleeing suspect in the fix of her determined, shock-adrenaline-fueled gaze. The suspect ran, clutching the small child to him.

Madison staggered toward the fast food restaurant at the freeway rest area. She could see the suspect yelling, waving the gun around in the air inside. Madison crouched down with her back against the hard wall below the fast food restaurant's window. She felt between her legs to realize the bleeding was profuse again. She slid down the half-wall, flinching at the sound of the suspect shooting out the restaurant's lights.

"How many guns has he got?" Madison uttered, struggling to reload her pistol. She quickly checked her weapon and released the safety catch.

Madison leaned over to look into the bottom half of the restaurant door made of glass. Customers lay face down on the floor. Madison bent her leg around to kick the door with the flat of her foot to open it slightly. Shots smashed the glass out of the door.

Madison struggled to get back up into a crouching position by using the half-wall below the windows as a back support.

She ran, bent over to go behind the restaurant. When she got to the staff entrance door behind the restaurant, she pulled on the handle, but it was locked. Madison looked around for something to give her an edge in this situation when, to her dismay, a car pulled up at the drive-thru ordering column.

"Are you open?" the driver asked into the receiver.

"No!" Madison shouted.

In the restaurant, the belt pack for the headphone and the microphone unit that the drive-thru window clerk wore crackled. The suspect fired at the restaurant staff on the floor lying face down, injuring one and killing two in cold blood. His aim lifted to center on the car at the drive-thru. Bullets struck the driver's side door. The car sped forward, colliding with the corner of the fast food restaurant, causing a partial building collapse.

Madison slowly stood upright. Past the debris and shuttered windshield, her partner, police officer Bevin Carter slumped dead in the car. In a selfless act of bravery, Bevin had recovered enough from his injury to pursue them to the restaurant and distract the suspect for Madison.

"You idiot!" Madison cried. Madison stood up. Her blood had turned to liquid-fuel rage. She was out of control, ready to do things that normally her rational mind would take control of. She checked her gun robotically. Her eyes stared wild. Her stance solid before the employee entrance of the roof-tiled fast food joint. Madison lifted her weapon to shoot the door open.

Bang, the door flew open of its own accord. It opened outward, knocking Madison over. She fell into the area behind the door as the suspect forced his way out with his helpless, tiny hostage. The child screamed a strangled cry, her chin quivering. The suspect looked back with a surprised look. He fired a couple of aimless shots back at her with his hands full. He clutched his hostage to his body like a human shield. The shots he fired at Madison made neat holes above her head in the prefabricated building materials. Puffs of dust and plaster flakes landed in Madison's hair.

She was exhausted, her mobility restricted. Semi-conscious, she had to get up, but she couldn't find the strength. A child's face appeared in Madison's darkened mind. Another floated in, followed by more. They inhabited the swirling void between her consciousness, thinly pressed against her closed eye lids. A darkness pricked with crimson flecks. Soon, a honeycomb of images, multi-layered, grew solid in her consciousness. Madison gasped, which was half-helplessness, half-realization that these kids hounding her closed-down mind were back as they always did, night after night. A projection of her purpose, a nightmare in stillness, a mismanaged willingness of hers to try to change the inevitable.

These kids, all of them, in all the post office posters across America had been missing for too long. *How obvious does it have to be? They are gone. What is it you are fighting for exactly?* the spokesman of doubt reverberated in her mind. "A lost cause." Madison sat on the ground. The restaurant wall supported her back.

"No, no," she uttered. *Another romantic egotistical hero of law enforcement trying to hold back the tide. When you finish counting the stars in the sky, there are real people who are alive to save. People who need your help.* "I will never give up on my lost ones. Never!" It didn't seem possible for such a loud voice to come from such a medium-sized body like nothing had knocked her out temporarily.

Madison stood, unsteady. She checked her pregnant stomach, then without checking if anyone could see her, she fished around inside her pants, then pulled out her hand. She looked for fresh blood on her fingertips, whipped her hand on the outside of her pants, and staggered into the darkness in the direction she thought the suspect had taken his hostage.

Edith's grandson, Mark, cringed, barely able to forgive himself for coming to his grandmother's birthday party. *There's nothing as embarrassing as an elderly person at a party or in public not realizing that perhaps their singing voice was once bearable, but over the years, all the politeness of family friends and strangers who patiently listened to that person's operatic acapella karaoke had not discouraged the impromptu diva to suddenly break the calm of a Christmas family gathering or a christening with a rendition of Ave Maria, he thought. A rendition that sounded like someone strangling an animal systematically to produce the effect of a recognizable aria. No not discouraged, but in fact the opposite—polite clapping and praise had encouraged such behavior.*

Tonight was such an occasion. Edith was eighty, and nothing, and no one, was going to stop her performance. Her family gave gifts and had all contributed to the dinner party by bringing plastic tubs of secret-recipe potato salad and the like. Now they sat, a captive audience in the living room of Edith's out-of-the-way ranch house. Mark would refuse to clap except being bombarded with all of the family stink eyes was proving challenging in making his refusal a reality.

Edith had opened her presents. She sat by the window, tired from all the commotion. Her daughters cleared away the dinner things and tried to get Edith interested in a DVD they had rented. Mark was grateful that she'd stopped her singing. Grandma Edith had just nodded off to sleep in her favorite chair when the suspect shot open the front door of Edith's house. Mark and her daughters tried to hide, but they had all been relaxed and they didn't stand a chance.

Chapter 22

She sat on her couch going over a box of snapshots, choosing which ones she would select to be fixed into a family album. The thought of Bevin's missed text still wreaked havoc on her mind. Madison had discovered Bevin's text message on her phone after the shootout. 'Acquisition the car from public. Coming to cause destruction. Get this guy, Madison.' *I failed when I was needed most, and I should have known Bevin wouldn't just lay there as soon as he managed to get up.*

She had been so focused on making sure that child got away from her demented captor. How could she ever shake the feeling of helplessness that scoured her mind as deeply as the sparks had on the side of her car as she'd tried to swipe him onto the off-ramp toward the stinger?

She shook her head, turning back toward the snapshots. She scrutinized her face on another photo taken a long time ago. She wanted to rotate the mirror to look in the back facet that magnified the image to see if the eighteen years that had elapsed had changed her appearance so much. Only very recently had she come to terms with how Anton had taken his own life, days after that visit.

She picked up the photo of Chris housed in a frame on her study desk. She compared their appearances. The likeness was uncanny. There was no doubt Chris was Anton's son. She clasped her hands to close her eyes, as she did on countless occasions, to thank God she had decided not to go through with terminating her pregnancy because when she had heard of Anton's suicide, she had thought it wrong to kill the innocence forming inside her. She remembered the doctor's impartial response when he had told her the morning before she was forced to sign on to the Homicide Division all those years ago, "The blow you sustained in that incident," meaning Mitchell's kick in the stomach, "has probably killed the fetus anyway." Madison had never forgotten that remark because of its hopeless lack of respect. Something she had carried into her work every single day of her distinguished career.

She cleared away the box of snapshots to go to the window. She opened the window. She loved the first heavy rain after summer because it washed the city streets clean. Madison inhaled the aroma of what had been dry streets that had been lashed with rain after such a long absence.

"Out with the old, in with the new," she muttered.

The rain cleansed the stench from store entrances, sidewalks, and alleyways. The stench of urine, spilled garbage, dried blood, and odors of the city's sins that stained outdoor places, insufficiently scrubbed clean by city maintenance workers. Soon, gutters would be streams that washed Santa Monica clean to make it fresh for Thanksgiving in a month. When it rained like this, the older streets grew darker, giving the city an unsurpassed atmosphere of reflected lights, risen against the sea and blinking beacons of ships. An atmosphere that only someone who called the city home knew and felt lower, more central to the heart below the sternum at the top of the stomach. An ambience that compelled photographers to reach for their cameras and writers to lift their laptop lids or mess up a room to find a pen before the breathtaking moment or inspiration had passed with the onshore flow like bigger cities in California it teetered on. Fault line edges and brightly painted houses with turrets that sloped up steep hills changing in style as diverse as the tolerant races that coexisted in its boundaries' damp uniqueness.

Her move to Florida upset Madison more than she would have shown Chris. It had been three short weeks since she had attended the stuffy meeting in Washington D.C. arranged by the congressional board of prison reform. She still wasn't sure why the congressional summit had chosen to invite her to speak. The single credential she possessed was a near-to-its-end-of-term ten-year stint as Santa Monica's chief of police. A title, which in its time, due to her success in keeping crime figures at an all-time low, had been extended to encompass an authoritarian overseeing of L.A's newly-appointed police chief who had inherited, jointly along with San Francisco, the worst crime figures in California.

Madison's status as police chief extraordinaire had been accomplished by the excellent team she had put together to assist her in a truly meteoric rise to the top. The only plausible explanation Madison could come up with was that her latest book *The Reformation* had nudged long-standing bestsellers from their exalted position of number one on the New York and Los Angeles bestsellers lists, whose readers were more than aware in actuality that prison needed to become more of a deterrent in order to whittle down the swelling crime rate in America's largest cities.

"Obviously ... someone with the power to make such decisions read my book, decided I'm brimming with expertise, admired my ability to manipulate crime-rate reports, put two and two together, came up with six, and thought I was the perfect person for the job," she had surmised the evening when she had sat at a restaurant table to tell her son how she had to move for her career.

"A bit like how you came to be a cop from the get-go," Chris had answered, smiling before he had taken a swig of his fizzy bottled water.

"Probably yes," Madison had replied with a blush.

"You know it shows we have a good mother-and-son relationship if I can still make you glow with embarrassment," Chris cajoled before he put a loaded forkful into his mouth.

"Relax, hold off, I'm getting the tab for this one. Shellfish is very expensive. Hold the charm."

"So is being selfish. That was genuine. I'm within budget, so to speak. Not all students are financially embarrassed."

"Yeah, just this one, particularly underlined," Madison teased, moving her finger horizontally in the air.

"No, seriously, Mom, I had a good day painting at Mr. Tenison's house. This is on me ... to celebrate your promotion."

Madison aborted the course of the piece of cutlery on its way to her mouth. "Promotion? What a load of ... broken oyster shells is that?"

"Mom, how you ever got from being a sad, lonely nerd, tapping on a keyboard, to being the chief of police is beyond me. You're F.O.S. You know, or at least I hope you know, you're going to Florida to lend your supervisory skills to the building of America's ultra-modern, all new, nothing-like-it, maximum security prison based on the ideas in your book that I still maintain is overly long." Chris pulled a mocking face and wagged his finger.

"That's a criticism I've heard so many times from you, and it should be a criticism, I wish, I could apply to your term papers," Madison replied while she wiped her hands to throw down her napkin.

"Touché, nice come back." Chris laughed to throw himself back from the table.

"What's F.O.S exactly?" Maddison quizzed.

"It's short for something, first word being full."

"I get it, and—"

"Mom, it is so glaringly obvious you're scaring me. This governing body will make you a spook that goes around setting up prisons all over America. They intend to do away with the antiquated buildings and systems to switch over to something this fine country's citizens have never seen before. Your book prison, and pardon the pun, I say that with conviction."

Madison stared at Chris long and hard. "Chris, has anyone at university offered you a hand-rolled, longer-than-normal cigarette to try that you liked and continued to use? Now, you're really F.O.S. What you're proposing is preposterous, son. My book is hypothetical, a suggestion, a novel. It's fiction."

"A hypothetical, fictitious suggestion the government is viewing at a screwy vantage point."

"Do you want desert?" Madison asked, realizing her son was as idealistically passionate and radical about opposing the government's motives as she was at his age.

"No, I kind of lost my appetite."

"Oh! Come on! I promise to tell you who they've chosen to take my place as chief of police."

"No, I have to get going. Let's get the check."

"Oh! Another, so soon after Cindy?"

"It's none of your business, but one of many, actually."

"Chris, women really don't like guys who play the field while they're dating." Madison could see Chris was trying, unsuccessfully, to control his tongue.

"You liked Dad didn't you?"

The color drained from her face as a painful tightness wrapped itself around her throat. She reminded herself to breath as she dredged up the past to figure how Chris felt he understood her relationship with his father. She visibly swallowed.

"That's different, Chris, and that's a topic I'm not prepared to go into right now."

He tipped his head back to look skyward before purposely closing his eyes like he was processing her relentless resistance to anything to do with his father. He reopened his eyes, loosening his jaw, and made eye contact with her again.

"You're perfect to work for the government, Mom, because you always got your standard line in place, ready for use," Chris snapped, raising his voice. He threw a hundred-dollar bill on the table and charged out of the restaurant.

Normally, the scene Chris had caused in a public place would have embarrassed Madison because his outbursts were getting more frequent, but the streaks of discoloration that traversed Ben

Franklin's face interested her more. She fought with herself, deliberating whether to or not, but in the end, she picked up the bill, placed it into a napkin for analysis, and paid with her credit card.

Madison pulled down the window when rain began to splash in on the paint work. She remembered her relief when she had gotten the results back from forensics that the streaks on the hundred-dollar bill had been caused by detergent bleach, resulting from it being put through a cycle in a washing machine. Madison couldn't contemplate Chris rolling a hundred dollar bill into a makeshift snuffer for coke or speed. She studied her reflection in the bathroom mirror while she applied her night cream, satisfied she had raised the reason to go on in the correct manner. She finished getting ready for bed, read for forty minutes or so, then fell fast asleep to dream of Florida.

Chapter 23

The frat party's drunk host lay on a bed upstairs at 9 p.m., hugging a bucket a guest had found in a closet by the kitchen. Most of the guests hadn't even arrived yet.

"How many do you want?"

"Enough to get me through the weekend."

Money crossed palms with a paper package in the lantern-lit yard.

"Danny, are you coming or not?" Chris yelled out into the yard from the backdoor.

"Yep! I'll be right there," Danny called back, stuffing the package into his coat pocket.

"Is he cool?" the apprentice dealer asked.

"Who, Chris? He is about as cool as a hemorrhoid on a cycling vacation in August."

The dealer patted both his pockets flat.

"Relax, his mom is just the chief of police for Los Angeles County." Danny laughed.

"If this stuff isn't what you claim it is, maybe we'll notch up another plus on his mother's score card."

"Danny!" Chris called out insanely, losing his patience.

"Coming," Danny yelled back, firing his fingers like guns at the dealer.

He joined Chris in the kitchen. They both watched another guy from the fraternity, who they didn't like, pour a bottle of vodka into a plastic garbage container that was a quarter-way full of swollen, faded slices of citrus fruit. He popped the cork on two wine bottles, then added them to the container also.

"Just pepping up the punch for when the ladies arrive," he shouted out loud, copying a radio disc jockey's patter, except for an intoxicated slur. "And now for the piece la resistance, to make sure we all get laid tonight, an undisclosed amount of blotters are gently stirred into the mix."

"Did he just do what I think he just did?" Danny asked Chris.

"He did. That's not funny. That's downright irresponsible. Some kid's gonna be the designated driver, have one cup to get in the party spirit, and they're gonna end up tripping on the freeway. I'm pouring that shit down the drain," Chris said, still looking at the punch preparer's antics but standing beside Danny.

"No, Chris!" Danny cried out to no avail.

Chris had already moved forward to pick up the garbage can of near toxic waste that his fellow frat boy had inappropriately christened as punch.

"Ah! Our first intrepid explorer who wishes to cross the desolate, hallucinogenic plains of his own mind," the punch stirrer joked.

"You're like a character from a crappy computer game influenced by the psychedelic sixties," Chris blurted out, lifting the trash can.

"Are you going to drink from the garbage pail? What are you doing?"

"The right thing," Chris answered. He locked his arms over his head, trembling with the voluminous weight.

"Stop! You'll upset the spirits."

Chris lowered the garbage container to rest the base on top of his head, which gave slightly to bend inward, not because he was intrigued but because he was undecided whether or not to carry out what he intended to do. "That's the plan."

"What spirits?" Danny asked, falling for the drunken punch stirrer's ploy for time.

"Pig told me when his parents bought this place they got it cheap because of what happened here."

"What happened here?" Chris demanded, pretending to stumble toward the sink and threatening to lose his grip on the container's balance.

"All right, I promised I would never tell, but two criminals were slaughtered in this very kitchen. One gunned down, the other, the author of his own misfortune."

"When?" Chris asked.

The punch stirrer rolled his eyes, calculating how long his friend Pig, who was still unconscious upstairs, had lived in the house. "They moved in when Pig was a babe in arms."

The story and the time frame pricked something in Chris's memory. "Who told you that?" Chris yelled volcanically.

Danny thought it was all part of the drunken game they played, being overly dramatic, but he didn't realize Chris hadn't been drinking.

"Incredibly, the kinky female cop who survived the ordeal, who the press never named, used her cufflinks for a cardiac arrest on this very floor."

"Oh! No! You shouldn't have said that," Danny exclaimed and put his hands over his eyes.

"My mom's a cop. You know that, you ..." and with that Chris relieved the ache in his neck and the dull pain in the rear of his skull by emptying the contents of the garbage can over the storyteller. Chris hopped forward on one foot, trying to regain his stability. He swung the container down to his calves to stop himself from falling into the soaked storyteller. "Here! Only, mix drug and alcohol cocktails for your own consumption in the future, you idiot," Chris yelled out, throwing the empty container at the stirrer as well.

Lemon slices slid off his hair before the trash can struck him, knocking him over. He stuck out an arm to steady himself against the counter.

The sticky, dripping-wet storyteller pulled himself straight again and took a sip of a glass of punch that had earlier been empty. "And the moral of this story, children, is, always hold an empty glass in case of emergencies."

Danny launched forward.

"I'll give you a punch you'll never forget," Chris threatened, held back by Danny.

"Come on! We were supposed to pick up the girls ten minute ago."

"Yeah! Let's go. This punk will kill himself before he kills anyone else. That's for sure."

"Oh, you ooze sexuality when you're angry. Make love to the lemons. Come on, give me the money shot," the storyteller taunted.

Chris turned to go for him again, but Danny held him back a second time, which made him give up, much to the disappointment of the sparse crowd of partygoers who had gathered around the entrance and exit to the kitchen.

A few minutes later, Danny sat beside Chris in Chris's car on their way to collect the girls who lived in dorms on campus.

"That guy has always bugged me. Who invited him anyway?" Chris asked.

"Pig, of course. They are both perfect examples of the word 'imbecile.' You, on the other hand, have got to try not to take every derogatory cop remark too seriously. Our generation reveres, but at the same time, despises any authority."

"It's just weird how that adolescent campfire exaggeration he fed us corresponded with something my mom wrote in one of her yawn-a-minute books."

"Right, let's put on some sounds," Danny suggested. "I remember that chapter clearly. I didn't know it took place in this particular house. What's this?" Danny asked, picking out a CD. "Oh! 'Paranoia Attack.' Perfect."

Chris had a full car, leaving a line of traffic that picked its way up the narrow road to reach the party house. He gaped toward the house, cursing under his breath. "Fire works! Are they crazy!? That will bring the cops up here for sure," Chris exclaimed to Danny beside him.

Someone must have fired up the barbecue on the massive sun deck built on stilts and in a drunken stupor had placed the paper grocery bag he could see filled with fireworks without telling anyone. Partygoers in the kitchen jumped out of their skin when a 'rocket-shocker' slammed into the window, cracking the glass. It hit the sun deck in a blaze of motion to tear around until it was spent. A blue, yellow, and red profusion of flares exploded out of the barbecue.

Chris wasn't sure whether to run toward the house or away from it. A loud bang of several fireworks combusting together caused the dome barbecue lid to take off over the sun deck's railings and fall eighty feet with a clatter and a rustling of leaves into trees that dwarfed bushes below. Randomly erratic showers of magnesium lit up the sun deck with sporadic bursts of noise that scintillated, then fizzled back into darkness.

"We're going to get up there to find people staggering around with their faces blown off!" Danny cried.

The young women in the back of the car made disapproving noises at Danny's remarks.

"Danny, you sure know how to ingratiate yourself with the opposite sex," one of the women in the car yelled out.

"I'm merely synchronizing my mood to coincide with Piss, I mean Chris. Hey! That's his new nickname 'Pissed Chris.'"

When they got to the house, most of the male partygoers, previously assembled, were ecstatically overjoyed to see carloads of coeds arrive. They elegantly departed the stationary line of vehicles by taking either Danny's or Chris's hand and lowering their feet to the ground once the boys opened the back doors for them. Similar to starlets arriving at a gala premier, the coeds vacated each car in the same style, despite the fact that most of them wore jeans and sweatshirts. The illusion was still quite effective.

Chris escorted the last overly inebriated girl toward the party's entrance before he turned to go back to his car trunk to pull out a six pack. He assessed the trunk's contents. He took out the beer and searched for his satchel that he finally found tucked away in the corner of his trunk. He had decided not to take his satchel into the party because he had seen one almost identical to his next to a chair in the lounge. This kind of affair could get spectacularly messy, so he pushed the trunk shut.

The music system's droning bass requisitioned the walls to amplify its range, leaving the youth under its influence, mixed with vast quantities of booze, to go from conversation-contrived to attention-seeking shouts.

"I'm heading into the yard."

"They're getting stoned upstairs if you want."

After he picked up the fireworks, he made sure no other ones were around that could go off. At least, the glass hadn't shattered. Chris found Lucy, the girl he hoped would become his next steady relationship. She stood in the middle of the lounge, shotgunning a Budweiser can and shaking it vigorously before piercing at its base causing its contents to exit at a phenomenal pressure and speed. Chris put his arm around her while she sucked the spurting beer can dry to applause around her.

Chris found fraternity and sorority drinking games vulgar. "A pursuit more suited to minions set free from the squalor of temporary housing parks," he would say to those who frowned on his dislike of such practices.

He assumed Lucy had led a sheltered life and for her this was a chance to live on the edge, so to speak. He wanted to kiss her cheek in greeting but was concerned she might belch in his face. Her colorful expression led him to believe she was about to hurl.

"Do you want to leave and go shoot some pool?"

The music's pounding monotony at full volume in the lounge made him ask her again.

"Yeah! I want to go to the pool," she answered.

Ah, even better, he thought.

He steadied her as they went into the yard. They passed some loungers where other students made out to the gate in the wooden fencing.

"There's a pool next to some tennis courts out there," Lucy announced in her own drunken way.

A flash of eager, late-adolescent lust made Chris grab Lucy to kiss her. When they got out to the pool in the backyard, the dim lighting became less effective. Tom, one of Chris's frat boys taking part in the drinking game in the lounge, had reached his alcohol limit, a quota exceeded with regurgitating alarm. The site and smell sent most of the party into the backyard where Chris held Lucy. Outraged students fled from the vomit.

Lucy complained she didn't feel too good. She broke away from Chris toward the crowd in the yard. The party had moved outside. The scene before Chris and his new friend was reminiscent of an orgy organized by the federation of the visually impaired where partners' names and the name of body parts had been attached to everyone's clothing in 'Braille.'

Lucy turned back to Chris. They took each other's hands without speaking. They encountered a subconscious transmission between them. Both decided to head for the pool for some privacy. No sooner had they stripped down to their underwear to enter the outdoor pool's heated water than a collective decree took place to shift the entire party to the swimming pool. Now, they considered that the most amusing thing possible was to throw students in who were sober, the most well-dressed, or the least likely person to agree to jump in of their own accord. When the first big splash happened behind them, they broke from their embrace. Being in the water was going to get tough. Soon, bodies would be flying everywhere.

Chris pulled himself up onto the pool's edge. Then, he helped Lucy up. They shivered in the autumnal night air as fully dressed freshmen against their will hit the water and disappeared.

"I'm not feeling so good, Chris," Lucy repeated again.

"Do you want to go back into the house?"

"No, if someone has puked in there, it will definitely get me started. I'll be okay, but can you take me back to campus so I can get some sleep soon?"

"No problem," Chris replied. "Be right back."

Chris went into the house to search for a blanket. He figured she'd forget about leaving if they had a chance to play around under a blanket. Anything, remotely towel- or blanket-like would be at a premium, so he snuck in to grab one before anyone else did. He had rolled Pig off his bed in order to get it. He did not want to use any of Pig's parents' bedding. He hoped but knew others would not do likewise respectfully.

By the time Chris had found a blanket inside and made it back downstairs, the novelty of throwing clothed people into the pool had worn off. Most of the stampede were inside the house looking for towels or sitting next to the real flame, fiberglass log-fire in the air-freshener-scented lounge. The pool would be peaceful once more, but Lucy wouldn't get back in and he didn't want to get in again either.

Heading back to where he'd left her poolside, he said, "God, that house is going to be a real mess in the morning. Pig's dead when his folks get back."

"I dare say he is," Lucy replied. Chris pulled a blanket edge free from Lucy's grip so he could huddle up close to her in the blanket. "This is nice. The stars overhead."

Before long, Chris was kissing Lucy more persistently. Chris maneuvered her back to lay down on the blanket that covered the paving slabs that created the poolside patio. Chris's hand began to wander under the red-and-black-checkered blanket.

"Stop that, Chris!" she protested.

"You're nothing more than a tease," he barked. He got to his knees, stomping off for being denied access to her more sensual regions. "I'm going back to the house to find me someone less frigid, a real woman who wants what I have to offer. I've been hanging around you for a week for this. Even your lips are too cold to kiss. It's like kissing a dead body." Heat flushed through his body as his laugh took on a nasty edge.

Chris was already at the wooden gate near the house when she cried out, "I'm feeling sick. Come back, Chris! Please!" When he glared back at her, she entered the pool's soothing warmth once more.

Chapter 24

Chris answered the phone he had just found between a zebra's legs in his dream, but it continued to ring. The trill demand that emanated from the phone beside his bed had manifested itself in his sleep as his eyes shot open. His incredulous stare threw him into a dazed funk. *Who would call me at ten in the morning on a Sunday?* He wrestled with the thought, his muscles frozen in place as he prepared to scold whoever it was, even if it was his mother. She knew he normally didn't rise before two in the afternoon on a Sunday, especially after a party.

He covered his head with his pillow to block out its persistent intrusion. He lifted his hand limply next to his pillow and plopped it on the phone, unwilling to lift his head. He tried to formulate the best words to use to answer as his thoughts reeled around his head. Mostly, his concern if this fresh hell would let him fall back to sleep after he lit into them revolved around his head.

Nobody else in the shared house he lived in had stirred. A heavy blow to the front door from downstairs confused him. Maybe someone had got up early to move some new furniture in?

The crash of glass made him bolt up in bed dropping his phone as his pillow fell to the ground. He searched the floor for something to wear, the smell of chlorine still on his wet underwear on the ground next to him. A multitude of thoughts collided in his foggy reckoning as to what had caused it, from an intruder to Danny forgetting his keys.

Cautiously, he got up to cross the room in a pair of dry boxer shorts he managed to find at the end of his bed. Treated timber coming apart told him someone was kicking the front door down. *Did I piss someone off? Apart from the guy with the blotters the night before? Or did I forget to pay the rent?*

"Chris, get up now!" his mother screamed in a way that scared him. He broke into a cold sweat, fighting the urge to run.

He was glued to the spot, busy trying to make sense of the situation but unable to think coherently. The floorboards moved from her rapid approach up to his room.

"Chris!" she screamed. His mom kicked open his bedroom door. She practically took it off its hinges. She stopped to glare at him. "What are you trying to do to my life?" she demanded in a tone Chris had never thought possible from a human being, an animal, an untamed animal, perhaps.

"If it's about the booze or the fireworks last night, I can explain," Chris said, completely unsure what had provoked her to a state he didn't think she or anyone was capable of reaching.

Before he could realize what was happening, his mother was scratching and slapping him in her fury. She cursed at him.

"Mom!" he pleaded, deeply disturbed by what she was doing to him. He had scratches on his face that went down his neck.

"Oh, no! What have I done? I've given them exactly what they want," Madison cried.

Chris stood before her, shaking. His racing heartbeat battered his chest. His eyes involuntarily generated tears that he tried desperately to clear so he could see his mother's next move to attack him, though he was incapable of retaliating against the one he loved the most.

He reverted to a little boy, helpless, cute, afraid. She opened her arms to beckon him. He entered her embrace, fearful of her sudden insanity. His mom crumbled into despair, unable to voice the source of her anguish.

"Mom, what's wrong? What do you think I've done?"

"You are your father's son," she moaned, stilted. Her forced restraint pelted adrenaline through his whole body while his overwhelming dread nauseated him.

Chapter 25

Her son avoided looking around the courtroom as the hollowness in her chest weighed her down heavily. She suppressed her incessant urge to shift uncomfortably on the bench, favoring falling into a deep, vigilant attentiveness although her slumped shoulders couldn't be helped. The whole duration, members of Chris's fraternity testified against him. He kept his attention on the cuffs that chained his wrists together.

Even the numbskull Chris had emptied the receptacle of lethal punch over got on the stand to donate his five cents worth of damnation. He embroidered facts of that evening, trying to sway the jury to a verdict they were contemplating anyway. He told the court how Chris had returned from the pool in an irritable mood, bragging how he had permanently dumped Lucy and he didn't seem to be under the influence of merely alcohol.

Madison had postponed her move to Florida, indefinitely. Chris avoided eye contact with her. She knew him well enough to identify his disappointment in her for failing him. She hadn't conclusively proven to the jury that Lucy had felt sick, choked, then drowned alone. Madison wasn't sure if her son was a killer like his father before him.

She had been ready to pass out when she had determined that the address on the report was the same address where she had shot Tony Mitchell to death. The same house where Jane had lived and Jane's father had died. How could life present Madison with such a strange twist of fate?

Pictures of scratches on Chris's face and neck were presented to the court. Evidence Madison had created in reaction to her son's circumstances that convinced the court of her son's guilt. Madison had caused the scratches not the victim, but the photos were used to add an extra layer of condemnation. Madison had even produced his skin to forensics from under her fingernails later that day when she had attacked him in her fury. All it did was guarantee she would have nothing to do with the case from then on based on her testimony about what he'd told her about Lucy rejecting him and that others saw him come into the party and look for someone else to hit on. Most people involved were of the opinion it was her attempt to cover up her son's heinous crime, not a depiction of the actual truth. Madison studied the bruises on Chris's face from the other side of the courtroom. With each of his appearances to confront justice, the result of his beatings became more severely apparent.

It was not the only evidence clearly obvious. Local news channels reported on the killer's skin under his mother's nails, but in the rush of the scandal's speculative sensationalism, it was lost to be ignored. The tide of opinion in Santa Monica had turned against her and her son. Everyone accepted he was guilty. Now, they just went through the motions to reach a conclusion. On many occasions during the trial, she had been warned that she was in danger of being in contempt of court for shouting out when she was sure a mistake had occurred in the proceedings. It was grueling for her to witness the loyalties of those around her being tested to destruction.

Before they reached a verdict in the sixth week of the trial, a court injunction in the proceedings allowed the release of a second independent coroner's report that Madison had insisted on that could conclusively prove Lucy James had choked on her own vomit before she had drowned. At last, the case was finally uncovering the truth of what really happened.

She arrived at the courthouse to find out the case had been adjourned. She raced through the corridors of state power to the detention room where defendants waited to be called into the court. She wanted to tell Chris.

First, she inquired why the case had been adjourned. A chaperone courtroom sheriff told her blatantly, without beautifying the news, even with a hint of satisfaction in his voice, that another inmate had beaten the defendant in the case to death in his cell because the defendant's mother had exposed the inmate's third strike and he would be going down for a long time. He speculated that the defendant's mother must have been a lawyer or something.

Madison's world was sucked in the same way a hole the size of an apple does when a plane decompresses at high altitude. Everything slowed down. Even the pocket book she dropped seemed to stop in the air before it hit the floor, as did the folder of papers on the case she also dropped. She turned, the suspended world breaking her ability to steadily walk out of the courtroom as she stumbled forward tuning everything around her out. She kept walking until morning became nightfall.

Chapter 26

The strain of having bought these plots sometimes caught up with her, reminding her of how she'd justified her reluctance to accept the empty feeling that had come with the passage of time and the meaning truth brought to her. It spat in her face as she reckoned with Anton, his lack of relationship with Chris, and her sordid actual father and dealing with her disgust. A couple of years earlier, Madison had won a court case to get her father taken off the life-support machine he had been attached to in the prison where he had been kept. When the prison doctor had pronounced him dead, she had paid to have his body flown to Santa Monica where she had buried him next to Anton. Now, she had buried her son next to them both before she left to design a new prison for the government.

One of Madison's more peaceful pastimes was to sit on her favorite bench in the cemetery on temperate days. She would listen to passersby inaccurately guess with confident authority the name of flowers cared for in beds on either side of her. She had heard self-appointed gardening experts enforce their knowledge by calling foxgloves lupines, hyacinths, and even hollyhocks. She felt compelled to call out, "You're wrong, they're foxgloves," but she never did. She found the peace of the cemetery too precious.

On this particular visit, after she had prepared herself on her favorite bench, Madison moved through cluttered lanes of monumental statue tributes of bereavements: cliché, solid angels and cement-mold, Greek urns. Her son, the father of her son, along with his grandfather, her father, lay beneath a neat line of polished marble headstones, not the most expensive package available, but there again, not the cheapest. The three men in her life lay interred at rest. The safest place they could be for everyone's sake.

She remained their dark family secrets' keeper, and in doing so, had become the reluctant, victorious predecessor of truth.

She had survived two men of pathological violence and one young man whose innocence she still questioned. Nevertheless, he would always be her son. Blood made her visit their graves. The blood that flowed through her veins, and that which remained spilled, a stain on her identity, on the conscience of her recollections. For the second time in her life, she had to accept what was being offered in order to escape. Santa Monica would not forget her son's trial.

She checked her PalmPilot high on the hill overlooking the city. Nancy had emailed her from Washington D.C., preliminarily confirming a date for her departure to Florida. Madison stared out across the mesh of streets people called a city, resolute that nothing and no one could ever break her spirit. For the first time in her life, she was emotionally indestructible and whole. She finally had all she needed. A detailed approximation of who she was, excited by the future, haunted by the past, and in control of her destiny. She was finally, after all the sacrifices, attached to her name, alive at last, fearless and free.

She took the book she had just read out of her bag. A book about the fifteenth-century English Queen Elizabeth I that had inspired her. She peeled off a ring scotch-taped to her bookmark Anton had given her as a joke so long ago. She read a passage from the book and slid the ring on her wedding finger. She passed some temple column pillars on a grave copied from those on Social Security cards, identical to those that stood around the apartment complex she had lived in for so long.

Beneath this land, the corpses are all truly free, she thought.

Over a fence, an orchard whispered legends of its fruit to illuminate the four bright corners of this Earth against the cemetery's boundary wall. Madison kissed the ring on her finger before she headed home.

Chapter 27

They passed the heavy construction machinery mounted on flat beds in line with big rigs that churned gigantic, cylindrical tumblers of ready-mix concrete on their backs, giving her an expanding feeling in her chest. She leaned forward to the front seats, eyes glowing.

"Is the building schedule true to form?" Madison asked the director of operations who sat in the passenger seat of the car they traveled in.

"We might lose a month or two to hurricane season," he answered, taking a swig from a fiber-sleeved cup of franchise coffee.

Madison sat up in the back seat. Her face was close to the back of the headrest his slick hair touched. "Wasn't that calculated into the schedule from the beginning of the project?"

"Obviously not." The director of operations laughed. He winked at the driver who found his lack of professionalism a source of amusement.

"What's your name?"

"Chris Montgomery. Why?" he snapped. His voice intensified, and he shot Madison a flat look, narrowing his eyes.

Madison's face flickered with some weakness saying his name, as the memory of her son always momentarily disabled her emotionally. "Because, I will do my best to see to it that you are removed from my task force. Attitudes like yours are two a penny. No wonder we are running behind and losing money," Madison answered calmly as if she was commenting on the weather outside the car.

Moron, she thought.

Her quiet confidence seemed to upset him more than anything else. "Excuse me. I don't think you know who keeps this project on the move. Well, let me introduce you to the way things run around here. Floridians keep this going, so your Californian, nose-in-the-air 'my waste has no odor' attitude doesn't work in our neck of the woods. Now perhaps, you ought to apologize to Senator Reed, myself, and while you're at it, you can apologize to my driver too, before I stamp a black mark on your ass and your congressional user manual. It's still a man's world in these parts, Your Highness," Montgomery rattled off like he was reprimanding a self-esteem-impoverished secretarial assistant.

Senator Reed coughed, loosening his tie.

Madison's reputation had preceded her. "Stop the car!" she ordered.

"You be careful now. This is my car," Montgomery warned, turning to point at Madison.

She tapped the driver on the shoulder. "Do you want to go with him? I said stop the car, Chri ...!" She couldn't bring herself to say his name, even though it had been nigh on eighteen months since she had buried her son. "Mr. Montgomery will be leaving us now! I will give you twenty-four hours to resign. After that, if I don't receive your resignation, you're fired," she informed him.

The driver slowed down before he pulled over in view of the prison under construction.

Madison leaned over Mr. Montgomery in his seat from the rear of the car so she could open his door. "Now, get out before I become less lenient. You don't want me to change my mind about the resignation! It would be very embarrassing for you to get fired on the spot."

"But this is my car. I refuse to leave. I offered to give you a ride to tour the site, remember?"

Madison reached into her purse for a congressional expenses checkbook. "What year is it?"

"It's this year's model, isn't it?" Montgomery asked the driver.

"Yeah," he replied.

Madison pulled her PalmPilot out of her purse. "Let me see. Book price for a new, used Lincoln," she mumbled to herself. She wrote on a check in the checkbook, then tore it out carefully. Then, she spoke in a bubbly tone, rushing through her words, "There. Now get out! This car is government property. This will not affect your severance pay." She handed over the check, her stomach fluttering. *Us Californians!* She laughed, her eyes wide and rounded, unblinking.

Montgomery pressed his lips together and took a hard, obvious swallow before a steeling, slow breath. He stalled with hesitant steps getting out of the car. He stooped to look in at the senator who sat next to Madison with a grave face refusing to get involved. He looked left, out of the closest window to him, when Montgomery realized he was not going to look at him and moved away.

Madison got out of the car to take his seat in the front. "I quite like my new car," she said to him in passing. She got in and lowered the window. "I want the owner documentation delivered with your resignation," she ordered out the open window. "Drive on!" she added with a wink to the driver.

They drove off to leave Montgomery standing by the side of the road with a check for his car in his hand.

They were building the prison on the very last few thousand acres developers could squeeze out of the Everglade Delta since the land was put up for tender. Nobody was sure what it was designated for. When building began, after approved planning permission, information had leaked out to conservationists about the project who had rallied with locals to try to stop the building of the prison from happening. The announcement had kept housing prices in a twenty-mile radius down after they had climbed considerably in recent years. Now, they proposed to build the prison.

Couples with families were not keen to live in the shadow of a convict zoo. Every resident received a brochure that reassured them that no matter what they had heard about the building of 'Portcullis' near their homes it would be the safest maximum-security prison in the world, unlike no other operated by a democracy in the free world. A lot of local gossip circulated that the prison would be an unofficial human cattle farm where prisoners would be used to test new advances in medicine and related weapons technology.

Another rumor had it that the prison was being built without cells, that inmates instead lived in rooms similar in design to hotel rooms. Each with their own bathroom, shower, digital TV, telephone, and DSL Internet access where they were sedated for years on end so they didn't even know their own names or recognize their own reflections ... hence, the presence of walls inside made from sheets of indestructible, mirroring material. The men and women who built it perpetuated most of these fairy tales, concocting weird, wonderful fantasies derived from its rudimentary blueprints through days of steady labor.

But nobody could have speculated, even with the most bizarre imagination, what its creator had envisaged for its final, organizational formation. After Congress had scrutinized the proposals offered for an integrated back-to-basics revolution to completely reform America's prison system, Madison Paige's 54,760-word report proposal was accepted and implemented.

Assigned to the post of 'Correctional Attorney General,' she would have access to a limitless budget to reinvent the meaning of punishment, penitence, and incarceration to improve an inmate's chance of perpetual rehabilitation, with a commitment to further the safety and protection of law-abiding citizens against those who federal policy deemed temporarily criminally insane. A title administered without room for definition or legal representation once proof of guilt was ascertained or room to be open to interpretation, forthwith.

Chapter 28

Months passed, and the following spring, Madison received a letter from Santa Monica's governing board's judicial office informing her that her son's unfortunate death in custody had prompted a whole reexamination of the unresolved question of his role in Lucy James' death, and in light of her service to the people of Santa Monica and the corroborating coroner's statement, they had returned a not guilty verdict. Madison read the letter. She likened it to an apology from a corporation for an unsatisfactory warranty notice they had issued in conjunction with a faulty appliance she had purchased long ago. Spare, emotionless, and all business. The unsympathetic letter struck her as a poor substitute for her son's life.

She shut her eyes, letting the letter fall back on the table with her other mail. An envelope with paper could be so bruising. She wished he had died in a war. She wanted a letter stating he died in the service of his country's insufficient legal system. A testimony to the rules of detainment must stipulate that, unless convicted, those awaiting justice must be segregated for their own safety. If she changed anything in the American penal system, this would be the foremost goal of her term as attorney general of corrections.

"It only took them two years to absolve my son from blame," she exclaimed, stuffing the letter into her jacket pocket.

She checked that her makeup hadn't run or smeared from her reaction to the letter in the ornately framed mirror in her lounge before she left her new subsiding house that was gradually sinking into its swampy foundations. Cracks had begun to creep across its walls, while the recently laid turf that made the lawn had died from constant flooding from below.

Today, she would attend the prison's hyped, official inaugural ceremony. While she sat in the car on her way to the public-relations exercise, she reviewed the busy weeks ahead. The task she faced was to choose her captive audience, to select the most hardened criminals in America's crumbling prison system to transport them, and then settle them into their new surroundings when the process she had developed with Harvard's Practical Behavioral Psychology Department would begin.

When she arrived through the freshly oxidized metal gates, she wasn't prepared for the circus that had set up by the foundation stone Senator Ned Reed was going to unveil with her that morning. Cordoning ropes hung from freestanding brass poles on either side of the ruby-colored carpet that led to the inscribed foundation stone that read: "This foundation stone was unveiled by Senator Reed, the next governor of Florida, the Sunshine State for the opening of 'Portcullis' correctional facility, with a set date of July 15, 2017." The inscription was so egotistically self-serving that she planned to have a signpost map placed in front of the foundation stone as soon as possible. Underneath the governor's self-praise, a boxed caption read 'Portcullis—A New Prison For A New America' chiseled in the rock for prosperity in larger letters than the rest. This was the only thing on the foundation stone Madison agreed with, even though she found Reed's achievements inspirational.

A crowd of topical, importance-fueled reporters charged toward Madison's car when one journalist who had interviewed her the week before recognized her look of disbelief from her car window. She pulled away to avoid them. She opted to park around the back of the prison, seeing as a cable news network van with its antennae at full mast had taken her allotted parking space.

The microchip implanted in her mammary sack meant the prison's outer doors opened on their own before she reached them. A joke circulated among the male staff members who had the same kind of chip inserted in their scrotal tissue. Portcullis had no keys. Their motto was: "Do you have the balls to enter Portcullis?" Once inside, only a full x-ray machine to scan the staff member's body from head to foot allowed them to enter the prison's inner sanctum.

Unless certain selected individual staff members cleared to pass had vital signs that were normal, including a regular heartbeat with a lack of excessive perspiration, the next sequence of hydraulic-powered security doors would not open. Staff members were bound by a clause signed in their employment contracts not to work out before their shift or to cycle to the facility. The computer system handling security would issue a financial penalty automatically when more than three violations of "over stimulus" on entry resulted. She'd laughed at the response from prison employees who were overjoyed that this form of technology also did away with time-consuming drug tests as she considered the cost-cutting benefits to her overall budget. *The money will be better spent elsewhere*, she thought.

Madison stopped in the expansive main forecourt inside the prison's central community area, quirking an eyebrow and beaming. Low marble walls contained eighty-seven-thousand square feet of landscaped gardens. Round recreational tables surrounded comfortable chairs, their centers speared with striped awning umbrellas. A flick of a switch could put in place a power-assisted roof in case of rain or remove it to let sunshine flood into the forecourt during drier weather spells.

She tried to foresee initial impressions of prisoners, who would be the originating inmates to arrive at Portcullis, to find it resembled a fancy shopping mall in an affluent area of the town or city they were once at liberty in. She had fought legions of opposition in and outside Congress to get her proposed prison design. Her defensive response to their criticisms was her belief that if you treated prisoners like human beings they were more likely to be obliged to acknowledge there was an alternative to the corrupt state of mind that steered them there to begin with.

She intended to make them enjoy their stay for a short duration. That way, when it was threatened, it grew into a circumstance they valued to the extent that a change in behavior could avert them from being transferred back to a more traditional institution with harsher conditions than normal—where they could be eligible for a staggered duration of up to a year in solitary confinement. She wanted every prisoner who arrived at Portcullis to be aware that their presence there was a privilege that could be revoked at any moment's notice, depending on the way they conducted themselves.

An overwhelming sense of being vindicated, particularly for the hard work and sacrifice for a specially modified secure helicopter on standby, hit her. It would be deployed in the event that someone would have to be removed. The containing cell built into the chopper's cargo bay housed screens behind indestructible glass panels that showed motion picture trailers of up-and-coming concerts and menu choices inmates they left behind could expect in coming weeks. Then, short film clips enlightened them to what they could expect indefinitely at the conventional prison they were going back to. The chopper would circle Portcullis for an hour, repeating its onboard movies, until it would touch down back on the prison roof.

If the prisoner correctly answered a multiple-choice questionnaire, structured to determine if he or she knew why they had been removed, they would be transferred to a separate building in the experimental correctional facility to encounter 'Phase Two.' If they had no idea why they had been removed from 'Phase One' of Portcullis, they took off to go back to where they had come from. Every prisoner was expected to go through this procedure, even though they thought it was they who were the exception, getting special treatment for being unruly at the new, cushy vacation camp of a prison. They didn't realize it was part of the procedure for them to be graded for their ultimate form of psychological punishment. A procedure that could only be effective if the prisoner in question was continually disorientated to never know what was going to happen next.

If they were quiet and unconfrontational, they remained in the luxurious out-to-pasture state of Phase One until the governing computer program threw out their time for euthanasia, depending on that prisoner's cost to the taxpayer. Dormancy in character sped up the death sentence process. The prisoner was informed seven days before an appointment for physical retirement was made, so they had time to adjust to the decision that they were in Portcullis's opinion, "Terminally dormant beyond help."

They could fill out forms to donate their healthier organs to those in need. Male prisoners were encouraged to offer their sperm samples while female prisoners could leave eggs for Portcullis's in vitro archive. When international humanitarian groups were contacted about Portcullis's proposed experimental protocol for approval, Madison's visual presentation addressed the groups at the beginning with the slogan "We, at Portcullis, believe prison should come from within to live in our prisoners' minds, not in the bricks that hold them."

Madison climbed a staircase that appeared from a steep, flat slope of metal her breast-implanted chip activated, revisiting the hurdles they'd jumped through to lead to this moment. Escalator-type steps emerged from the unscalable slope, pushing through slots in the alloy hillside so prisoners could not gain access to the nerve center of Portcullis. The stairway would only project its steps to those who had the implanted, harmless security chip.

Madison entered the main control room. The stairs retracted back to become a flat, slippery slope of alarm-censored aluminum behind her the second the pressure of her body weight distributed around her shoe sole's surface left them. Inside the control room, known as 'The Dungeon,' Madison chatted with technicians who ran a diagnostic on the recently installed, modified sprinkler system with double nozzle heads that were equally fixed at the same length apart across the prison ceiling's every square foot. She showed her gratitude for helping make this all possible.

The sprinkler's conventional nozzle would disperse water or foam on any kind of fire in the prison automatically when one was detected. The more unusual nozzle was used for a completely separate purpose all together. The prison architects, who designed the only system of its kind in the world, called the nozzle 'The Fumigator.' In the event of a prison riot, 'The Dungeon' could neutralize the irate inmates by blasting them with 'Corrintium gas,' the crowd-control predecessor of tear gas.

Whereas irritant substances were effective in riot situations in the past, 'The Fumigator' expelled an instant inert-knockout, personal deterrent gas . A two-hundred-and-fifty-pound male who had spent countless hours training his body to a peak of physical strength and fitness would collapse unconscious at the slightest gas inhalation from 'The Fumigator.' When inmates, or whoever, was present at its release, regained consciousness, the side effects would include paralysis, hallucination, and a potent, long-lasting tendency to experience extreme paranoia.

At that point, prison attendants—formerly referred to as guards—would conduct an immediate standby shift change. They would assume a status, not so much as one who dealt with security but more with duties that dealt with insecurity. They would with the aid of a varied amount of authentic props at their disposal, such as lifelike body parts and fake torture devices, intimidate the immobile inmates by convincing them that they were close to death. This would be easy under the gas's influence because they had all received instant physical retirement euthanasia sentences. A computer-generated probability model calculated the possibility of a similar disturbance orchestrated by inmates who had previously experienced such a realistic lockdown. It generated a below ten-percent-chance likelihood of a reoccurrence taking place.

Madison made some excuse from 'The Dungeon' why she could not attend the unveiling ceremony via her cell phone. Final adjustments had to be made. Governor Reed would surely be more concerned about how his hair looked on camera than he would be about the prison's curator's absence as he strangely referred to her.

The systems analyst, whose ultimate decision it was that such a lockdown should be implemented, came on shift. Madison enjoyed being around the young, very attractive, and extremely intelligent graduate from Yale's criminal psychology unit. . Kim would be the kind of woman Madison would like to travel the world with or be close friends with until they could sit and play cards for the rest of their retirement. Often they had discussed their private lives with each other while they had prepared various prison procedures.

After they greeted each other, Kim started a conversation. "What are you doing this weekend?"

Madison, who reclined in an anatomically contoured office chair, watched the foundation stone's unveiling on a surveillance monitor. "I'm busy, busy, busy. I'm buying a house," she answered, not taking her eyes off the ceremony.

Kim stopped what she was doing to watch what Madison was interested in. "If you don't mind me saying so, with all due respect, our governor is the kind of politician who ends up getting caught with his hand in the cookie jar and his pants down at the same time," she remarked, starting to laugh because what she had said was unintentionally confusing, but naturally comical.

The two women broke out into fits of laughter at the idiosyncrasy.

"It's not every day a spoonerism comes up good," Kim delivered with perfect timing.

"No! Well done! That was a very stylish faux pas," Madison returned wittily. "You know the more I get to know you, the more I like you," she added, thinking aloud.

"I was about to say exactly the same thing. Whereabouts are you snatching up real estate, then? Along the Delta?"

"No, Santa Monica, where I came from."

"You're moving back?"

"Not exactly," Madison replied. "It's a long story."

"Too bad it's not the Delta. You'd get to see the helicopters in action with Governor Reed, and he loved your novel. He was looking forward to celebrating the opening with you. He said they couldn't have done it without you. Of course, he toots his horn, but my guess is, you didn't escape the press," Kim said, her lip lifted to the right.

Madison sighed. She cringed thinking of how the press would run with whatever Reed said. *Maybe I should have attended.* She had hoped to avoid anyone bringing up her book to make the connection to her book and the prison a central focus by avoiding any direct questions. *Great!*

Chapter 29

A week after she obtained the legal transfer of ownership on the house, Madison figured other neighboring homeowners were paying attention in passing to the developments taking place in and around the spacious property in their exclusive neighborhood. When the 'For Sale' signage posted around its mailbox on the road outside the driveway vanished, it would be natural for residents to expect that before too long trucks would arrive to unload its next occupant's household contents. That made Madison smile.

Madison took the overnighter to LAX from Florida International. By the time she had rented a car to drive the ten miles or so to Santa Monica, the sun had lit the Saturday morning horizon above the mountain range. The wrecking crew that arrived at 7:30 a.m. stared at Madison sitting in a rental car in the driveway. The demolition team's foreman came late. Madison introduced herself to him to see if he would acknowledge that he had been late, but he didn't. She decided the bonus she planned to give the team would stay in her bank account.

"I thought the house was going to be a derelict," he mentioned to her, viewing the well-maintained building with some trepidation.

"It's derelict, believe me," Madison replied, shivering from the memories the house's appearance revived in her.

He read off a clip-boarded paper before he looked up at her with a confused grimace, his squinted eyes studying her. "And you want the processed, powdered building-material leftovers put in bags and delivered to your home in Florida?"

"Correct!" she confirmed.

A bulldozer was driven off the back of a truck trailer near them.

"Is it okay if I watch from my car here?" Madison asked.

The foreman, busy guiding the bulldozer down a ramp, caught what Madison had said. "Yeah! Fine! Only move it back a little bit," he commanded, wearing an expression of concern like she might not be firing on all pistons.

Madison sat in her rental car, preparing to decork a bottle of gold-foil-topped spume in celebration. She paraded her relieved joy on her face toward the wrecking crew as she waited for the first signs that the bulldozer could pick that place apart like vultures at the site of a dead deer. Madison raised her plastic cocktail glass full of champagne to her lips as the wrecking crew leveled the Mitchell's old house piece by piece. She imagined all the trapped spirits of its dead fleeing in dust clouds that swept across the mountains.

No new name would be painted on the family mailbox of the troubled house where the father of four, a teacher at a local school, was convicted of drug possession a few years ago, then further back in the house's checkered past, the murders happened. Madison would ensure that the leveled land would remain vacant for half a century to come.

When a truck delivered the pulverized, ground-down rubble powder in sixty-one builders merchant sacks a few weeks later, she moved it to the studio compound where the last final additions to Portcullis were being put together. A sculptor whose work stood in office-building forecourts all over Florida had completed his commissioned work's fiberglass mold, ready for pouring.

When the bags he was to include into the stone plaster to be used in his work arrived, less than a week would pass before two giant arms with hands attached emerged from the ground by the prison gates, shackled together by mighty stone chain links. Standing letters in the same material proclaimed: 'Our history was in shackles. What's to come is self-liberty imposed.'

The black-and-silver sheriff's surveilled prisoner transportation bus drove a perfect circle to stop by the enclosed telescopic gangway that would be used to move prisoners inside. Portcullis attendants came on to the bus with personalized shower bags that contained a face cloth, shampoo, soap, and a shaving cream can with a disposable razor, eliciting thirty-one despondent convicts' unrestrained smiles and happy tears. Madison had selected all of them from America's most high-profile death row facilities. They shared head nods at one another. The bag the wash kit came in had Portcullis printed on it, as did all the toiletries inside. Madison braced herself watching the surveillance screen in the control room. She'd waited for this moment a long time, and despite all the effort, she retained an important level of aloofness.

"What the fu ...!" one of the first inmates remarked when his shackles were removed so he could carry his fancy wash bag into the prison.

Many of them had been transferred before. They had never had their shackles removed in the past, and they had definitely never been given a wash bag that looked like it was complimentary from a high-roller Vegas hotel suite.

When each prisoner had exited the bus, they entered the telescopic gangway tunnel similar to those used at airports to gain access or exit to commercial airliners. Ahead, those at the front of the line were getting a stamp put on the back of their hands, as though they were entering a public place that required an admission fee.

"Is this in case we want to leave and then with this we can get back in?" one inmate asked, raising a laugh from others around him.

"Kind of," the attendant who stamped them, replied, also laughing.

Madison curled her lip.

Once they stamped each prisoner's hand, they were led into a small, plush movie theater. They sat in silence. Some shook their heads at the prison's strange approach. The light dimmed, and the screen came to life with an image of a drawbridge gate. "Welcome to Portcullis," Madison's voice announced, and she approached the camera on the screen.

"Orrr! I would devour her feline," a voice piped up from the back of the captive audience.

A ripple of laughter coursed through the crowd of convicts.

"You have, I hope, had your stamps put on. This is to replace outdated notions. Here at Portcullis, we do things differently. Here you'll be taken to our wardrobe department for you to select from a varied range of attire. Choose something you would like to wear. So far, I hope you have found your experience here pleasurable. On a more serious note, the substance you've all been stamped with is a radar pigmentation. This means it will not wash off with any solvents that currently exist. We are able to detect your whereabouts from space anywhere on the globe. And believe me, it's entirely accurate.

"In case someone here thinks they can escape without detection, the ink we've put on your skin is also an extremely slow, potent toxin that is now entering your blood stream. Should you get away, we strongly advise you to report for roll call at 10 a.m. every day, as we have the only known antidote to the poison we've given you. Don't be alarmed. If used correctly, it's completely harmless. But if it's not, it mutates into a strain of toxins far more lethal to human internal organs and blood than strychnine, arsenic, and cyanide mixed. Each morning at roll call, both your hands and feet will be stamped, in case you decide amputation will save you. Leave here, and the only thing that is certain during your escape is that you will die within twenty-four hours. As long as we can administer the overriding stamp, the procedure is completely harmless. If it's clear, remain silent. If it's not, raise your hand and shout 'aye' clearly."

Some inmates looked around, but no one seemed to be in any doubt that it would be a dumb idea to try and escape.

As Madison and Kim watched the inmates take in the Welcome video, Madison's breath quickened at the sheer silence. Over and over, her mind had returned to how these hardened prisoners would hear the prison's rules they had spent hours and weeks selecting. She relaxed the fanatical shine in her eyes and turned to Kim. "Now, it's about time the prison system spellbind the most hardened. Look at them sitting with rapt attention like they're watching a murder mystery."

Madison, you're so excited your words are running together," said Kim as she smiled back at Madison.

"Let's see how long these strong, silent newbies stay that way!" Madison returned her attention to the monitors following the prison's new inhabitants.

The interactive digital videodisc continued with Madison laying out the law of the land. "Good! Now, in this prison whatever you do will affect everything you experience. In two minutes, the doors will open. Remain seated. After some time, you will be invited to attend one of three nutritional sessions on offer in the forecourt. When our greenhouses are completed, you will grow and harvest all your own fruit and vegetables."

The Orientation Presentation Theater doors flipped open. Some inmates cautiously checked outside them before they stepped into the steel tunnel. There were no prison attendants anywhere to be seen. The tunnel had grown shorter. At one end, there were two doors. At the other, there was one wide door. Madison, surrounded by her team, observed the new inmates' first reactions intently.

"Which way?" an inmate asked those around him.

The group split up. A couple inmates tried the door to the right, the others, the doors to the left.

A prisoner put his palm on the door pad. It slid open to reveal the forecourt. He marched excitedly into the epically sized area, airing his astonishment at its beauty and sheer dimension. "Holy guacamole! I would commit a felony just to get into this place," he said to the small crowd that followed him into the forecourt.

The convicts at the other door got it open.

Madison thought, *Now that they know the sheriff's bus had departed, I wonder how they'll act.*

"Shit! It looks like they blew it already. We could easily walk out."

"It's a test, you idiot, to see if you really got what that bitch said on that commercial."

"Well, I'm tempted to go for it."

"Then, you would be as backward as they think you are."

"Well, what would you do?"

"I'm going back in for some food."

Reluctantly, the collection of tempted, undecided inmates stood back to let the door slide across.

"A test?" Kim asked, wincing.

"I know," said Madison.

Madison and the prison staff were actually confident nobody would really be so stupid to challenge their foolproof security techniques. The sad irony of the situation was their hands were stamped with normal, standard-black stationary ink. The illusionary confidence scams Portcullis used on its occupants had already begun.

Madison observed them milling about the forecourt. "Segregate the creepy one who spoke in the presentation about how he wanted to do something to me, or whatever it was he said," she said to the guards over the comms.

An address system announced that prisoner Eduardo 2 should report to receptacle 'A' for a blood-sugar examination. Eduardo shuffled slowly over to a row of cubicles that resembled instant photo booths. He took a seat in the one marked 'A.' Some lights flashed on a screen in front of him. An electronically produced voice told him that in order for the prison doctor to determine the extent of his diabetes, he must insert his tongue into the saliva sample receptacle.

He felt exceedingly stupid sticking out his tongue to insert it into a plastic tube by the screen. After another verbal request, he reluctantly leaned forward, chuckling at the outlandish nature of his predicament. He jerked his head back quickly when his tongue detected the foulest taste it had ever come in contact with. The prisoner thought the taste was reminiscent of rotting eggs mixed with decomposing flesh that he had smelled when he had worked for the coroner's office before he had taken someone's life in a fit of anger.

After a few short days, Eduardo and every prisoner in Portcullis realized what the cubicles were for. Soon, he informed everyone how the bad taste still remained in his mouth for a straight nine days, no matter how many times he brushed his tongue with his toothbrush or used mouthwash. When they used inappropriate language, or insulted the staff or each other, or even the prison itself, they would have to do the tongue-tainting exercise or suffer a more severe punishment, and he didn't want them to think he'd keep that to himself.

From their viewpoint in 'The Dungeon,' analysts soon reported to Madison that the more ardent criminals were asserting themselves, making alliances and enemies in equal measure at the speed viruses or germs multiply. When Madison received her first weekly prisoner's progress report, she realized what she had suspected from the start was coming to fruition. A three-faction split had occurred. The pack instinct had not been avoided, despite the extraordinarily relaxed resort surroundings of Portcullis. A struggle for power between three gangs had formed from the formerly unassociated prisoners, and it would not be long until the first death or casualty was being taken up to the infirmary of Portcullis. An infirmary that didn't exist. On paper to the prisoners, it did, but in reality, the sick or injured found themselves in a euthanasia suite. A simple, little sedative would be administered by way of injection. Then, before the prisoner fell asleep, his or her body would be incinerated down in the morgue.

The protocol of Portcullis seemed harsh, but there again, its inmates were the most violent inmates America had already sentenced to death. Now, society had a chance to fight back. It provided society with an extremely tight-budgeted chance to study, condition, and maybe even reform the illnesses that made these icons of fear kill.

Madison decided to nip the growing situation in the prison in the bud. Rodriguez 4, the most feared prisoner in Portcullis, had reportedly murdered women back in Chicago if they had decided they didn't want to lure clients to dingy motel rooms anymore, then give Rodriguez his ninety-five percent cut. His victims' bodies were found decapitated, floating in bags in the city's river. Since Rodriguez had been incarcerated, he had killed two prison guards at his last death row correctional facility. His present tally for carnage, if Madison included the three suspected, unproven slayings of fellow prisoners at his last transfer, added to nine resulting from incarcerated gang warfare skirmishes.

These possible, unconfirmed murders made him the closest thing to a daddy in the prison at present, though Madison anticipated someone with a more disturbing resume would end up at Portcullis. For now, she would concentrate on this particular inmate. Practically all the prisoners in Portcullis made a wide berth around Rodriguez 4 to avoid any confrontation with him. Overexaggerated stories of his almost superhuman ability to withstand prolonged beatings and numerous attempts on his life, which included a shotgun wound from a failed prison breakout, were relayed around the prison, taking the place of heroic folklore.

What Rodriguez 4 didn't realize was somebody else, who really ran the prison, had a similar, less publicized history of enduring tenacity, but she had learned to fight back with her mind not with her anger. A couple of gas-masked prison attendants came up behind Rodriguez 4 at the morning nutrition break. They sprayed an aerosol of 'Corrintium gas' in his face. He immediately went limp. The attendants lifted him from under his armpits to place him on an eight-foot gurney.

The rest of the prisoners continued to eat, not daring to witness what was happening to Rodriguez 4 in case of repercussions from 'The Dungeon.' They had learned that much so far.

Rodriguez 4 resisted his restraints in total darkness, held in a high-backed chair. His wrists were strapped to the chair's arm supports, his ankles to a cross bar, spanning the chair's front legs. He complained about discomfort in his neck. An automated hypodermic emptied its contents into his main vein. Madison watched the procedure on her surveillance screen.

Terror came over his face, and his body stiffening as he cried, "Is this going to kill me?" A euphoric look spread over his face.

"Your mother died, broke and alone," flew in a whisper over his head like a bird. He inhaled deeply. He looked freaked out. On a screen that covered the floor and the room's ceiling, a police photo of how his mother was found dead in her apartment came into focus. "She died of a broken heart because she failed to raise her son the right way," the surrounding audiovisual presentation continued. The whispering voice was best described as a heavenly being's judgmental, supernatural voice.

The injected drug took complete hold of him. Powerless, his toughness waned, physically, as a look of remorse took hold.

A child appeared on the screen with one of her legs healed-over in a blunt stump. "Rodriguez, I died in a war-torn country because men like you got into power. You're the devil you fear the most. Come with me. I will show you hell exists." To anyone not under the administered hallucinogenic drug's influence, the presentation would have seemed very tame and unreal, but with the drug, Rodriguez 4 would really believe he had died and that now this poor little kid was leading him to hell. Madison banked on it.

"No! I don't want to go," he yelled out, sobbing.

"That's what Eva Fitzpatrick said the night you killed her," the hobbling child said, looking back at Rodriguez 4 from a tunnel of fire. "You didn't listen to her."

Their extensive library collection of every conceivable character impressed Madison. Portcullis could stage such elaborate personal presentations by recording the child actor's part without dialogue onto a DVD, along with police photos of all victims and every inmate's family members. Then an analyst in 'The Dungeon' could put together a real-time experience for the inmate by using records kept on childhood, psycho-analysis, etc. By talking through a microphone in 'The Dungeon,' a software-enhanced analyst's voice could create any type of speech pattern that sounded exactly like a child, Satan, God, or could even be transmitted by microwaves to seem as if the prisoner were hearing voices in their head.

The child turned around to hold up a hundred dollar bill. "This costs the Treasury the equivalent of twenty cents to produce. Who is to say what it's really worth? Your whole life was a trick of the light. Now, your damnation will be the only real thing you've ever experienced."

Madison looked away from the screen at Kim who was talking close to a microphone.

"Increase the hallucinogenic gas for Rodriguez 4," Kim ordered.

"Good, keep it up. I don't want this one being mellow for a few weeks then coming back for revenge on the other prisoners," Madison interjected.

"When you kid yourself that you're not a loser like all those you look down on, you're not just a loser at the game of life. You are judged today a loser to creation itself because you believed in the illusion of wealth offered to you. Yours is the disillusion of worth. You valued federal linen slips of U.S. currency over your ability to decide whether another human being should live. Tonight, people will celebrate your demise. Tell me, how must that feel?" The child started to cry.

"That's the saddest thing I have ever heard: people celebrating someone's death."

"Keep it going for another half an hour. I want this guy to be too ashamed to look at his own reflection. Oh! And make sure he gets a few extra mirrors placed in his room," said Madison.

Prisoners had filled the forecourt when Rodriguez 4 walked in. He hadn't been anywhere near them for the better part of a week. They looked at him like they noticed he looked different. His posture had the stuffing knocked out of it.

He turned to the crowd of awestruck inmates. "What? What's wrong?" he shouted.

"He is faking it, pretending to be brainwashed. This sucker is too tough for this place. I was transferred from the other big house to here. I know this guy. This is not him," a prisoner yelled out.

The rest of the inmates eyeballed the prisoner who spoke like they were unconvinced Rodriguez 4 wasn't playacting for the surveillance cameras.

Rodriguez 4 glanced down to the floor and continued to speak. "I cannot forgive myself. You still have time. You don't know where you are. Be worried. Your souls are in prison, not your bodies. If any of you feel it's too much, at any time, my door is open. I will do my best to listen to your pain." He dragged his hands to his ears in great distress. "If mine is still not deafening me!" He shouted the last words the loudest.

His words fell on stunned silence.

"Fuck! What could they have done to break Rodriguez 4?" a concerned inmate asked those around him as a surge of humiliation extinguished any feeling of motivation he had reserved from all the reasons he'd justified his murders.

"I don't know, but this place gets a kick out of messing with us," another beside him answered.

Rodriguez couldn't agree more. He had hoped that the sight of all the other inmates would have helped him ease his mind.

The two inmates both stood up to go toward the cubicles before 'The Dungeon' instructed them to.

The prison's unofficial trading officer approached them. He held out two miniature travel mouthwash bottles. "These will cost a pack of smokes each," he told them. "You can pay now or later."

Each prisoner took their own mouthwash bottle, then headed to the cubicles to receive their sensory error treatment. He imagined all the prisoners back along the corridors, now aware that forced treatment became a daily standard practice, reducing men like Rodriguez into walking sinkholes of anguish.

Rodriguez 4 ran back to his room. He hid in his room, haunted by his past crimes' hallucinatory victims.

Chapter 30

It had taken a total of eight visits to a Cleveland courtroom to finally release the most sought-after prisoner Madison had on her list into her jurisdiction. She had never once thought about giving up trying to clinch the approval necessary for his transfer to Portcullis. For the most notorious infant serial killer in American criminal history, she had devised a whole new spectrum of protocols.

Marvin Reese had been a teacher for twenty years. In that period of time, he had personally seen to it that the amount of students of a modern-size classroom had by his hands found notoriety by being lost, feared missing, or endangered on post office bulletin boards. The kind of bulletin boards Madison still stood transfixed before, desperate for answers of how to tear away his layers to expose the core of his vile neurosis.

This fueled Madison's passion. She would inflict upon him and others like him a ten-fold of what they had inflicted upon each of their victims. She would murder their personality's impunity endlessly until she deservedly arranged the revenge she hoped the children would have found reasonably reimbursed their suffering.

Portcullis's secure twin prop flew him in before guards escorted him to his room in a deserted wing of the prison. Twenty-four hours a day, they magnetically locked his door. These were the maximum-penalty suites. Each room's walls were plasma screens, protected by bomb-proof glass casings. These screens would display digital photographs of his victims, day and night.

Madison caught up with the detail transporting him to his room. She stood beside him as they waited for the door to register its security request to open.

He walked in before anyone else. "You call this incarceration?" he said calmly, studying the room. He took a while to absorb each chubby grin of childhood he had extinguished. "It feels just like home," he commented with a sterile smile.

Madison noticed pure evil residing in his pale-green eyes.

"Yes, even though you're an animal, I can't bring myself to treat you like one ... I don't expect anyone, bereft of any shred of human decency like yourself, to understand that ... But welcome to Portcullis anyway."

"And you are? Though your face is familiar. Ah! The lady from the courtroom. So that's why you were so eager to sit in on my appeal proceedings. Who are you exactly? Let's see. You see yourself as Joan of Arc, burnt at the stake of your own mistake by the look of it."

"Tut, tut! A gross misjudgment on your part. No, I'm ... let me see since you enjoy comparisons so much. I'm the dominatrix of the last sad aspirations you possess. A reality check doesn't bounce. I feel sorry for you, Mr. Reese. Good luck," Madison replied, coldly autocratic.

"The ability to achieve orgasm by Susan Gottfried ... you might find it a lifesaver," Reese yelled after Madison.

"I want ultrasonic discipline for that prisoner to commence immediately," Madison ordered, striding down the corridor.

Kim joined her, having waited for Madison at her request.

"But he just arrived," Kim protested.

"Did you hear the way he just spoke to me?"

"Yes, but you're starting to take your work to a level that exceeds personal."

"Kim, unless you didn't notice, this prison is a structural testament to my personal commitment to thoroughly punish those who have transgressed the rules of morality. They haven't broken the law. They have broken the universe's heart. Unless you've been on the receiving end of that living form of death, it's hard to translate words into feelings. Open your eyes. Look at the children this guy butchered."

"You're right. I'm sorry! I think, these people at our mercy are human beings ... I forget they lost that right when they claimed another life. It worries me when I see things like this prisoner's arrival docket that states he has requested the American Civil Liberties Union inspect his conditions," Kim mentioned, studying a sheet of paper in her clipboard.

"How much mercy did he show his victims?" Madison asked, giving Kim time to answer. She didn't, so Madison continued. "So we have a guest who knows what he is doing. Relax, it's not a problem. When the ACLU comes knocking, they will be adequately briefed on our methods. Now, call up to 'The Dungeon' so we can give this abomination of nature a sample of the treatment he can come to expect at Portcullis," Madison stressed with the correct authority needed to alleviate Kim's concerns.

"Give room zero, zero, four 'Level two' noise abatement," Kim commanded into her micro-radio dispatch receiver attached to her blouse. "I'll fill out the appropriate forms when I get there." She offered Madison a subdued goodbye and left her in the corridor leading from Reese's room.

After Kim left, Madison made her way back to his door to listen to his cries the ultrasonic bombardment caused in his eardrums. The ultra-frequency punishment session stopped. Reese fell to the floor.

"What was that?" He struggled, holding his head and crawling over to the requester built into the wall by the locked door. "Help! I've suffered a seizure," he gasped into the requester.

Madison monitored his response from the surveillance point monitor by the outside of his room. She released the magnetized lock on his door. "One of many ways we probe to the center of your illness. If you cooperate ... are civil in action, both verbally and physically, you are rewarded. Break our code of conduct, Mr. Reese, and you will get to experience the vast array of our virtual torture chamber."

"You don't know what enormous pleasure it would give me for you to know that your demented technological detriments have triggered an actual medical meltdown in my metabolism ..." Reese could not finish what he wanted to say, still conquered by the ultrasonic bombardment.

Madison waited for him to recover enough so he could take in what she wanted to say. "Most of our disciplinary techniques have been proven to be harmless. The ultrasonic noise abatement therapy you just sampled was developed from a medical procedure that was designed to prevent strokes in susceptible patients, but it proved to be too painful. Apart from that, you can be rest assured you will definitely not be suffering from that particular type of medical emergency."

Madison watched him trying to pull himself up into a chair, but he collapsed during each attempt. Madison drained herself of any compassion.

"As you are in such a lucid frame of mind, Mr. Reese, I've never really had a chance to ask any of our prisoners what made them commit such atrocities ...Why did you kill so many young children?"

"Why would you even be interested?" Reese exhaled with a gasp of defeat, trying to get onto the chair.

"Maybe it's because the science of extermination has to really study the vermin for whom they are inventing products to kill, in order to do so, effectively."

"Do you really want to know why?"

"Yes, I cannot begin to understand."

"Oh! I disagree. What are you feeling now?"

"Pity, Mr. Reese. I'm feeling pity that you should end up here. Pity those children you killed never got to go home to their families. Please don't misinterpret any feeling of pity I might have as being in any way sympathetic to you. If I had a gun in my hand right now, and I could find a way for those cameras to malfunction, I would give the taxpayer a break with the same credence I'd give to squishing a bug in my house with the heel of my shoe."

"Yeah! There was some of that to it too. Your appetite for honesty compels me against my better judgment to harbor a fondness for you, Miss Paige."

Madison's face betrayed her surprise that he knew her name.

He continued, "When you're locked away to rot, there's not much to do but read newspapers. You have an appropriate last name, considering you've appeared in so many."

She ached to defeat him as he purposely strayed from the point so he could become personal. This was the only way, he assumed, he might fuel her anger enough so she lost her temper and made a mistake that would be captured on inadmissible, visible DVD evidence.

"You didn't answer my question," she steered him back to the conversation away from his tangential dig.

"Oh! That. That's simple. I didn't think it was worth mentioning. Since time began, man has scoured Heaven and Earth for the ultimate form of potency enhancement. I don't mind telling you, killing those brats, having the power of their lives in my hands, enabled me to tap into the kind of urges most men can only dream about. What an aphrodisiac."

Madison's body went rigid. Even though she stared at him, she could plainly see his infant victims' enlarged faces around the walls in his room. They called out for justice from their protected screens. "Surveillance, check five one," Madison said abruptly to the room.

She listened to her radio, and Kim informed her that the monitors that were now recalibrated to show the inside of Reese's room had gone blank while the main computer acknowledged Madison's voice command to run a maintenance check on the surveillance equipment installed in Reese's room.

"OK, thanks," she replied.

After sixty seconds, Kim informed her that Reese's room reappeared on the monitor, recording Reese lying face down on the floor and rolling over onto his back and the door sliding closed.

Madison strolled down the corridors that led to her office. She'd broken his nose so severely that she had ruptured blood vessels in the whites of his eyes. The diagrams she had taken exams in, prior to her getting approval to use ultrasonic punishment, clearly outlined that individuals whose nasal passages were restricted or blocked in some way were in danger of brain damage occurring. Physicians had recommended in their paperwork bombardees with existing proboscis collapse should not be subjected to this form of disciplinary treatment.

Chapter 31

A memo arrived on Madison's desk on an October morning requesting permission for a full inspection to be granted immediately. The American Civil Liberties Union intended to begin a process that would slowly bring about public condemnation of Portcullis—a prison they described as being devised by a 'Huxleyian member of the judicial torture regime.' They'd lifted the ridiculous caption directly from one of many pieces of correspondence Marvin Reese had sent them. The longing that Reese demonstrated to wage a propaganda campaign against her prison from the confines of his subduing suite hinged on how articulate he was and he had dulled his senses, subservient to his single-minded endeavor. The multiple suicide rate that the methods used in Portcullis had accumulated in a remarkably short period of time didn't help.

When Madison had finished reading the American Civil Liberties Union's request, she screwed up the paper it was written on, then furiously made her way to Reese's room. The door slid back.

Reese sat in an easy chair, reading a book. "Knocking is a courtesy I would not expect from such a brutal penal regime's leader."

"The request for an ACLU inspection has been denied."

"I can appreciate how you ended up the way you are," Reese calculated.

Madison restrained her temper to narrow her eyes to a squint so she could read the title on the spine of the book Reese had closed to place on the chair's arm. She made out that the book's title was *How I Came to Be*. Madison had written it about the period in her life when she had met Anton Winter.

"So, your daddy broke your heart, then Anton came along and did the same. It's no wonder you're a queen bitch to the criminality sector of this country's economy."

She left his room. The door slid closed. Madison had grown resilient to his constant personal provocation. She had taken enough of his attitude. His incarceration was not improving his way of thinking. So, she signed the release warrant for him to remain in the wing he resided in but to undergo 'Phase Two' of Portcullis. She'd kept Reese waiting for the crippling ultrasonic treatment to begin, but it would never come.

Tuesday ticked into Wednesday. Madison didn't visit him. His protest letters still arrived at the American Civil Liberties Union's headquarters. In the beginning, she had visited him every time an answer to his protests was redirected to Madison in the form of a request to inspect the conditions in which they detained Reese.

Now, every Monday morning, the computer in Madison's office automatically instructed her printer to run a standard letter that instructed the ACLU to contact Congress for approval of their request to inspect an inmate's quarters. Madison would sign, then fold the standard letter every Monday morning while she sipped her breakfast roast. When she had dropped it off at the prison's mailing room, she felt her week had begun. This procedure continued, whether she received requests or any correspondence from the American Civil Liberties Union or not.

She wasn't going to be played.

Reese reached the end of his tether. He had put his heart and soul into condemning Madison and her fascist correctional facility. He finished shaving. He dried his chin by dabbing a towel on the sensitive skin the razor had just scraped smooth. The knock at his door impelled him to remain dormant for a while, enjoying the moment. He couldn't remember the last time someone had knocked on the door of a room he was in.

"Come in!" he called out.

The door slid back to reveal an attractive young woman.

"Who are you?"

"An inmate of this prison like you," she replied. She stormed into the room without being invited. "Let's get on with it. We don't have long."

"Get on with what?" Reese asked, thinking they may have sent her to do his housekeeping.

"That's perverse, if they didn't tell you."

"Tell me what?"

"You and me, we are booked in for conjugal recreation today. I was inspected for it. Don't tell me you weren't. I was given a medical examination when I arrived, for what, I didn't know."

"So, you're saying we have been matched to have sex?"

The woman crossed her legs where she stood and blushed to turn away from him. "Do you have to be so blatant?" She smiled.

"It's been forever since I did it. Do you want to or not?" Reese could already feel something rising, causing pressure in his pants at the prospect.

"How old are you anyway?" she asked in a coy way.

"Forty-four, and you?"

"Thirty-nine," she told him.

"Did you request someone older?"

"Yep! Someone older who's in for multiple slayings, like I am."

"Do we have anything to fear from each other, do you think?"

"I hope so. That's what gets me going."

The two inmates moved closer toward each other. The door closed behind her. A voice from 'The Dungeon' announced surveillance inside the room would remain off for twenty minutes but would return if audio surveillance detected any violence taking place. When the inmates realized they had privacy, they tore off one another's clothing. She bit his neck. He enjoyed the pain. Before he pulled off her pants, she pulled a condom out of the packet. He closed his fist around her hand, holding the condom, took it, and threw it to the other side of the room.

Madison approached two guards on either side of a new prisoner being brought into Portcullis. "Can I have a word with him?" Madison asked.

The two guards did not reply but militarily took several steps back out of earshot.

"You do not remember me, do you?" Madison asked the prisoner.

"Should I?" the prisoner answered.

"Madison held out her hand to shake the prisoner's. "You were twenty-six back then."

The new prisoner looked down at Madison's hand with a surprised look on his face.

"I want to thank you," Madison continued.

"For what?" the prisoner asked, still completely ignorant as to who Madison was. She relaxed her posture and grew animated for a moment as the memory of hiding in the fast food restaurant crossed her mind. Her eyes brightened as she recalled learning details of the investigation over time.

"It's people like you, especially you, who got me to where I am today ... the fact you had to murder your mother, Edith, on her eightieth birthday and most of your family present at the house that night is the reason I am here today. It took me a long time, but today, I finally got you ... Welcome to my prison."

"So you know why I am here? What is it you are trying to say? I don't get it."

"Oh you will ... trust me you will ... You left me for dead at that burger joint that night. I followed you to your mother's house and led all units to your location before I passed out. I was pregnant ..."

"You ... it can't be!"

An excited flutter moved through her belly.

"We finally meet. I said to myself back then your soul would be mine, and I kept that promise to myself ... I even have a bottle of wine at home ... a twenty-year-old red wine in fact. I can open it tonight. Your only plus point is your child hostage was found alive in the house until I found out your own sister had thrown herself in front of the bullet meant for the child." Madison moved close to his ear. "You're mine now."

"Let me go! Let me out of here!" the new prisoner screamed.

While he wrestled his shackles, the two guards moved forward to restrain him.

Madison walked away with long, urgent strides.

Chapter 32

Elsewhere, summer rusted into fall. Closer to the equator in the Everglades, summer mostly slipped into fall. Months had expired since Reese had seen Madison. The young, female inmate never returned to his room for carnal recreation. In fact, nobody visited him anymore. He sat on the sofa, reading Amnesty International's track record from their web page.

It annoyed him that prisoners were denied access to chat rooms for obvious reasons. He wanted to see if Amnesty International could assist him in his male-oriented condemnation campaign against Portcullis. Although his treatment had been relatively subdued recently, he decided to see if he could, with outside intervention, strike a balance between the prison's harsh punishment regime and its more unconventional privileges.

The sensitivity medications administered through a series of aromatherapy spray dispensers, hidden behind the room's climate control vents, had begun to mellow his personality. He missed the woman he had enjoyed intimacy with. The children he had murdered still smiled from digital photos, taken when they had lived, shown on screens the size of pool tables around his room. They, too, started to wage their own war of attrition upon him.

He spent most of his days inside an enclosure of books he had built. A wall of titles that encircled him blocked his view from the tragedy of the crimes he had committed in what felt like another life. With each day that passed, the airborne drugs in his room stimulated his ability to feel until it became the most dormant part of his character.

Each morning, after he had woken up and each night before turning in, Reese would ceremoniously bow before each screen positioned around the walls of his room to address each child he had slain. He would hurriedly recite his own concocted version of a prayer that bore no resemblance to any kind of religious version with words in it, such as 'I'm sorry, I slashed your throat.' A prayer, he hoped, would in some way—when recited multiple times over years—absolve him from blame.

His need for forgiveness became the focus of his detained life, which he outlined in a letter informing various agencies of his intentions. He stated that in return for thirty-six months of pledging committed allegiance to his victims' memory, which he hoped would not be considered self-serving, he demanded that the creator-governor of Portcullis, Madison Paige, come to his secure room to award him a certificate of forgiveness signed by the families of the children he had killed. If they did not sign the certificate and guarantee it sealed and delivered by the end of the thirty-seventh month, he would have no choice but to embark on an outright hunger strike until the prison authority's medical officer pronounced him dead.

Madison came into 'The Dungeon.' "What seems to be the problem? I got a notification from the AI voice in my earpiece," she inquired, reading a prison progress report.

"It's not so much a problem. It's more peculiar than antagonistic," Kim noted, pointing to the monitors that gave them a view of Reese's room while she too studied a page of text.

Madison drew closer to the image of Reese sitting in the middle of his room. He wore a makeshift blindfold. Madison could hear him sobbing. "The Triansuline gas is working wonders. Don't worry. He's finally beginning to become introspective and grow a conscience. We will continue to let him confront his demons before we hit him with the Grand Slam," Madison explained. "It's strange how it affects every prisoner differently."

"Yes, I must say, I'm pleasantly surprised it has caused such a drastic swing in him. Perhaps, we can break this one at last. This will prove my methods work, and even the toughest psychopath can be reunited with their disconnected conscience."

"He sent me another request this week for forgiveness." She shared it with Kim.

Both she and Kim knew the request transcript, which was cross-sectioned and highlighted by analysts' interpretations, would be a nonstarter since none of the victims' families would ever consent to add their signature to such a document. She had to accelerate the conclusion of his P.T.P or Perpetual Transformation Program as a solution to the imminent problem his request posed.

The building brilliance of dawn's hues bled upward in absorbing variants. A process executed with the patience known only to the shift of planets. Reese sat upright. He pulled the dribble-wet, patch-stained pillow from the top of the bed with him. He stood up to cross over to the row of screens and start his morning ritual. After he knelt, lowering his head, still sleepy, he pressed his flattened hands together to blurt the resemblance of a prayer he had constructed. It wasn't until he had turned the corner that he realized the pictures on the screens had changed.

No sooner had he noticed than he was on his feet stumbling backward from the new image that occupied the screens. He clawed at his sticky brow, feeling a rush of faintness. The aromatherapy spray dispensers behind the ventilation grills had been steadily increasing their micro-droplet ratio all night. Now, the dosage of sensitivity drugs filled the room at the maximum dangerous level.

He looked away, covering his eyes, returning to stare at the replacement images, quickly trying to catch the plasma-filled screens off guard. No, his imagination wasn't playing tricks on him. His victims' faces that had watched over him for years had vanished. Now, a woman, a familiar woman, a woman he realized was the woman who had come to him for sex, long ago, sat on a chair with a child he estimated was between two or three years of age straddling the woman's thigh.

Reese charged to the communicator panel by his secure room's door. "Get me the Barren Fascist in charge! ... I'm sorry! ... Ask Mrs. Paige if she can make some time to see me ... Tell her I want to see her immediately," Reese stuttered.

"This is how forgiveness begins," Madison's voice calmly answered.

Tremors of emotional relief spasmed his torso. Before Reese could properly respond to the information from Kim, posing as Madison, he dropped to his knees. The airborne medication had tipped his evilness scale to mush. No conflict resided in him anymore, just a sense of peace remained as the last of his rage crumbled with the sentence "This is how forgiveness begins."

Kim watched as he fell to his knees. She had hoped the software control in the microphone had copied Madison's voice pattern exactly because Madison was away on business, arranging the transfer of another extremely violent serial killer to Portcullis. He'd missed the "You do not need to be reminded of those you have been forgiven for." it seemed since he'd collapsed inward.

Kim continued, "You are the recipient of two pieces of good news today, Mr. Reese. Congratulations are in order. The contraceptive patch we placed on your carnal recreation partner failed. We thought you might like to replace pictures of your past with a picture of your new family."

Reese's tear-stained face registered a look of confused, dumbfounded amazement. "I have a family." He sobbed.

"Is there a possibility you might consent to their request to visit you?"

Reese took a long time to reply, then with streams of fluid proof that he was reformed running down past his neck, he answered, "Of course, I must see them soon. Tell them, with your permission, they may visit me whenever they wish."

"Thank you, Mr. Reese."

"Thank you," he replied.

Kim wondered what words he wanted to flow from him that were stuck on his broken floodgates' current.

Chapter 33

Madison wasn't sure where the prisoner had gotten the sharp implement. He had not been in Portcullis an hour. Now, he punctured the archery in her neck with the pressure of his grip on her.

"I warn you, Mr. Ellwood, I'm trying to keep my vital signs from racing, but if you continue to cut my neck any further, the prison computer will read 'I am distressed' and will result in an automatic lockdown, so relax a bit."

"I'll give you another chance to look as God intended. If you don't answer my question, I'll carve you a double biopsy. Is the chip in your right or left?" Ellwood reached up and squeezed each of Madison's breasts with his free hand.

"I told you, Mr. Ellwood. I have no idea what you're referring to."

She had entered Ellwood's room to greet him—a custom others on the prison watch always deemed a risky, non-essential part of Madison's duties. The case to sue the former employee who had leaked Portcullis's security details to the media was ongoing. Madison, herself, had decided not to change any of the leaked procedures.

She figured that the analysts observing her from the 'The Dungeon' were watching every one of her moves. Madison's hands remained at her sides. They would have to wait for her signal to release knockout gas into the room the new inmate held her in before the main computer read her increasing pulse rate, then automatically initiated an entire inert prison lockdown.

"You realize your actions in the next few minutes will determine whether or not we decide if you should be eligible for immediate euthanasia?"

"You lovers of life, you're so dumb. If suicide weren't a sin, I would have done it a long time ago."

"What about murder? Isn't that a sin?"

"Not if God ordains that my hand should carry out his bidding."

"What does he tell you about me? Have I been judged?" Madison asked, wriggling in his tightening grip.

"You have not been mentioned in our discussion as yet," he answered sweetly by her ear, like the Alabama preacher he had been. "But should I be given the task of your salvation, I will fulfill the Lord's wish so your soul may be saved."

"I've been to heaven already, Mr. Ellwood. You see, I have died. I was sent back to do his work on Earth also."

The sharp-tipped implement in his hand broke the skin on her neck. Despite its consistency, a trickle of blood urgently made its way to the starched rigidity of Madison's shirt collar.

"When did you go to heaven ... if you did? What did you see? I'll know if Satan has made a liar of you," Ellwood said intently, testing her claim.

"When I died briefly ... there was no tunnel, there was light. I floated on voices. It was as if I was skydiving on a current of rushing thoughts, on a cushion of uttered prayers, locked in a vacuum. Then, an inspiration came into my head, similar to a localized sunlight beam, captured in the source of the blackest night. Pure tranquility endowed my soul ... You see, this prison is a result of my experience with life, death, and the glimpse of heaven I was given. What you might want to consider is you in that prison. What does it say about the voices in your head? Perhaps they come from the opposite end of the spectrum. I can help you with that."

Ellwood let go of her to push her forward. "You just shattered my reality, lady. You shouldn't go round doing that to people. Truth is the most powerful force on Earth. That's what I perceive God to be. That's why physicists and priests will never see eye to eye."

Madison turned to face him. "No," she yelled, foreseeing his intentions.

Ellwood thumped his solar plexus, sending the sharp implement deep into his chest. The self-inflicted wound burst his heart messily. A red, glistening circle immediately expanded across the top of the beige T-shirt he wore. He staggered, threatening to topple.

Madison rushed to catch him before he fell.

"Forgive me! You've been touched by the Lord. You can forgive me!"

"You were a good man. You were just suffering from an illness too severe for most to understand. I hope you will go where my humble forgiveness will take you." Madison ran her finger across the stream of her fresh tears to anoint a cross on Ellwood's forehead.

His eyes rolled upward. His body went rigid, then relaxed to embrace what for some was the unknown—where Madison had once been.

Her mind went blank. Her fading senses acknowledged the inert lockdown sirens. The main power to the prison cut out. The only sources of light inside the correctional facility's vast maze were chaotic crimson strobes that deliriously created their own form of frenzy throughout the prison. The analysts in 'The Dungeon' had prevented the shift change procedure from taking place.

"The inmates are all unconscious," one of the analysts reported to Madison. The effect of the vague fragrance that resembled pine cones produced by the chemicals used in the knockout gas.

Lying curved in the tumbler cylinder of one of the industrial dryers, Jose 6 realized the person they had chosen to open the dryer doors was not running to schedule.

What is holding him up?

They had equipped the prisoner who remained outside the dryers with a proper face mask close to his nose and mouth, protecting him from the knockout gas. In the prison laundry facility, five other prisoners hid, curled behind the water-tight sealed, industrial-sized dryer doors.

They'd concealed Kim's warm, crumbled body in the seventh. The cylindrical casing surrounded by electromagnets had acted as an insulating shield against the trauma of Kim having her breasts hacked off from the main computer's vital-sign sensors. They had calculated in their escape plan the sensors would be triggered by Madison's ordeal with Ellwood to cover any attempt they made to obtain the access chip to 'The Dungeon' should the spin dryer method have failed.

Things had worked more advantageously than they had envisaged for 'Stage One' of their plans. Luckily for them, Ellwood had not compromised their plans.

Jose 6 wiggled his body around to press his feet against the window in the industrial dryer door. He groaned with effort to thrust kick both feet on the glass but made little or no impact on it. He rippled his body, moving on his shoulder blades, using his heels, V-shaped from the hips. He bent his legs from the knees to forcibly straighten them again, but the door catch, like the tempered glass, would not budge. He expected the knocked-out prison attendant would be replaced by the next shift. Fortunately for the prisoners, 'The Dungeon' had left their plans wide open for them. His feet struck the dryer door harder the third time, breaking the door catch. He slid out of the industrial spin dryer's tumbler, feet first.

Apparently, the collapsed prisoner at the door's gas mask had proven to be ineffective. He'd fallen down and crawled across the floor.

Jose 6 went over to the unconscious liberator to jump on his face with all his weight. "You useless piece of crap. I should have known you couldn't do it for us," he hummed with a Southern drawl. After he had administered a brain-damaging penalty on the inmate who failed to open the dryer door, he quickly went about releasing the other prisoners cooped up in the rest of the dryers.

The group of prisoners cautiously made their way to 'The Dungeon,' stepping over knocked-out bodies, strewn all over the floors of Portcullis. The route they took meant they slid with their backs along walls, under cameras, then took turns to run distances from one blind spot to another to avoid being detected by analysts on monitors in 'The Dungeon.'

When they reached the steep slope of alloy that had retracted the steps to 'The Dungeon,' inmate Robert 4 held up a transparent polythene bag containing Kim's severed breasts. He twisted the knotted bag in his hands for the invisible beam across the slope's entrance to read the chip still implanted in the detached glandular tissue. While the metal steps to 'The Dungeon' mechanically pushed out from the alloy slope, the prisoners checked the sturdiness of homemade weapons they had fashioned in the days leading up to their email-organized bid for freedom. Somehow, the crude code they had devised had been sufficient for them to get the job done. A code they used in case the prison scrutinized their email before they sent it on to its intended destination.

'The Dungeon' door moved back into a slot in the wall. The two analysts in the keep looked up into the prisoners' faces as they sieged through the open door, striking fear into both of them. The marauding prisoners thwarted their attempt to engage 'The Dungeon's' fail-safe system by plunging their basic weapons into the analysts before they could release gas into 'The Dungeon' or hit the red mushroom button to lock it down.

After some brutal, impersonal score settling, the inmates were in control of Portcullis. The inmates in 'The Dungeon' worked as if they didn't have a millisecond to spare. They blasted down the shortest route to the nearest form of transport.

The other analysts got to Madison. One flicked a pore pressure syringe to give her a shot that would counteract the knockout gas's effects. She regained consciousness with an expression of relieved astonishment. It soon dawned on her she had cheated death, yet again. Her intuition took control immediately.

"Where is the shift change?"

"We didn't think it necessary."

"You broke from procedure. Something is wrong. Get me to 'The Dungeon.'"

"Relax! Until this gas wears off, you will feel increased levels of anxiety, that's normal. Everyone in the prison is comatose," Yorik, the newest analyst to the team, informed her.

"That's what worries me. I will rest when I know everything is how it should be." Madison went out to a main computer terminal built into the prison corridor wall. "Status!" she barked.

"All is well," the synthetic voice program answered, recognizing her voice. The prison schematics rotated in three-dimensional graphics on the screen.

Madison took in columns of numerical information that altered at high speed. "Stop!" she ordered. "Give me a thermal vital sign scan of 'The Dungeon.'"

The computer did so.

"I knew it. Always trust your instincts," she yelled, pacing down the corridor.

"What is it? What's wrong?" Yorik asked.

"The three security-clearance chips in 'The Dungeon' don't register any connection to vital signs. It confirms that a major breach of security is going on in my prison. The main computer will vet who is in 'The Dungeon.' And since I'm acting unpredictably, it'll slowly begin a power phaseout to certain aspects of the prison's main control room. If it doesn't receive any access codes to question its decision, it will complete a scan mode."

"Only authorized personnel are in 'The Dungeon!'" cried Yorik.

A few inmates ran over to the door to the 'The Dungeon' to prevent it from closing completely, but the pneumatics closing it proved too powerful for them. Improvised stoppers they placed in the doorway snapped. Michael 3 pulled his foot clear in time. The door to 'The Dungeon' closed.

The lights went out. Surveillance equipment went dead. The five inmates in the control room seethed at the withdrawal of services to 'The Dungeon.' The escape route they had organized went dark on the screen.

Webber 1 hit the console with his fist. "What the fuck's going on here?"

The inmates spotted powerful shotguns hidden under the console. Two prisoners pumped cartridges into the twelve-gauge chambers, then fired at will at the closed door, but it effortlessly withstood the pounding. The shotgun blasts hitting the reinforced door were deafening in 'The Dungeon.' Some stray shot rebounded, striking one of the gunmen in the stomach, prompting them to relinquish firing.

Madison stopped to assess the situation.

"What was that?" Madison uttered, breaking her stride with her arm up for the others to stop behind her.

"It sounds like apes trying to escape from a cage."

"No, it sounds like shotguns ... We may have trapped some nasties in 'The Dungeon'... Quick, where I'm taking you now doesn't exist. If you tell a single soul, I will see to it your careers are ruined for the inevitable future, and that's not just in here."

"Okay!" Yorik answered. "What have you got to get us out of here alive?" He stopped to look at the other analyst's watch by hijacking Julie's wrist. "Because in about eighteen minutes, we are going to be surrounded by groggy inmates with nowhere safe to hide," he estimated.

His pessimism urged her on. Madison led them down a network of corridors until they reached what looked like a dead end. Madison went over to the last terminal built into the wall. She tapped out something on the keyboard.

Yorik leaned over her shoulder.

A voice command from the main computer addressed the requesting programmer. "Who wants to initiate protocol 004-Y? Please identify."

"Me, Madison Paige. Code 4909617KRIS."

"Voice recognition complete. Please try again later when you are calmer. Your heart rate and blood pressure are above the recommended level for security clearance. You are under duress," the computer voice command added, denying Madison's request.

She turned to rest her back against the prison wall. "I need you to massage my neck," she said seriously to the female analyst. "You must work on my arms," she continued to Yorik.

The ludicrous scene bilked the prison's suitableness in her mind. Here she was, the head of a maximum-security prison standing in the corridor of a locked-down facility with two of her assistants soothingly rubbing her neck and limbs like her last request was a ménage à trois. Madison took some deep breaths but couldn't help finding the image of them soothing her into a more relaxed state incongruous and potentially needing adjusting at a later time. For now, she focused on her breathing.

Yorik felt for her pulse and highjacked Julie's watch again. "Your heart is beating fast, but you are good to go," he told her.

Madison addressed the main computer a second time.

"Access accepted," the synthetic female voice purred calmly. The wall in the dead-ended corridor moved aside to reveal a thick armor-plated entrance that also drew back to allow entry.

Madison ran into the room that lay behind the false wall. The two analysts followed her in disbelief. The room was an exact copy of the original 'Dungeon.'

"The key to its effectiveness is its secrecy," Madison informed them.

Yorik noticed a rack of shotguns on the wall, more prominently displayed than in the initial 'Dungeon.'

Madison powered up the system in the reserve control room. She wanted to contact the prison's outer buildings, especially the recreation room, of the standby shift change that remained on-duty at the prison in case of an all-out lockdown. Their lack of curiosity as to what was going extremely concerned her. When she got no response from their command post, she activated that sector's cameras.

She stepped back from the screen with a gasp. "No, no, no, no, no!" she expelled quickly. At some point in the inmates' planned escape, a separate team of prisoners, who had a working knowledge of plumbing, had rigged the climate-control vents to divert the knockout gas into the standby shift's recreational room with lengths of pipe from the skills' workshop where prisoners could learn a trade. They had sawed through the carrying pipe of the gas to add a T-junction section that they had extended to reach the main air-conditioning tube that went to the recreation room.

Madison grabbed a shoulder strap pack of shotgun cartridges. "This leaves me no choice! We're going to have to settle this the old-fashioned way," she told the two analysts, lifting a shotgun from the rack.

"Can't we seal ourselves up in here? We can wait for outside help," Yorik suggested.

"No, this is our ... my responsibility. I want it resolved before the news breaks outside ... You can both come or stay. I'll understand," Madison answered.

The female analyst took her ammo, then reached for a pump-action weapon.

"I'll stay here to guide you through the prison," Yorik feebly informed them.

Madison stopped with her back to him. "Yeah! You stay here to dry out the isosceles triangle of pee that is tainting what you imagine is your Herculean manhood. Come on!" she ordered.

Yorik took his gun and shells, then followed them out nervously.

Madison closed the reserve 'Dungeon' behind her with a password. When they reached the main promenade area, some prisoners with stronger constitutions than others stirred from their imposed slumber without looking in their direction. Madison blasted everything that moved at the edge of her line of vision.

"It might seem harsh, but if the tables were turned, they would do likewise in a blink," Madison explained. "If it moves, shoot it!" Madison advised.

Yorik stared back at the inmate she had already shot. He had to look away from the instant autopsy of the dead inmate's blown-apart chest. By the time they got to 'The Dungeon,' Madison had shot five because they had twitched or rolled over in their sleep. Yorik and Julie hadn't shot anyone.

As Madison, Julie, and Yorik approached the arch of the entrance to 'The Dungeon's' forecourt, an inmate came out of hiding and dove onto Yorik who was closest to him. He tried to pry the shotgun from Yorik's grip to kill the three of them, but as a small man in stature, Yorik pounced on his back, clutching the inmate's neck as if implanting himself into him and cutting off access to air from his windpipe with the shotgun.

Madison lifted the stock of her shotgun to bring it down forcibly on the back of the prisoner's neck as Yorik let go momentarily. It all happened so quickly, even Madison hadn't expected Yorik's grit. The prisoner slid off Yorik's back sideways.

Yorik spun around, training the shotgun on the limp inmate.

"There's no need," Madison shouted, but Yorik was so wired he fired directly at the prisoner's head. Specks of blood appeared over the three colleagues' clothing and face, like a conjuring trick.

Yorik yelled an incomprehensible scream of fearful anger. Julie's face was fixed in shock. A strong hand gripped her ankle. She screamed, trying to clumsily get the shotgun around to the object that had snagged her. She fired without hesitation, detaching a prisoner's arm from the elbow. She tried to kick the severed limb from her ankle, but it gripped tightly.

Madison and Yorik approached her at either side to unload their weapons into the writhing prisoners around her. Madison checked around the central prison area for a gray electrical box. She found it locked in a service storage cupboard. She opened the electrical box with another computer password. She pulled out some contained fuses in a row in the electrical box.

"We should try to find a way to storm 'The Dungeon.' Time is running out!" Julie told Madison.

"No need! We are getting out of here now. When the next shift comes round, we will send them in. If those people are so keen on being holed up in 'The Dungeon,' then we leave them there. I have disabled any chance of it being reactivated. We can control the prison from the emergency version of 'The Dungeon.' I think to starve to death, dying in your own crap, is probably more terrible than a shootout. I'm satisfied the situation is contained. Besides, we won't get any money out of the board for a manicure."

After a week, it was as if nothing had happened, except the original 'Dungeon' was still closed off. Rumors of what had happened that day circulated, but Madison had achieved her goal. The outside world knew nothing of the skirmish in Portcullis. When Madison was convinced they had enough, she appeared on the monitors in 'The Dungeon' to inform the remaining inmates that if they agreed to surrender the weapons they had in their possession a swift conclusion might help each one of their individual cases. She never got a reply. Finally, the decision was made to use a SWAT Team to break into 'The Dungeon.'

Fifty-one days had passed when explosive charges removed the door. The smell of decomposing human flesh filled the prison. Everyone who had occupied the main control room was dead, genuinely disappointing Madison.

She found herself in a strange situation in that people involved in Portcullis praised her for the way she had handled the incident, but she felt respect for the prisoners who had never given in. She had achieved her goal, yet again, so had they. They chose to die rather than surrender to the prison. This realization changed Madison's approach to her work for the rest of her career to the extent that any prisoner she felt would prefer to lose their life, instead of following her guidelines, was to her, in some way, an equal, someone whose conviction had finally given them a true creed. Madison would never get over losing Kim, along with the other members of her analytical team, and she wouldn't forgive herself for it ever having left them like sitting ducks reaching for water they would never reach on time.

Chapter 34

The door to Reese's room slid back. The woman with the infant in the picture on his walls sped into the room. Reese stood up, smiling from the armchair to greet her. His child's mother slapped his face hard. He took the rebuke by leaning over to look past her at his daughter following her into the room.

"She gave me purpose, made me want to try for the only time in my life!" the child's mother sobbed erratically. Reese was trying to listen to her, but their child who he was meeting in the flesh for the first time in his life awed him. The sensitivity drugs had completely stripped away his tendencies.

"Don't touch her!" the inmate mother yelled in his face.

He got annoyed at her after a delayed response. "What's your problem? We made this child together. Isn't it bad enough that we've got to raise her in this place? Look at her. She is the most incredible thing I've ever seen," Reese confided, kneeling down to match his approaching daughter's eye level.

"You don't know anything about this place! It's a setup! They wouldn't tell me why you were in here. Did they tell you about my crimes?" the inmate mother screamed, her face disfigured with distress.

"No, what did you do? Why are you in Portcullis?" Reese asked, his arms hanging limply at his sides before he lifted a hand loosely, palm up.

She drew in a supportive breath. "I killed my sister's kids, one niece and two nephews. Now, tell me why you are in here so I might try in my wildest imagination to come to terms with this prison's governing board's decision," she voiced, losing control of her ironclad façade. Her oxygen intake fluctuated, restricting her vocal cords with a visible need to break down.

"I killed ..."—Reese could barely speak his crimes—"I killed children also." He labored to form the words in his head into speech. "But ... but, why would you want to know? ... What decision?"

"Molly, our daughter, will be sent for euthanasia for our crimes next Sunday, and I will be following closely behind her by my own hand," the inmate mother replied calmly, like the pressure to verbalize her heartbreak had gone. She reached out for Molly's hand. "Come on, I don't want you near this thing!"

Molly took her mother's hand, and they turned to leave Reese's room.

The information the female inmate had given him still had Reese reeling. He shuffled to the armchair in need of support and comfort. He wanted to run toward Molly's leaving infant frame, but the reality of Molly's mother's words had immobilized him. His room door slid shut, as did a shield in Reese's mind.

He suffered something similar to a self-induced stroke. He was, for the want of a better expression, imprisoned in his own body.

The inmate mother led Molly down the Portcullis corridors where Madison waited in an empty holding room for them. When they got there, she gave the inmate mother a change of clothing.

"Did it affect him?" Madison asked. The inmate's saddened demeanor from her task surprised her.

"I thought he had turned to stone on the spot. So, I'm completely off the euthanasia list from now on for doing this?"

"Completely," Madison verified.

"What about Molly?" she asked.

"Molly will be going to foster parents, outside of Portcullis. She was, after all, an egg donated from our archive."

"So, nobody goes unpunished. He gets his comeuppance as do I."

"Thou shalt not kill should be underlined within the Ten Commandments."

"It is in here," the inmate mother sighed, releasing tears as she lowered herself to kiss her daughter goodbye.

Chapter 35

He stood behind a yellow line painted on the admissions building's floor, waiting to be called forward to place his personal belongings onto the sunken, stainless-steel dish molded into the counter. His family's cries when the verdict was read out in the courtroom still rang in his ears. The Department of Corrections' twin prop only took an hour to reach Portcullis. From the horror stories that had filtered through the criminal community, he knew he faced a tough sentence. And he might never leave this prison alive. A conclusion that was statistically proven. America's crime rate had plummeted since all prisons in the country had adopted the methods used at Portcullis.

He put some dollar bills held together with a money clip into the dish. He dug deep into his pockets for a bunch of keys. His fingertips raked the smooth surface of quarters, nickels, and dimes. He pulled his closed hand out of his pocket and dropped the coins that clattered noisily into the stainless-steel dish set into the counter.

"They let you keep currency and personals in bail-denied detention?" the admissions officer asked with sincere concern.

"Yeah! Why? No one seemed too bothered," the Portcullis freshman replied.

"Jesus Christ! Come through the opening there. I wanna see what else they let you keep. God knows what they think they're running down there."

The new inmate shambled around to an x-ray detector at the end of the counter. As he stepped into its paneled confines, he flipped a coin. He had not given in, making a bet with himself that he would not make it through his sentence in the maximum-security prison.

"Steady on, boy. Don't try nothing stupid now!" the admission officer told him some feet away behind the protective screen.

"I'm just flipping this coin on my chances," he explained. He flipped it again.

He looked up at the somersaulting quarter. Heads, he would make it through to rehabilitation. Tails, his ashes would end up in an unmarked marble P.O. Box shrine in the prison's cemetery on the edge of the Everglades.

He caught the coin on the back of his fist, shielding the coin with his other cupped hand. He then lifted his hand to see what side the coin had landed on. Evident relief relaxed him when he saw the head in profile of a woman. In his mind, a female was the weaker sex and didn't pose a big threat to him.

What he didn't know was that woman was Madison Paige, the founder of Portcullis. This was the newly minted 'Women Who Have Changed Our World' circulation. And to her, luck was a fallacy for the foolish who were gullible enough to take it upon themselves to extinguish an innocent person's life.

Don't miss out!

Visit the website below and you can sign up to receive emails whenever A. Joseph publishes a new book. There's no charge and no obligation.

https://books2read.com/r/B-A-KDAMC-QNCAF

BOOKS 2 READ

Connecting independent readers to independent writers.